NapPily
in BloOm

Nappily in Bloom

Trisha R. Thomas

St. Martin's Griffin
New York

Published in the United States by St. Martin's Griffin, an imprint of St. Martin's Publishing Group

NAPPILY IN BLOOM. Copyright © 2009 by Trisha R. Thomas. All rights reserved. Printed in the United States of America. For information, address St. Martin's Publishing Group, 120 Broadway, New York, NY 10271.

www.stmartins.com

The Library of Congress has cataloged the first St. Martin's Griffin edition as follows:

Thomas, Trisha R., 1964–
    Nappily in bloom / Trisha R. Thomas. — 1st ed.
      p. cm.
    ISBN 978-0-312-55764-5
    1. African Americans—Fiction.   2. Married people—Fiction.   3. Domestic fiction.   I. Title.
    PS3570.H5917N375 2009
    813'.54—dc22

                                                                                2009012522

ISBN 978-1-250-62391-1 (trade paperback)

Our books may be purchased in bulk for promotional, educational, or business use. Please contact your local bookseller or the Macmillan Corporate and Premium Sales Department at 1-800-221-7945, extension 5442, or by email at MacmillanSpecialMarkets@macmillan.com.

Second St. Martin's Griffin Edition: March 2020

10   9   8   7   6   5   4   3   2   1

To my mom and all the mama and papa bears out there,

this one is for you.

I would rather trust a woman's instinct than a man's reason.
—*Stanley Baldwin*

The sound of water running through the walls, as if the pipes will burst at any moment, wakes me from a hazy drift of sleep. Darkness turns a creak into an echo. A brush of my own skin sounds like footsteps in dry grass. Every subtle shift in the wind gives me momentary hope—only to be dashed by the knowledge that I am probably going to die here.

I curl my aching body tighter and decide there's little to do but wait, hope, and continue to pray. I've made so many mistakes in the past, but nothing to deserve what's happening to me now.

My throat is dry, and I'm hoarse from crying out for help. The lump on the back of my head aches and feels like it's growing larger by the minute. I've told myself to stop with the feeble attempts of scratching at the wood. Splinters sting underneath my nails, burning raw. But I can't help myself, stopping for a few moments, then back at it again. "Somebody, please . . . can you hear me?" I shove against the heavy wooden cell destined to be my casket if I don't get out. I've always been a survivor. No one to depend on but myself. Always believing there is a way, even when there isn't. I've forged ahead and made my own path, even when doubt has clouded my vision. Until now. No way am I making it out of here. *Stop it.* No. *I will see my daughter.*

We all dream of being loved. How is it that from the time we suckle at our mother's breast, we know there is no greater gift or reward? At such a tender age, even before we're through wetting diapers, we know love. As I sit and wait for the end, all I want is one more chance to love and be loved. I'll get it right this time, I swear. I won't waste a minute, not even a second, pouting about the past. Only moving in the present, the here and now.

Doesn't everyone deserve a second chance? Everyone? No, not everyone. I will see the one who did this to me, whether in heaven or hell, and make him wish he'd never set hands on me.

If only someone finds me, God only knows I will be a different person when I leave here.

I promise . . . I promise to be better and do better, please, if you just give me a chance, Lord.

Dear God . . . this prayer will probably be my last. Hear me now. Whatever path you have chosen for me, I will follow. Whatever my destiny, I will accept.

The Bigger They Are

When Satan attacks, he doesn't sneak or hide. He makes sure you see him coming. His sheer pleasure comes in the terror and fear that spread and eat your spirit, spill acid into your gut, and disease into your body. It is called worry.

I opened my eyes to try to stop the vision. My soul was heavy. I'd already spent half the day worrying about Airic and what his affair with my assistant would do to my reputation. Now it was time to release the burden. He'd caused the pain, and he alone would have to deal with the ramifications.

He'd asked to meet in a public place—as if I were a threat and not *him*, the very one who'd tried to crush my spirit. I walked into Risou, the upscale restaurant in the Perimeter shopping district of Atlanta, looking impeccable. I'd spent a good thousand dollars between the spa and salon and dropped the ten pounds I'd recently gained, to make sure there was no proof of my stress. I wouldn't give him the satisfaction of witnessing my devastation.

He stood up, wearing an aqua blue shirt and tie under a dark suit that made him look respectable, though I knew what kind of treachery he was capable of. He was out to destroy me. What else could explain his behavior?

"Thank you for coming." He pulled out a chair at the table. The dim lighting of the restaurant made it feel like evening when it was only eleven thirty in the morning. I was grateful the lunch crowd had yet to arrive.

He wasted no time with small talk. "All I'm offering is a compromise. I want what's fair—that's all," he said.

"Fair? I don't see you on television every night. I don't hear your voice on the CDs, books, and tapes I've sold. How is it fair?"

"I've been a substantial part of your life over the last two years. If it wasn't for me, and the investments I made, you wouldn't be worth half of what you are now."

"Money doesn't define me. Our union was not based on money, so why should this dissolution be based on money?"

"This isn't a philosophical debate. The math is all we're dealing with. You have a substantial increase in your net worth since our two-year marriage. It's a simple, basic fact." Airic shifted his weight, leaning back in his chair.

The waitress sat two cups down and placed the French press filled with more fresh coffee between us.

I waited until she was gone. "But you forfeited your right to our marriage and its benefits when you decided to sleep with that low-rent whore." I took a delicate sip of the hot coffee, doing my best to hold the cup steady despite the gentle tremor I felt in my grip. "And of all times, you *know* I have a new book coming out in a few weeks. I will not be embarrassed like this."

"You don't have a choice. I've got proof of what you did. I don't want to have to do it, but I will go public. You could be charged with fraud, a federal offense. Tampering with a court-ordered document. You paid someone to change those DNA results. You won't bounce back from this like you do from everything else."

This brought about laughter I didn't know I was capable of. I laughed until my ribs hurt. "I don't think it can compare to you and your little girlfriend's sex tape. Besides, who did I hurt? You still have your precious Mya."

"Only after putting Mya through another DNA test. You're spiteful and evil. I don't think I can ever forgive you."

Again, I had to try to mask my amusement. "Airic, please, you can't touch me. However, I will do whatever I have to in order to protect myself." He'd forgotten who I was, Trevelle Doval. I grew up fast and hard, and the one thing I remembered and would always keep as my mode of operation was to get them before they got you.

"Do you really want to find out?" he asked, shaking his head. "You are some kind of stubborn."

"I am a survivor. I have worked too hard to let you destroy everything I've built because you couldn't keep your dick in your pants. Whatever you do will only bring about more embarrassment on yourself." I forced a smile, but I was breaking into a million pieces.

As they say, the bigger they are, the harder they fall. But no one is ever referring to physical size when they make that statement, but rather resolve and circumstance, hopes and dreams. The bigger those dreams, the louder it can be heard around the world when someone knocks them off their stage. One thing for sure, I wasn't going down easy.

I'd been blessed with a second chance. Not many can make that claim. A daughter I'd thought died at birth was put before me like a gift from God. Only the highly favored received those kinds of blessings. I'd come to accept this honor. Some were ashamed of their good fortune. Not I. My potential was only beginning. I commanded audiences of tens of thousands who wanted to hear me speak. I was God's vessel. I owed my legion of faithful followers respect by proving His power and grace.

Airic would need more than idle threats to put a period on the end of my sentence. I was in survival mode. "Why do we have to fight, Airic? Why can't you see the error of your ways and ask for forgiveness?"

He leaned in. "Stop it. All right. You don't care anything about me. You're just trying to save face because your new book is coming out. Image is all you care about." He was silenced by the stares of a few patrons. The restaurant was filling quickly. "You want to stay in a loveless marriage? Is that what you're saying? Because I can't do it anymore."

"Yes. You're right. That's exactly what I'm saying. I have an empire to maintain, and I can't do it as damaged goods. Divorced. Cast out by my own husband. Do you know how it felt to get that DVD in the mail, put it in my player, and see my husband—my husband." I tried to stop my lip from trembling. "I didn't do anything to deserve that."

"I was hurt when I found out what you did. It was my way of lashing out to hurt you back. Chandra didn't mean anything to me. She sent the DVD after I explained we couldn't ever see each other again. She thought it would break us up and send me straight into her arms. . . . Well, she was right about the first part."

"Are you saying it was only once?" His silence lasted a second too long. My stomach curled into a tight ball. I couldn't stand the way I sounded—pathetic, weak, powerless. "You two deserve each other. God bless me." I closed my eyes. "I can't stay here." I picked up my clutch, securing it high under my arm.

He took a hold of my hand. "Wait a minute."

"Don't touch me. You lost that right."

Airic followed me out of the restaurant. It took the valet a second before he recognized me.

"Ms. Doval, may I get your car?"

"Not yet." Airic spoke in my place, putting up a dismissive hand.

"Please, thank you." I handed my ticket to the young man.

"I think we have to admit this was a long time coming, whether it was Chandra or something else. Chandra is not the reason we're here."

The mention of her name one too many times made a surge run through my veins. Before I could stop myself, I slapped his face with one hand and swung at the air with my purse with the other. I struggled while his long fingers managed to clasp around both my wrists like rope.

"Stop making a fool of yourself."

"I'm the fool—you're right about that. I've been a fool since the day I believed you loved me."

"I did love you," he huffed, still trying to catch his breath. He straightened his tie and wiped the sting on his neck where I'd scratched him. "I did. I tried to make it work. You think I want this . . . what's happening between us? Did you ever stop and think how it made me feel not being able to sleep in the same bed with my wife? In the world of Trevelle Doval I was trying to fit in, think of how the things you did affected me, for once."

"You know why we can't sleep in the same bed, you know my past, how could you throw that back in my face like this?"

"I am willing to go to therapy with you to work through this. Damn, you are so stubborn!"

"God is my therapist, and you need to repent in your heart for betraying my love for you and our marriage. If you are serious about reconciliation, you need to call that . . . woman and let her know your intentions for her and I mean now."

"I've already told her it's over. She knows it's over. You're the one who doesn't seem to understand English."

"I want to hear you say it. I want to hear both of you." One thing I knew for sure: Voices don't lie. Words lie. Inflection and tone do not. I would hear her voice on the other end of the phone, and I'd know. I would hear his, and be certain. I needed Airic to be my husband, and for all intents and purposes, I still loved him. So help me God, I wished I didn't, but I did.

"Call her." I pulled out my phone and shoved it against his chest.

He shook his head and took his own phone off his belt and dialed. She must've answered on the first ring. "Listen, we're through. Is it clear?"

I snatched the phone from his ear and heard her pretentious innocence. "Okay," she said gently. "Whatever you say, Airic."

I couldn't answer fast enough. "No, you scheming little tramp, it's whatever *I* say."

Airic pried the phone back and pressed the button ending the call. A fleeting moment of happiness beat through my heart. Key word: *fleeting*. He pushed his hands out to keep me from coming closer. "I want to work this out. I'm trying, but if you can't be civil, this will be the last time you and I have anything to talk about."

"Civil? The fact that you're still standing after what I saw on that video—oh, I'm civil. I should've cut your throat."

"Enough." He leaned in close. "I'll stay in the pretense of a marriage for one more year. The price is five million dollars. Between me and you, you're getting off cheap." He waited for me to agree, but I couldn't utter a word.

I felt like such a fool for not having made a prenuptial agreement. At the time, there was love that could fill a fountain and overflow a river. I would've given him the shoes off my feet, the shirt off my back, and then went out and worked for more. He knew I'd been abused and prostituted from the time I was twelve years old. He knew my struggle, where I'd come from. It was no mystery that I was a fighter and would never let someone take advantage of me again. I would not pay for his false love.

The valet drove my white Jaguar to the curb. I marched over to the driver's side, handed him a tip, and slipped inside. Airic remained. I rolled down the window. "You won't see a dime of my money. In fact, you'll be lucky to have two nickels to rub together when I'm through with you."

I could hear his last words. "You don't want to do this."

Oh, but I do want to do this. I jammed on the gas and didn't bother looking back in my rearview mirror. I dialed my producer and told her I was going on hiatus, effective immediately. I couldn't speak the word until my heart was cleansed. The devil had taken residence in my house, and it was time to get him out.

Arrangements

Venus

I saw the limo parked out front as I pulled into the lot behind my floral boutique. I must admit, of all the careers I'd dreamed and wished for, arranging flowers was not one of them. Me—the staunch educated professional determined to step over the corporate brass one stiletto heel at a time—turned quiet small-business owner of a quaint yet sophisticated florist shop. I needed something to do while holed up in Atlanta, waiting for my husband to come to his senses and move us back to Pacific Coast time, a subject not to be discussed without one of us walking away angry.

I gave up the good fight and hunkered down, got comfortable in my southern digs just like the rustic plaque hanging over the back entrance read: GROW WHERE YOU'RE PLANTED. I did exactly that. I stopped defending my native California pride, and admitted that living in Georgia was far better in the ways of brown folks. Where else could you buy a business for the equivalent of an online shopping spree? Didn't matter that the business was failing miserably before I came along. I could see the place had good bones.

I put on my marketing cap and pushed up my sleeves. Never underestimate the power of a flyer. I made sure everyone knew the place was under new ownership, and that I was to go the extra mile.

The showroom was serene and sophisticated with comfy furniture and gorgeous bouquet arrangements. Most who entered forgot what they'd come for while enjoying the ambience. We served tea and cookies, and sometimes champagne, depending how big a budget they were working with. But the back of the place was another story. Chaotic was the best way to describe the minefield of boxes filled with flowers, ribbons, bows, and mountains of greenery. I heard rummaging behind the stacked shelves. "Vin?" I didn't take another step until I got an answer.

"Who else? A burglar who likes the smell of roses?" Vince joked about being part of the package. I seriously wanted something in writing saying he'd stay with In Bloom for the first year. My corporate background liked to see things in black-and-white with signatures underneath. Vince promised nothing. He silently accepted his new boss, and I silently offered incentives like homemade peanut butter cookies, since I'd heard him complain that nobody made them decent anymore. I *do*, and it was cheaper than a raise.

"There's somebody in the front area waiting for you." He squeezed my shoulder, attempting to be gentle and playful, but Vince was a gym rat. Every muscle that could be piqued and perfected sat on display underneath his too-tight T-shirt and amazingly formfitting black jeans. As appealing as that picture should've been, the reality meant he'd rather spend his time staring at himself in the mirror while he lifted weights than sharing a pizza with a friend. When Jake met him, he wanted to shut the party down. Vince was toned, tanned, with testosterone dripping from his pores. Then it dawned on Jake that the man worked in a flower shop. How much of a threat could he really be? *Right,* I agreed. Pointing a gaydar finger was the easiest way to have a male buddy like Vince in your life.

"I saw the limo out front. Who is it?" I peeked out and didn't see anyone. I dropped my bag and straightened myself out a little. The white cap I wore with a ponytail pushed through the vent in the back made everyone think I was just the help, which was fine by me. With ownership came problems. Solicitors were shooed away by saying the owner wasn't in. On the few occasions when bill collectors came, they were easily thwarted by saying the owner had just left.

"It's a lady and her daughter." Vince shrugged his shoulders. "Nothing new there."

"People don't shop for flowers in a limo, Vin. Did she ask for me specifically or did they ask for the owner?"

"She asked for you specifically. What's the paranoia about? You in the witness protection program or something?"

"Funny."

"Well, are you?" he asked with serious consideration. I got the idea he may know a little something about people hiding for their lives.

"No, but I have made a few enemies in my time." I moved past him. I walked out and stopped in my tracks. The woman turned around. I threw my arms out. "Ohmigoodness," I stammered. "Judge Hawkins, how are you?"

"It's so good to see you," she whispered near my ear. "Look at you." She pulled back to get a fresh view. "How's Mya and your husband?"

Vince was waiting, arms folded over his wide chest. He leaned on the archway, making sure everything was copacetic.

"You've met Vince," I said. "This is the Honorable Judge Delma Hawkins and—"

"This is my lovely daughter, Keisha."

The young woman put out a slender hand to me. "Nice to meet you, Venus. My mother's talked about you often. She thinks the world of you." There was no resemblance, with Keisha being near six feet in heels and Delma being only my height in three-inch mules—which meant short.

"Really?" I tried not to make it sound too implausible, but honestly, the last time I'd laid eyes on Judge Delma Hawkins, she was about to grant full custody of my daughter to Airic Fisher, her biological father. That wasn't the behavior of someone who thought highly of me.

If not for the intervention of a defrauded DNA test, Judge Delma Hawkins would've handed my daughter over to the enemy wrapped with a bow. Looking back, I realized we hadn't made a strong case for ourselves. Jake had been accused of his accountant's murder. I had spent a brief time under psychiatric evaluation after accidentally overdosing on antianxiety medication. Not to mention various other legal mishaps under both our belts. I guess anyone could've made the mistake of assuming Airic would've made the better parent. I tried not to hold it against Judge Delma while she stood in front of me, beaming with proud excitement.

"My baby's all grown up and about to embark on a new life. She's getting married. I absolutely had to bring her to you to handle the flowers. I heard about this quaint little shop of yours."

"When's the ceremony, and what kind of budget are we working with?" I was trying not to stare at the Rock of Gibraltar–size ring on her daughter's finger. I may even have drooled a bit.

"Honey, she's marrying Gray Hillman, senior partner at Shark Boyd, a prominent entertainment law firm. The sky is the limit, that's what your man said." She cut her eyes at Keisha, following up with a lopsided frown. "Mr. Moneybags wants only the best for my Keisha, because she's worth it."

"Mom, I think we've already discussed this." Keisha stroked the length of her long silky hair. "Money has nothing to do with our relationship."

"Yes, we've discussed it. Did you see the limo out front?" Delma pointed. "He arranged for a full day of limo service so we'd get all our errands done without stress. Then we're set up for lunch at the Calloway Gardens to do the sampling. After that, straight to the spa and salon just so Keisha can try out a few hairstyles and nail colors. Does that sound like someone who isn't trying to buy love? Being lavish and boastful."

"Mom, please. You can't complain about it, then sit there giddy, enjoying the ride."

"Hey, I'm not complaining. I'm just saying . . . stop trying to pretend money doesn't make the world go round. If he was broke, we all wouldn't be here," Delma huffed, finally getting her point across. "Shoot . . . I haven't had this kind of fun in . . . well, ever. This is going to be a spectacular wedding, one like you've never seen."

"What about your own wedding, Mom? That was really special and beautiful."

This seemed to quiet her. The puzzled look on my face asked the question: *Who?* I couldn't imagine who the victim could be.

Keisha answered, "It was cute and intimate by candlelight. The most romantic ceremony. She married Hudson, her clerk. They're the cutest couple," Keisha said with great pride.

Delma remained silent.

"It's like they're schoolkids when they're around each other."

Delma finally spoke. "I guess that's what marrying for love will get you—cute and intimate. Back to you, let's stay on task here. Focus on the time line." She plopped on the couch with her legs coming together only at her ankles. She picked up a brochure and fanned herself. "Anything to drink around here?"

"Champagne." I moved quickly to the back for a bottle of Veuve Clicquot. Whoever Keisha was marrying had deep pockets, and I was only too happy to oblige.

Minutes later, we were toasting and signing order sheets and Delma was writing a check from what she called the "sugar daddy account."

"So, I'll take it from here." I reached out and patted Keisha's hand. "You're going to be a beautiful bride." She was long and lean with gentle features.

She stood up, a bit wobbly. "Too much champagne. Your restroom . . ."

"It's all the way in the back. Watch out for those boxes."

As Delma scooted toward my chair, I could see in her eyes there was something heavy on her mind. "There's something I have to tell you. I wouldn't expect you to know this, but I just wanted to come right out with it."

"Okay." I tensed up for whatever bomb she was about to drop.

"Well, there's no easy way to say this, so here goes it. Keisha is Trevelle Doval's biological daughter."

My mouth refused to move. My face shook side to side like a silly cartoon character. "How can that be? You knew this all along, even when we were all in your courtroom?"

"I know, I know. I'm not proud of the way I handled things in my courtroom last year. The only reason I had even considered giving your ex custody of your daughter was because Doval tried to force me not to." She put up a hand as if she'd already spoken to God about it, so enough said. "Ya see, she was a prostitute. But you knew that—the whole world knows. It's her bragging rights to say, *Ooh, look at me. I'm a sinner, but now the queen of the self-righteous.*"

She caught herself going off on a tangent. "I worked in the district attorney's office at the time. I happened to be driving in the downtown area when Trevelle gave birth to Keisha in the back of her pimp's car. She just left her there for dead." Delma stared straight ahead, as if she'd rehearsed this story many times. She held her chin high, like she was on stage doing a one-woman play. "What I saw that night would indelibly be a part of me. The good part was finding Keisha."

She took a sip of her champagne, then poured some more. "I found Keisha and raised her as my own. Trevelle Doval never even mourned the loss of that child, just left her there. I would've never divulged my secret. But then the biological father felt it his duty to mix us all up in one big pot of mess. He was a married white police officer, supposed to be protecting and serving. He was serving, all right. Got a fifteen-year-old pregnant."

I covered my mouth with shock. A married white cop and a teenaged Trevelle. Unfathomable. The woman who'd made a name for herself through pointing fingers of indignation at others? I still couldn't speak.

Keisha emerged from the back with her cell pressed against her ear.

"Goodness, the man doesn't give her a minute on her own," Delma whispered quickly. Then back on the more important subject. "I just want you to know that Trevelle could be a thorn. If anyone could be trusted to keep her out of the details, it would be you. Whatever it costs extra for your wonderful wedding coordinating skills, I'm willing to pay."

"But wait." I was reaching for Delma's sleeve, drowning in the 101 questions that were fluttering in my head.

Delma scooted away to tend to Keisha, so the questions would have to wait for another time.

From that point on, it was hard to look at Keisha and not think of Trevelle. Scandal. Intrigue. I wanted details. I wanted to know how Trevelle reacted when she found out . . . and why this wasn't in the news like everything else about that woman. I could barely focus on the job at hand.

Delma downed her last corner of champagne. "It's going to be beautiful. My baby's getting married," she announced, as if we hadn't been discussing old secrets.

They hugged, and I thought I'd cry, too. I could only imagine what they had been through. Had Keisha known Trevelle was her mother? The ties of love were strong with these two.

Delma gathered herself, wiping her eyes. "I don't stand a chance at the actual ceremony." She moved toward the door, following Keisha out. The swish of her thick panty hose suddenly stopped. She turned to face me. "I want you to know I tried to make it up to you."

"What?" I'd heard her, but didn't understand.

"I pulled as many strings as I was able to try to get your adoption passed—you know, last year."

"Thank you. I had no idea."

"Just so you know. I tried."

It was quiet and still, as if the last hour had been a dream. I plopped down onto the vintage sofa, which could have used some extra stuffing. All I could do was say, *Whoa.* My mind was spinning with the emotional overdose.

Delma had reminded me of all I'd tried to forget. I had stopped myself from thinking about the past few years and the deluge of disappointments. Jake and I had suffered through the birth of our stillborn son, then fought tooth and nail to keep Airic from taking our daughter. The final heartbreaker was not being able to adopt a ten-month-old little boy named Ralph, whom I'd fallen in love with, and wanted dearly to take care of.

Once again, the same issues on paper pegged us as *at-risk parents*, and we couldn't get approved for the state adoption. If the baby hadn't already been in the state system, I could've adopted him privately. I even tried the foster parent route to get him that way. By the time I'd finished the drawn-out paperwork, another family adopted him. I was devastated. Between the stillbirth in my seventh month and losing Ralph, I simply couldn't deal with another loss, so I put the whole notion of another child out of my mind.

I had my sweet daughter Mya to be grateful for, even if I had to share her with Airic. I watched the black limousine pull away.

"Sounds like a windfall," Vince said from behind. "But you're going to have to work for it. Only thing you won't do is officiate the ceremony."

"I'm going to be officiating, all right. Like Tyson versus Buster Douglas. This should be interesting." Delma had basically hired me to keep Trevelle at bay, as if I were any match for that woman. I'd barely saved my *own* daughter from Trevelle's claw, and now Delma wanted me to save hers?

With Friends Like These

Trevelle

The concierge called out to me as I tried to rush past. "Your mail, Ms. Doval. It's been piling up for the last few days." I slid my sunglasses back on. I didn't want anyone to see the black smudges underneath my eyes.

"Thank you." I took the stack of bills. The constant bombardment of invoices and credit card statements stuffed daily in my box was Airic's department. Late notices were beginning to show up now, to the point where I refused even to stop by the desk. Not that I didn't have the money. The Doval Ministry was a multimillion-dollar empire.

I moved swiftly to the elevator. The condo had all the amenities—doorman, concierge, and valet. But along with all this service was a lack of anonymity. Everyone knew your comings and goings. I got inside the elevator and resisted the urge to give in to the fatigue after the doors closed. Elevators had cameras, and I was determined not to let anyone see me rattled.

My floor had only two units—the other unit belonged to a male couple, Dr. Joe Perry and Donte Clancy, both plastic surgeons, highly regarded in their field. Had I known what was going on, I would never have moved in. I'd done my part by sprinkling holy water on their door. I'd offered a prayer of salvation from their affliction. Needless to say, prayer can't fix everything, especially when the parties involved don't want to accept the blessing.

The elevator stopped at the fourth floor, where the gym was located. Speak of the devils—at least one of them. Dr. Perry was perspiring with a towel around his neck.

"Good afternoon." His heart rate had yet to calm down, so he rested both hands on his hips.

I nodded, but kept my eyes forward. I didn't need to absorb any more negative energy. I would spend the evening praying and meditating. By morning, I would be cleansed and rejuvenated after my terrible meeting with Airic. I wished I could understand why he betrayed me this way. I understood why Chandra McKinney wanted to take everything I had. That was the easy answer. Chandra said she felt like I had everything—and I must admit that I did.

She could barely read, let alone type a decent sentence. I gave her a job because she needed guidance and direction. I offered her my hand when she needed a lift up. Three months in, I found out she'd been stealing from me. Jewelry—my diamond tennis bracelet was the first to come up missing. Then it was the engraved cross with almost three carats total weight down the center. I tried to ignore the larceny. I understood the mind of someone who stole, feeling cheated from all that society has to offer.

I drew the line when I caught her trying on my Christian Louboutin taupe heels that took six months to get on special order. That was a whole other level of disrespect, to slip her stank feet into my shoes. I sent her packing. Three days later, the tape arrived.

The elevator stopped while I'd drifted into murderous thoughts of Chandra. Dr. Perry stood, holding the doors open with a hand. "You can't get any higher," he offered lightly.

"Yes, you can. It's called heaven." I strode past him. We took our opposite directions.

Inside my home, I locked the door with the double security latch. I hadn't changed the locks, holding on to hope that Airic would come to his senses. Now I was certain he had lost his mind, and I didn't want to be so easily accessible. I picked up the phone and pressed maintenance. "This is Ms. Doval. I'd like to request new locks, immediately."

"Yes, Ms. Doval. We can schedule that service for Thursday."

"What part of *immediately* do you not understand? Tomorrow morning is the latest I will wait."

"Yes, Ms. Doval. Is there anything else?" He didn't sound fazed in the least.

"Well, what time? What time am I scheduled?"

"Is eight o'clock too early?"

"Which part of *as soon as possible* did you not understand? Of course eight is fine." Honestly, I was surrounded by numskulls.

"How many keys will you need?"

"I'll need three sets of keys." I counted one for Marcella, and . . . just in case, I was thinking, in case Airic came to his senses. *Stop it.* It was so hard. Anger made you take the first step, but the journey was difficult, when you were letting someone go. Someone you trusted and loved. Flip-flopping: *I love him, I hate him.* Why couldn't he just do as I said? I'd tried to teach him the right ways of maintaining a relationship. Neither of us had a good record to speak of. I'd never been married, and Airic had been married twice before. But at least I had the Bible's teachings as a guide.

"Are we done here? Then fine, see you in the morning," I told the maintenance man.

I bent over to take off my shoes and saw a few pieces of mail that had fallen when I threw the stack on the glass table. I zeroed in on the thick white envelope with calligraphy script and knew before I picked it up: Keisha's wedding invitation.

As if I were some common acquaintance. Some guest expected to buy one flatware setting from the gift registry. I tore it open:

> *Delma J. Hawkins and*
> *Mr. and Mrs. Titus Hillman*
> *Request the honor of your presence*

at the wedding ceremony of
Keisha Hawkins & Gray Titus Hillman
March twenty-first, two thousand and nine . . .

The rest of the details began to bleed together. I had no right to be angry. No right to feel left out. I had no right, no right—yet I picked up the phone and dialed Keisha, filled with jealousy and a few choice words. Before the phone rang, I hung up.

I dialed again, hung up again.

No right, I kept telling myself. But the nagging voice was overpowered by the unmitigated truth: It was my only daughter's wedding. My only child.

"Missus?" Marcella came from the laundry room. She put down the basket of linens she was carrying. "Missus, oh please, don't cry." She rushed off and came back with wads of tissue.

Her solid hand rubbed my back comfortingly. "He will come back. And if he doesn't, you don't need him."

I blew into the tissue. More than anything, I wanted her to remove her hands from my body. If it required me to get myself together for that reason alone, I would do so with quickness. I blew once more. "I'm fine. Really. Thank you. Tea. Please."

"Right away." She pushed off on her rubber-soled shoes and headed to the kitchen.

I placed the phone back on its charger. I would save my conversation with Keisha for when I was stronger, because in all honesty, the one I had to confront was Delma J. Hawkins, the woman who'd stolen her from me.

"Missus, you have company."

I turned around to see Airic standing a foot taller than Marcella. She looked uncomfortable.

"Thank you, Marcella," I said, to ease her mind and excuse her at the same time.

"If you need me . . ." She gave me a knowing eye before she left Airic and me alone, closing the door behind her.

We stood facing one another. Silence. Had Marcella known what either one of us was capable of, she never would've left us alone.

⊙⊙

"What now?" My arms crossed over my chest for no other reason than to get ahold of myself. I still wanted to rip his eyes out of his head. "Say what you have to say."

"I don't want us to end."

"I know—you mentioned that, but in the same breath you asked me for five million dollars. So which one do you need? Me or the money?"

"You." Airic sounded like a prisoner with no real choice in the matter, since the confession had already been signed. Only thing to do now was await sentencing.

"Okay, then we'll stay together."

"Just like that?" His questioning tone said he didn't trust me. We were even in that regard.

I raised and lowered my shoulders. "What else do you want to hear?"

"Nothing, I guess."

"I do have one caveat. If you ever raise your eyes or so much as glance at another woman, I will cut off your—"

"Stop it. I get it."

I pushed the intercom on my nightstand. "Marcella, please get Mr. Fisher's room ready. He'll be staying."

He left with his shoulders hunched, defeated if not downright crushed. I don't know if Airic really understood why our sleeping arrangements had to be that way, but it's the only thing that made sense. I didn't know what I was capable of while ensconced in a bad dream. Afraid I'd pick up something and hurt him, not able to tell what was a real danger from within my nightmares. Especially now, while I was seething over his betrayal.

I'd killed a man once. The man I killed all those years ago had beaten me one too many times and destroyed my spirit long before the first punch. I would never be that person again. No man would raise a hand to me, let alone crush my heart with unkind words and ill intentions. I'd vowed a man would never lay violent hands on me and live to tell about it. I made that promise years ago and had made good on it. Thank God I was living my new life through the Holy Spirit, or Airic would've paid dearly. The embarrassment alone was reason enough.

From the Grave

Jake

Jake counted his blessings: He had a ridiculously large house, and was grateful to have paid cash for it up front.

He had his freedom, something he knew most people took for granted. He understood fear and uncertainty and never took for granted the value of each day, savoring the highs right along with the lows. The threat of spending your life in jail for a murder you didn't commit could do that to a man, humble him to his knees.

He saw his wife peek in his home office to say good-bye. She wore an IN BLOOM T-shirt with white jeans that were fitting kind of close. He rose and beckoned for her to meet him halfway for a kiss. He'd gotten home late from the Atlanta Hawks basketball game while she was already sleeping so they really hadn't spent any time together.

The Bluetooth headset in his ear signaled a call. He held up a finger before their lips could touch. He looked at the phone ID. "I gotta take this call, babe." He blew her a kiss and watched her round bottom exit. She'd put on a few pounds, he noticed, and he appreciated the change. Still, the jeans might be too tight for public consumption. He hadn't decided whether to trust the old school dude she was working with just yet. Men, gay, straight, or indifferent, all had one thing on the mind, booty. Respect was the only thing that could conquer the urge. He didn't know if Vince knew who he was dealing with.

Legend had been calling all week. Now it was time to put a lid on it and squash the subject for the last time. "Look, I'm through with L.A. That's all I have to say about it. You want to sell your interest in the company—do it. I got nothing for you." Jake pushed the button to end the call. He kept the conversation short.

He was sick of Legend whining about being burnt out on JP Wear—the company Jake had started nine years ago—when all he had to do was show up and be in charge. He'd handed it over on a silver platter, having signed the urban clothing company over to protect it from lawsuits. The arrangement suited both of them just fine. Every six months, Jake received a nice check toward the full buyout price, while Legend kept the business running smoothly.

It wasn't enough money to make him a rich man anytime soon, but it kept mouths fed, lights on, grass cut, and his wife satisfied. At least he hoped so. He was content, but any man who thought one person happy in a two-person deal was enough was dead wrong.

It was Legend again. "What now, man? I've already said everything I got to say. I like our arrangement. I'm not coming back to L.A." He paused briefly to listen for the garage door to open and close, then said what was really on his mind: "If you didn't spend all your time chasing tail, you might have some energy left to run the business. Seriously, though, why the need to drop this thing like it's hot? What's wrong with our arrangement?"

"I can't stay here." Legend's voice lowered almost to a whisper. "I need to leave Los Angeles. Hell, take a trip outside of these here United States, and yesterday wouldn't be too soon."

"You messed with the wrong man's wife or what?"

"Were it that simple." Legend sometimes sounded like a thespian on a stage. He had the dramatic flair and good looks. He mostly used them for seducing and conquering women, as if the sport were a dying art. There was no fun in simply bedding them; he had to make them believe he was a leading man, their knight in shining armor.

Jake leaned forward in his chair. "You need to tell me what the hell is going on. Straight up, no bullshit."

"Need face time. Technological advances won't do. I can be out there on the next flight." Again Jake had to strain to hear. He was about to be dragged into some mess, but Legend was his friend—one of the rare and few. Friends were hard to come by and even harder to get rid of. Like an arranged marriage, commitments were made. Time was vested.

"I'll pick you up at the airport. Just tell me when, I'll be there." Jake hung up and leaned on his elbows.

His wife wouldn't be happy about Legend's visit. Hopefully whatever Legend needed face time to talk about wouldn't take more than a day. He didn't like being the buffer between his best friend and the woman he loved. Most would assume the two had some secret relationship go bad. But Jake knew better than that. There's was a genuine disdain for each another—bad blood, bad chemistry—and he was in the middle, always trying to keep the two from touching, and setting off an explosion.

The doorbell chimed loudly through the empty house. It was too early in the day for salespeople or Jehovah's Witnesses. He meant to talk to the Homeowners' Association about the supposedly private gate that seemed never to close. The fees weren't high, but he was one to expect what he was paying for.

Jake saw a man and woman standing at such a distance, he wondered who'd actually rung the bell. He swung the door open. "Yeah, how you doin'?"

"Mr. Parson." They looked like a sharply dressed black couple here with an invitation to their church. On the contrary, the visitor flipped open his badge case. "I'm Agent Peterson, and this is Agent McDonald."

"Tonya McDonald," she said, offering a handshake as if they had just met at a networking seminar.

Jake read the badge closely. "Federal Bureau of Investigation . . . What can I do for you?"

"We'd like to come inside, if that's all right?"

"Not really. Like I said, what can I do for you?" Jake stood firm.

"Mr. Parson, we have something you're going to want to see, and I seriously believe you will want to sit down for this one." The male agent held up a portable DVD player as proof of his statement. "It won't take long."

Jake stepped inside, allowing them to follow. Agent McDonald remained standing while her partner took a seat and opened the player. Jake wanted to stand, but as soon as he heard the voice sail from the screen, he took a seat. On the clear tiny screen was the man who'd killed Byron Steeple, or at least one of them. He'd remember their voices until the end of time. He heard it in his dreams. If he was thinking hard enough, he could hear the two of them while he was standing in line at the grocery store, behind him when sitting in a dark theater, occasionally on the other end of the phone. He'd learned it was all a figment of his imagination. But this time the voice was real.

"Try these—they help." Agent Peterson handed him a huge set of headphones.

The interviewer wasn't on the screen. With the high-tech headphones, Jake could hear him clearly. "You work for the same company that employed Byron Steeple. Besides that, what was your connection?"

"No connection. I didn't know him. I work at JP Wear, in the warehouse. Since when is that a crime?"

"DNA at the scene of the crime, yours. Come on, all you have to do is tell us who hired you to do it. Why take the fall when it wasn't even your idea. Make a deal and walk away."

Jake slung the headphones. "What the . . . Don't even try it." The DVD player would've gone flying, too, if the agent hadn't gripped it tight in his lap.

"Jake." Agent McDonald spoke calmly, pulling her dark ponytail from one side of her shoulder to the other. "It's not you we're after. We do need your help, though."

"I had nothing do with Byron Steeple's death. Nothing." The man had been long dead and buried and was still causing havoc in Jake's life. *When is this nightmare supposed to end?*

"This isn't about his death. He was a clever money magician. He knew how to make money disappear, but he wasn't only stealing from you, but from just about every midlevel criminal from here to L.A."

"Oh, so now I'm lumped in with the criminals."

"On the contrary," Agent McDonald said, "You were the only one who actually operated a real business. He laundered money, and he began slicing off the top for himself."

"Please understand, this is very serious. We have never been able to locate the money, or the disk that would show us exactly who his customers were."

"I can't help you. I don't know a damn thing about this, and honestly don't want to know."

"Mr. Parson, what happened to your cell phone, the one you had on the night Byron Steeple died?" The square-head agent had said very little since he arrived. He'd obviously been holding the highest card in the deck, and he played it.

Jake shook his head, thinking back to that night and wishing he could make it all disappear. He had dropped his phone somewhere in the crucial seconds of holding Byron's limp body. "So what do you want me to do?"

Shaken Not Stirred

Venus

"The fountain has to be eight-tiered. Not six, not four. Uh-huh, uh-huh. Well, unless we're breaking some kind of fire code, how high it stands is not an issue." Before I could close out the call, the call-waiting chimed in. I saw it was Judge Delma and was going to let it ring, but since she was about to pay my rent solid for the next six months, I couldn't avoid talking to her.

"In Bloom, how can I help make it a fantastically floral day?"

"Venus, I have another urgent favor." With Delma, everything seemed to be urgent. The nerves of a mother-of-the-bride were usually the first to go.

"That's what I'm here for." I tapped my pen, ready to take direction.

"Do you think— well, is it possible for Mya to be the flower girl? It would be such an honor, but truly the little girl who was supposed to do it now stands taller than me, with breasts to match."

"It would be an honor. Yes, I'm sure Mya would love that," I said, mostly thinking of Jake's disapproval. But what the heck, none of my friends were having any nuptials anytime soon. What little girl doesn't enjoy dressing up like a princess and tossing rose petals all over the floor?

"I appreciate everything you're doing. You've been so diligent."

"I appreciate you, too."

Mostly I appreciated the check I'd just deposited. Jake didn't like to talk about it, but he considered my little business a serious drain on the resources. Partly true, but doesn't every business need a little start-up capital? After this job, I would be in the black and able to prove to him everything was coming up roses—excuse the pun.

I hung up after the last call, realizing I was going to be late picking up Mya. "I gotta get out of here."

I heard Vince filling vases behind me. "You know you're better than all of this."

I turned around and gave his shoulder a squeeze. His broad arms were more intended for a boxing ring than for playing in roses and daisies, obviously not his intended career choice.

"Sometimes you don't know what you're meant to do until you fall headfirst into it."

"I'm just sayin'. You seem more like the type could've been a CEO making big dollars."

I grinned ear to ear. "I was just thinking the same about you. Why don't you ever talk about your life before this one? What did you do before you came to this great peach of a state?"

"Put it this way: I was in the wish-making business. You made a wish, I made it happen."

Chills ran up my arms. For some reason, I knew Vince wasn't talking about a new pony or other childhood wish. "I better get moving. Mya is waiting."

Mya called for me when she saw me enter her preschool. "Mommy!"

"Hey, baby." I kneeled down and waited for her to push past the other children. She flew into my arms. "How was school today?"

"Good. Look what I drew." She held up her work of art—two wild splashes of brown and black. My hair, I assumed. In the center was a spot of red. My lips, I also assumed. "It's you, Mommy," she said proudly.

"You definitely got the hair right." I kissed her, then took her hand. I signed her out and walked through the throng of parents picking up their kids before the clock struck 6 P.M. One minute after, and there was a ten-dollar charge added to the bill. Worse than a late credit card payment, they continued adding up until double zeros appeared on a pay-or-quit notice. Good care costs good money, so I did my best to follow the rules.

"Wait, Mommy." Mya loosened her grip and took off toward the playground, where some children remained calm and happy with no idea about late fees.

I followed Mya to the iron fence where she stood, her hands wrapped around the bars. "Bye, Jory!" she yelled. "See you tomorrow."

A mop of blond hair and big dark eyes, cute as he wanted to be, rushed to the fence, landing directly in front of Mya. Before I could comprehend what was happening, they stuck out their lips and smooched between the octagon wire.

"Mya! What're you doing?" I took a hold of her hand, pulling her backwards.

Jory waved then rushed back to the jungle gym while Mya pitched a small fit.

"Stop it, Mommy." She tugged her hand away. "You've got about three seconds to turn your fast behind around and start marching to that car, do you hear me?" In that instant, I had turned into my mother. It had always worked when she did it. "One, two . . ."

When we were secured in the car and driving off, I finally exhaled, not quite over the shock. "Mya, don't you ever do that again."

She blinked confusion.

"Don't give me that look. Kissing a boy . . . Geez, what kind of place are they running?" Then I heard her hiccupped sob.

"I'm sorry, Mommy."

I pulled out of the gate of the preschool then pulled over. I reached in the backseat and stroked her cheek. "Oh, sweetie. I know you see Mommy and Daddy kissing, but that's because we love each other. Adults are allowed to kiss, not children." Somehow that hadn't come out right. "It's okay to love, just not with your lips." There, that was better. I'm sure I'd bought ten good years of not having to deal with the birds and the bees.

I must've traumatized the child. By the time we pulled into the garage, Mya was sound asleep. I carried her inside while her long legs and feet brushed against my calves.

Inside was the distinct sound of men's voices echoing through the high ceilings. I carried Mya to her bed, pulled off her shoes and socks, and decided she could sleep just until dinner.

I went downstairs to see who Jake was entertaining. Outside of the rare visits from his brother, Jake didn't have any visitors. His home, he said, was off-limits to the music-industry guys he'd met since moving to Atlanta. I was curious. And then I heard that voice and stopped in my tracks. *Legend.* The booming overarticulated words of a man I'd pretty much hated at first sight. As much as Jake loved him, I felt the exact opposite.

I paused near Jake's office, but he'd already heard me coming.

"Babe, is that you?"

"Hello," I said, cautiously stepping into the doorway. "Legend, what a surprise."

"Well, if it isn't the most beautiful woman in the world." His neat and long dreadlocks were pinned back like a girl, but the rest of him was all man: overbearing, sarcastic, and extremely full of himself.

I hugged him back, not as hard. The kiss on my cheek made me want to run screaming to the shower.

"Legend's staying—"

"For dinner," I finished. "No problem. I've got some cutlets in the fridge." I turned to rush out.

"No, babe, for a couple of nights."

"Oh, okay. Like a boys' sleepover," I said, knowing anything referring to nonmanly behavior would get under Legend's skin.

"More like, we have a lot to talk about and there's nothing like the privacy of a man's home." Legend opened his hands like the surveyor of all things great. "And it's lovely, by the way. Did you decorate it yourself?"

I knew it wasn't a compliment. Legend worked for me at one time while I worked for Jake. In other words, I was his boss. He did his best to cut me off at the knees at every turn. When he found out Jake had fallen for me, he did his best to destroy that, too. So now he was trying to pounce on my happy homemaker existence, mocking my sandstone-painted walls and dark hardwood flooring. He'd probably taken note of the coordinated silk screen paintings on the wall like a catalog shot for Pottery Barn.

"As a matter of fact, I did decorate it myself. Unfortunately, I never got to the guest bedroom, so you'll have to sleep on the floor." *Like a good doggy should,* I wanted to add.

Jake intervened. "You'll have a bed, man. But let me tell you, keep messing with V and I'd advise sleeping with one eye open."

I sneered and left, vowing not to let Legend get to me. Just two nights, three days. I could do it. At one point I'd had to stomach him every day.

⊚⟊

That night after dinner, I tried every position to fall asleep. The stress of knowing Legend was in my house and had full access to everything I loved dearly made me toss and turn. Having him as a guest was like inviting a vampire inside, knowing you were going to get bit before sunup.

The first bad sign was the way Jake had come to bed, pent up and angry. The way he hadn't bothered with niceties like a kiss or nuzzle before going straight for the gold. I hadn't been ravaged in some time—not to say I didn't enjoy it. But then, there's that fine line of feeling used. That moment of sadness when you realize you could've been Helga the bearded lady as long as he'd found the warmth between your thighs. Thrusting in and out, he found his salvation and wasn't concerned about bringing me with him.

All the while, I tried to make sense of the pieces of conversation I'd overhead before they heard me coming and stopped talking. *Serious . . . double jeopardy . . . new trial.*

Jake was such a fierce protector. I couldn't understand why he couldn't see straight through Legend and his destructive personality. He was bringing all the baggage Jake specifically wanted to get away from. He fell asleep quickly after his less-than-stellar performance. I nudged him. He didn't budge. "Baby," I whispered near his ear then shook his elbow. "Babe."

"Tomorrow, okay. Whatever it is, tomorrow."

"Not tomorrow. Now. Wake up. I want him out of here. Okay?"

"Okay, babe. Okay," he said before turning over.

I wished I'd made him pinkie swear.

Whispers in the Dark

Trevelle

I'd enlisted a good and dear friend to do what he did best: spy. Whoring wasn't the oldest profession, as so many believed. The truly oldest profession was finding another's weakness or strength and using that information to one's advantage. Even Moses sent twelve spies to the land of Canaan to explore the potential for success. *Tell me what I should do.* Moses asked those men for crucial information that would change lives. What I'd done was no different.

I simply needed to know if Airic was being honest with me about not seeing Chandra anymore.

Eddie Ray was a big ole teddy bear who wouldn't hurt a fly, but he was mean and relentless when it came to getting information. *By any means necessary* was his motto. Airic's car, office, and bedroom were all wired for sound. I had my suspicions, but I wanted to be wrong.

"Let's meet as soon as possible," Eddie reported on my voice mail. "You're going to want to hear this for yourself."

Just the thought of what I was going to hear made me angry. I was about to give Eddie a call back when the next message played.

It was my editor's assistant. "Ms. Doval, please call Monica Jackson as soon as you can. It's important that she speak with you."

The publisher hardly ever called, but my new book was about to be released; maybe there was some last-minute detail. I called right back. There were very few people who could demand a call back and get one; those three were clear. Lawyer, agent, and editor were top of the list.

"Hello, Trevelle. Good to hear your voice. Are we excited yet? Book launch three weeks and counting." She sounded unusually cheery.

"Very excited," I said, although I couldn't summon it in my voice. I was too exhausted from trying to stop my world from crashing around my feet. If she had good news, I needed to hear it like nobody's business. "So what's going on?"

"Well, there's been a slight change of plans. The numbers aren't coming in for preorders as we expected. Normally you know we do the full tour and ad spots. But with the booksellers not behind us—" She paused to offer this as gently as she could. "—we're going to have to launch with a little less bang."

I pushed my chair closer to my desk to rest my elbows and massage my temples. "Unbelievable. How much less bang are we talking?"

"Basically, we're going to leave it up to your viewers for support on this one. The budget was pulled for the ads and tour. I'm really sorry."

This was a death sentence. If the book didn't receive front-door space, it may as well have been left in the box and set on fire. "I don't understand how this happened. This is ridiculous. I reach thousands of people on television, I have a huge following, why aren't the preorders higher?"

"Honestly, they don't think it's going to sell. Remember . . . the title, we tried to get you to change it, and you fought hard to keep everything as it was? *You Have the Right to Refuse Service to Anyone: If a Restaurant Can Do It, So Can You.* The booksellers are saying it's a bit cold and confusing."

"Who doesn't understand? It's clear as it can possibly be. Women are constantly giving themselves away as if they have an obligation to serve these men that have little or no respect for them. That title speaks the basic truth . . . you have a right to refuse service, period.

What is there not to understand?" The room was getting hot as the sun shone on this side of my penthouse. I fanned myself with an envelope. "Then change the title, change the cover."

"I wish we could go back and make the changes, but the book is already printed, and as it stands, we don't have enough preorders to warrant paying for front-door space or any other caveats." My editor sighed as if talking to a child who didn't understand the big picture. So why continue to argue. "Let's just make the best of it. Hopefully you can use your forum to market the book and sell them at your church functions."

"I don't do church functions," I snapped. I actually pulled the phone away from my face to make sure this wasn't a bad dream. "Monica." I said her name to be sure I was talking to the same woman who'd promised me the world if I left the small imprint where I'd started off and signed on with her publisher. The same woman who told me that she would take care of me and we'd make sweet music together. "Listen to me, and listen closely: I will not accept defeat on any level. I spent a year writing that book. A year of my valuable time. We are not promised a tomorrow. None of us are. This book will be successful whether I have your support or not."

I hung up and moved to my luxurious bed and fell face-forward. I didn't want Marcella to come rushing if she heard my scream. It was all Airic and Chandra's fault. If they hadn't hurt me in the worst possible way, my thoughts wouldn't have been so negative. If I hadn't spent the last few months stressing over our marriage, I could've been publicizing the book like I was supposed to. Now what?

Negativity and resentment foul up the soul. Why would God grant me promise and victory when I'd spent every waking moment with a vengeful heart? "I forgive you," I said into my pillow. "I forgive your lies."

I immediately felt better. I honestly felt like a weight had been lifted off me. I rose up and moved to my television. I pushed the button of the DVD player so the disk would come out. There was nothing written on it except the manufacturer's name. No evidence or proof of where it came from. I pressed it to my chest with my best idea yet—genius, in fact.

I put the disk in a large envelope. I sat at my computer and wrote a nice little note signed by Anonymous. There was nothing like a little free publicity. In the old days, it was called scandal. Nowadays it was the only way to be seen or heard.

Delma

Delma wasn't usually a nervous ninny. She handled other people's lives just fine. She was a municipal judge for goodness' sake. However, this union of her daughter's with Gray Hillman had her heart racing. Dry mouth, headaches, and night sweats after dreaming too hard left her exhausted during the day.

Hudson had asked her a dozen times to speak her mind. She and Hudson had known each other twenty years before falling in love. If anyone knew her, it was her husband. He pressed on: "Tell Keisha about your dreams. She'll understand. Holding it in is a health risk." He was referring to the heart attack scare a few months back. Turned out to be heartburn, caused by stomach acids, caused by stress, caused by the day Keisha announced she was marrying a man she'd known all of sixty seconds or less. Her daughter was her life. Always had been. She didn't want to disappoint Keisha by acting petty. They'd been through enough after the truth came out about Trevelle Doval being her biological mother. Making waves was not on the list of things to do.

So she hugged her daughter and prayed that her concerns were imaginary. A trick of the mind. Jealousy, perhaps. The only thing she knew for sure was how she felt every time the man came within a few feet of her.

Gray Hillman wasn't your average man-species. Anyone could see that, and not because he was well-dressed, confident, spitefully good-looking, and smelled good. Nor was it his flawless creamy bronze skin and affable smile. These physical characteristics were merely a ploy to make you believe he was harmless.

In her early days as a district attorney, it was always the unassuming types who'd been the most unnerving. The obvious ones didn't scare you, because you knew what to expect—you could see them coming a mile away. It was the type who could put on a good face, the boys next door, Ted Bundy types who shook you to your core. Their sympathetic smiles and good looks masked heinous criminals underneath.

Admittedly, she'd run every background check upwards and sideways on Gray Hillman, only to find a spotless record. Not so much as a parking ticket. He was a shepherd of good fortune. He looked good on paper as well as in person. Delma couldn't say one bad thing out loud about the man. He was a catch by any standards.

Add to that the fact his grandfather owned a good portion of southern Georgia, which turned out to be a convenient location for an oil pipeline. The Hillman name had become synonymous with real estate. The second generation owned hundreds of acres of land, selling it off in bits and pieces. There was no end to the Hillman brood creating new money, until one day a catastrophic hurricane destroyed the pipeline. Along with the destruction came a megalawsuit that led directly back to the Hillman fortune.

Overnight, they'd lost it all. While the rest of the offspring fell into drugs and lazy drifting, Gray Hillman followed his passion to practice law. Delma knew it took perseverance to get through law school. So he was smart, handsome, and self-motivated. That's why it pained her to be so uncomfortable around him. Her instincts spoke loud and clear, and would not be ignored. There were snakes in his closet, and she prayed they didn't get out to bite her sweet daughter.

"Mother, are you ready?" Keisha stood at the bedroom door, keys in hand with her overly large handbag on her elbow. Delma didn't understand this new fashion statement. The smaller the pocketbook, the sexier a woman appeared. She was no guru on the subject, but that much she knew. Now it was the bigger, the better. Little did they know they all looked like they were going off to war with their duffle bags filled with life's weaponry. Nothing sexy about carrying around baggage.

Delma had to stop herself. Lately, all she did was criticize, analyze, and marginalize every single thing. Maybe it was time to take the estrogen her doctor had prescribed. "I'm ready." She slipped on her comfortable flats.

"Are you okay?" Keisha reached out a hand and pressed it to Delma's forehead the same way she used to when Keisha was a child. Cherry cough drops and Campbell's soup were a main staple in their house. Delma had loved taking care of her daughter. There had been no greater joy.

"Didn't get enough sleep, but I'm fine."

"Do you want to postpone, Mom? It's okay. Nikki is going to meet me there, too, so I'll have her opinion as well."

Delma wouldn't dream of being absent while Keisha picked out her wedding gown. Regardless of how she felt about this wedding, it was her baby's time to shine, and she was going to be there to the end. Just like always. "I'm fine. Let's go."

Something in the Way She Moves

Delma

Keisha spun around in the long white gown, her bare shoulders smooth as the day she was born.

"Look at you. Just look at you." Delma took a cleansing breath and tried to count backwards until she could no longer contain it. She was sick of tears, the constant influx of emotion she'd given in to every time her daughter took one more step toward the altar.

She couldn't help but fight back the flashbacks of Keisha bloodied as a baby in the backseat of that pimp's car, where Trevelle had left her. That memory haunted her now. Delma had to make a snap decision that could have cost her career if anyone ever found out she took the baby for her own. Delma couldn't leave that child, not after all the suffering she saw throughout her life in the court system, with children being placed in the hands of incompetent women who would only perpetuate the ghetto reality generation after generation. Well, she was going to save one in her lifetime, really save one, and that was Keisha.

The gown made her radiant beauty blossom. Keisha was smart and successful, at the brink of the happiest day of her life, yet Delma was in turmoil. No way could she contain or share her emotions with anyone in the room. It was like a reservoir filling up to capacity, with the water having nowhere else to go but spill over the dam and gush everywhere uncontrollably. "I love you, baby." There went the floodgates again—it was really borderline hysterical, happy and sad all at the same time.

"Mother?" Keisha was scolding now. "You're scaring me." Her words only made Delma hiccup and sob more.

"You're just so beautiful. You're getting married."

"I'm about ready to start crying myself," Nikki said, fake-dabbing her eyes. She was Gray's assistant but also Keisha's NBF or "new best friend," as they'd explained. "What happened to your old best friend, or OBF?" Delma wanted to know. She had three other bridesmaids: Jasmine, Yolanda, the girl with the nose ring, and Sara—the one with hips that could take flight and who only dated rich white guys. Where were they on this special day? It seemed everyone who'd meant anything to Keisha was slowly being weeded out. Delma's greatest fear was that she would be next.

"Miss Delma, don't think of it as losing a daughter—think of it as gaining a son-in-law." NBF sat patiently next to Delma and stroked her back.

"Wise words." She patted the young woman on her knee when she really felt like pinching her. That was the dumbest thing she'd ever heard. Who was ever happy to be gaining an in-law? Especially a son-in-law who sucked all the available air out of a room the minute he entered. She had to get herself together. This air of defeat was uncharacteristic for Delma J. Hawkins.

She moved to Keisha and straightened out the six-foot train. "She's getting on my nerves," Delma said quietly, but loud enough for Keisha's ears. It was all too much. These new people in their lives were closing in on them. Hadn't it always been just the two of them and they did just fine?

Had to be all her fault. She'd made the first move by marrying Hudson, her law clerk of twenty years, giving the impression that she needed someone besides Keisha in her life. Giving the impression that she wanted distance and space. She'd married Hudson because she was tired of waking up alone each morning and couldn't

see fit living shacked up like hippies. She and Hudson had been com-
rades in the trenches for twenty years. Hudson was her rock and
support, getting her through court dates of baby mamas versus
knuckleheads, day in and day out. Most of all, he loved her like nobody's business. They deserved to take the next step.

Keisha and Gray's relationship was completely the opposite.
They had no history, no stories. Real friendship took time.

"Miss Delma, I have some tissues in my purse." Nikki dug around,
pulling out a fresh pack of Kleenex.

"I'm fine, child." Delma said, fighting off the urge to release the
sorrow building in her chest.

"Mother, if you weep on this gown, I'm going to have to buy it—
and I'm not sure this is the one."

"Oh yeah, that's the one." The voice came from over Delma's
shoulder. She turned around to see the man of the hour. He flipped
his cashmere jacket from one arm to the other, then clapped his
hands in appreciation. "You are radiant. Tell me that's the one."

"Gray!" Keisha crossed her arms over her chest as if she were
naked.

"Please." He grinned, shaking his head. "Tell me you're not believing in some old-school superstition. Next thing I know, you'll
have us jumping the broom in dashikis and crowns of cloth. No,
baby." His honey-clear eyes filled with amusement. "We're in the
here and now, and it's all good. By the way, knowing how beautiful
you look, I could die tomorrow a happy man."

"Gray, don't talk like that."

"I'm serious—you look amazing."

Delma stood up, though it had taken a moment to get fully
straightened. "There's nothing wrong with tradition. The groom
waiting to see his bride look like a bride until the actual wedding
day is a good respectful tradition." She leaned side to side, then gave
herself a lower-back massage.

"Mama D, it's old-fashioned and archaic, and you know it. Keisha picked out my tux, yet I don't have a say in what gown she wears? Come on, you see how it's a little sexist? Shouldn't the groom have a tiny bit of say?" He squeezed two fingers together.

Keisha nodded, slowly dropping her guard and lowering her arms. Gray had a way of talking that made everything look easy. Everything he said sounded like it made complete sense. Delma was sure he could sell ice to Eskimos with a 1,000 percent markup. The combination of good looks and a killer smile was intoxicating, and the worst thing about it: He knew it.

"You're right, Gray." Keisha faced him, taking the full flare of fabric with her. "Your opinion is really the only one that matters. What do you think?"

"Like I said—amazing." He smiled with approval. "But let's see the rest of our choices."

Delma's stomach lurched, pulling into a knot. She shifted left and then right hoping to alleviate what might've been a simple case of flatulence. Stomach problems had been regular . . . ever since the engagement.

Nikki stood up. "You're not going to be needing me, then," she said, taking a peek at her cell phone. "I have an appointment, and it's clear across town. I better get a move on." She blew a kiss in no certain direction and then tried to hug Delma. *Tried* is the operative word. Delma wasn't feeling all the fake and phony love in the room. "One big happy family" felt like a noose around her neck.

"An appointment, is that what we're calling dates nowadays?" Delma asked. "More of what I'm out of touch with, I guess."

Nikki's eyes shifted side to side. "A date? I didn't say I had a date."

Having spent enough time looking for the truth in petulant defendants' faces, Delma knew when someone was trying to shake her. "You spent the entire afternoon talking about the gorgeous new man who just happens to be a prince in his country—what was the name of it again?" Delma snapped her fingers a couple of times for recollection.

"No . . . I wasn't serious." Nikki cut her eyes toward Gray, then back to her smartphone. "I have a hair appointment. Really, Morell Evans is like the Prince of Hair. If you're late, he makes you very sorry." She hurried, picking up her satchel and straightening her too-tight pencil skirt. A cool breeze was left by her swift exit.

Delma was an expert observer. "She's a sweet girl, way too sweet to be single." Gray Hillman was uncomfortable with the subject. His practiced, unfazed expression only confirmed her suspicion. Those two were the ones with history and, Delma would bet, a few stories to tell.

Keisha spoke, but kept her eyes on herself in the mirror. "I don't know what that was about. You're right, Mom. She was giggling in the phone like a schoolgirl. When I asked her who she was talking about, she said her prince—literally—and went on to tell me how they met and his mega-millions' worth from an oil-rich part of Africa."

"I heard the exact same thing." All the while, Delma kept a peripheral watch on Gray. He seemed to find the wall more interesting than the conversation. "Wonder why she's changed her story. What do you think, Gray?"

"The only thing I care about is the precious minutes wasted discussing my assistant's love life. Time is always money, my love." He approached Keisha and kissed her bare shoulder. "And though you are priceless, I really have to get back to the office."

"I thought you wanted to see my choices," Keisha protested, bustling the full skirt of the gown. "Now I don't know which dress to choose. I'm going to be worried that you won't like it more than this one."

"Then the choice is made, isn't it?" He brushed against her ear. Their reflection in the mirror was wedding-portrait ready.

Delma's stomach lurched and bubbled. "I . . . going to the restroom." She took a step and realized her water-swollen feet hurt. In fact, her head, eyes, neck, shoulders—hell, every part of her body—wilted with fatigue and exhaustion. Pretending was a lot of work. Pretending to be happy when she was not. Hudson had begged her last night to just come out with it, tell the universe how she felt and be free. Not a chance. She'd even drawn a mock line across her lips to vow her silence.

"Bathroom," Delma squeaked out before moving toward the center of the bridal salon. "Bathroom," she said this time to the consultant sitting at the round glass table.

She eyed Delma over her spectacles. "Oh, yes, past the back wall, through the center of the salon."

Delma looked up where Keisha and Gray were still huddled. She'd have to pass them to get to the restroom. "Please, this big ole place only has *one* bathroom? Is that what you're telling me?"

Arlene raised an eyebrow, curious but not swayed. "The stress of weddings can do that to you. Bathroom." She pointed.

Delma waddled carefully, keeping her head down.

"Mother, are you all right?"

"Fine, sweetie."

The walls were thin as paper. Delma could hear Gray's voice and then Keisha's soft agreeing laughter. His influence over her daughter was toxic, as if Keisha had lost all the good sense Delma planted in the child. What had happened to her independent, no-nonsense daughter? Led around by the pinkie by this man, like she'd swallowed silly pills.

She should speak, as Hudson advised. Say her piece and then go on and let the chips fall where they may. Say what? Delma had to ask herself—exactly what was it she wanted to point out? The fact her daughter had fallen in love with a real man who wasn't afraid to make decisions and take the lead. The fact Gray Hillman had too much testosterone. Too much take. Not enough give. The type unwilling to bend. "His way or no way" usually ended in the wife being beaten down and squashed to fit neatly into his box of wishes.

Delma flushed, washed up, and situated herself. She leaned in to the mirror and observed the redness in her eyes from lack of sleep. The deep lines curved around her mouth. She was tired. Even having taken a month off from work to help organize the wedding hadn't helped. Hudson had convinced her it'd be like a vacation, a much-needed vacation. More like a perpetual nightmare. Morning to dusk, it was all about Gray Hillman.

"Mother, you all right?" The knock was a surprise. Especially since she'd felt invisible. Surprised that Keisha had even noticed she was missing.

"I'm fine, sweetie. Be right out."

When she opened the door, to her amazement the room was clear of Gray Hillman. She smiled to herself and wondered if she'd made him disappear with the will of her thoughts. And if she could do it here, could it work anywhere—say, on the day of their grand nuptials? Just a thought, wish, and a prayer—and poof, like smoke . . . he could disappear.

Bad News Travels Fast

Trevelle

Airic and I sat together in silence, reading the morning paper. We had very little to say to each other besides the necessary good morning, hello, or good night. Still, I had a feeling it was going to be a good day. After all I'd been put through in the last twenty-four hours, I deserved something to go right.

"More coffee, missus?" Marcella was already pouring before I could answer. "And for you, sir?" Airic put his hand out to defend his cup. He drank only one serving of coffee and didn't like to readjust the milk and sugar once it was perfect. So of course, the hot coffee landed on his hand.

"Damn it." His gritted teeth were enough to make me smile.

"Sorry." Marcella rushed to get a towel.

"Get him some ice," I said, still perusing the paper. "That works to keep it from blistering." I gave up on the newspaper and picked up the remote control to the built-in television. I flipped from one station to the other until I saw the caption. POPULAR TELEVANGELIST'S HUSBAND CAUGHT ON TAPE.

"Oh my goodness." I turned up the volume. "Oh my gosh, what are we going to do? My life is ruined!"

He took the remote and turned it up even louder. His face flushed with anger.

"The tape is definitely Airic Fisher with a young woman named

Chandra McKinney. The young lady was three days shy of her eigh-teenth birthday, according to the date stamp on the tape. Authorities are looking into filing statutory rape charges."

I covered my mouth in shock. This time true, paralyzing shock left me stammering, "What . . . what are they saying? Of course she was eighteen. I hired her—she filled out an application."

"She must've lied about her age," Airic said woefully. "My God." His face fell into his hands. "You've got to show them the applica-tion, where she lied."

This was not supposed to be happening. This was not the plan. I stood up and paced.

Airic reached out for my hand. "I'm so sorry. I don't know how all of this has happened, how everything could've been so perfect one moment and then fall apart the next."

"If everything was so perfect, you wouldn't have slept with her in the first place. This is your entire fault. Everything is your fault."

Marcella made a point of letting the dishes clang in the dish-washer rack when she closed it to remind us she was still in the room. Her eyes darted in our direction. "You need anything else, missus?"

"No, we're fine."

She left quickly, not wanting to hear the rest of our heated argu-ment. I faced Airic directly. "This changes everything. We can't rec-oncile under this type of scrutiny. I have a million-dollar empire to think of. If I'm seen as a wife who would stick by a man who likes young girls, I'll be ruined like that." I snapped my finger. "You know I love you. You know I do, but this changes everything. You're going to have to move out, just until this blows over. Then we can start over."

Airic calmly walked over and poured his coffee down the sink. As he was walking past, he said one last thing: "I'm glad it's over. None of this is worth it. There won't be a new beginning, because I'm sick of you."

For some reason, it hurt me to the core. I reached out to touch his shoulder, and he jerked away.

"I beg your pardon. How are you going to act? You're the one who slept with an underage girl. Am I the one who sent that disc to the news media?"

"Who knows? Maybe you did. I've seen you do worse things. I know who you really are underneath your white angel robe. I know you're a lying, manipulating control freak who can't stand when things don't go your way."

With that, I reached for the butter knife that sat on the kitchen table. Airic twisted my wrist until it fell to the floor. When I tried to swing my fists, he put out his arm, knocking me off balance. My head hit the table. Pain sprang from the side of my face, and I cried out. Airic tried to help me up.

"Stay away!"

Marcella ran in to see Airic leaning over me. She went into protection mode. Her short arms came down with powerful blows. "No, stay away from Missus!"

Airic pushed Marcella, trying to get away from the attack dog. She began cussing at him in Spanish. I stayed on the ground with my arms over my head. Airic made his escape. Marcella had surprising strength. "I call *la policía*." She rushed off before I could stop her. As if I needed more drama than what I'd already created for myself.

Within minutes, the security guard from downstairs, accompanied by two police officers, entered the penthouse.

"Since when do you not knock before entering someone's home?" I had a pack of frozen peas pressed against the side of my face. Every time I tried to rise up from the chaise, my head went into a dizzying spin. "Oh God."

"Call an ambulance," one of the officers said to the security guard.

"No, I'm fine."

"She's very dizzy," Marcella added. "Maybe you need to go."

"Where's your husband, ma'am?"

"He's in his room packing. We had a fight. It was an accident."

"Mister." Marcella pointed at Airic's bedroom door. "He hit her," she said with conviction. "I see everything."

"Did he hit you?" the square-jaw officer with arms big enough to swing on asked gently. His hands rested on his belt, too close to his gun.

"I would like for you all to leave. Please. Please, everything is fine. Really, we've settled everything. It was an accident."

Airic was rolling a small suitcase behind him with his overcoat in hand. He looked from the officers to me lying on the chaise like a damsel in distress. "Oh, what now? Telling more lies? She attacked me with a knife. I defended myself by pushing her away. That's all."

"Sir, you want to put your hands behind your back." The thick officer said this with pleasure, grateful for Airic's arrogance.

"Wait a minute. I just told you what happened."

"It was an accident. Please, don't do this." I must've sounded like the same old story officers always hear once they showed up for a domestic abuse call. Always crying it was an accident or he didn't mean it or *I fell*. And I really had fallen, only with a little shove as he defended himself.

I felt so guilty for all the trouble I'd caused in that moment, watching my husband being escorted off in handcuffs. Yes, he'd slept with my assistant. Yes, he'd threatened me—extortion, if you wanted to give it a proper name—but he didn't deserve jail. It was a filthy place. I'd spent enough time ministering to inmates to know nothing good happened in those places. Murder, rape, or abuse of a child were the only real offenses that deserved that kind of treatment.

Marcella followed the men to the door, then gratefully shut it and locked the bolt. She dusted her hands off and then said a small prayer in Spanish—either that or a curse.

I knew immediately what I must do.

She saw me trying to reach the phone on the glass coffee table. "No, no, you stay." She handed me the phone.

I held the phone to my chest and prayed for the room to stop spinning. I dialed. "Eddie, I have a situation. My husband, Airic Fisher, has been arrested. Please handle his bond. Make sure he doesn't spend a night in jail."

I listened for only a moment and didn't like what I was hearing. "No, not now. I don't care what those tapes have to say. Right now, I'm just praying for a minute of peace." I closed my eyes, and the swirling in my head quickened. I leaned over the side of the couch and threw up. That was the last straw for Marcella. The paramedics arrived quickly. I was carted off in a gurney with the sound of cameras clicking. I'd wanted attention. Sometimes you just have to be careful what you wish for.

Knock, Knock—
Who's There?

Venus

Like clockwork, every other weekend Airic showed up, no matter how many dreams I'd had of his demise. No matter if I lied and said Mya had a birthday party to attend, Girl Scout meeting, or tummy-ache, he was ringing the bell by 6 P.M. Friday evening, exactly as the court order stated. I dreaded these visits. He would ring the doorbell while Trevelle sat in their white Jaguar, keeping watch in case the ex-rapper and crazy mama made any false moves. Although I had to admit, lately Trevelle had fallen down on her job. She'd been a no-show for the last few visits. I was beginning to think there was trouble in paradise. I wouldn't be surprised. That they'd lasted two years was shocking.

Mya and I sat in the living room, waiting for the doomsday bell to ring. She played on her toy piano, and I played with her hair. Correction, there wasn't much playing involved. This was serious business, requiring much attention to detail. Every strand of hair required spritz, gel, and deep stroking. I didn't dare send her alone with Airic in her natural state, for fear he or his wife would stop off and get her a kiddie perm while they were out. Perfect hair was a requirement for Trevelle—hers and everyone else's if they were going to be in her presence. Needless to say, my unrelaxed hair made it hard for Trevelle to maintain more than a second or two of eye contact with me. In fact, on the days she was coming I made it a point to forget the conditioning gel altogether, giving my hair a large moon eclipse effect just to get under her skin.

I didn't want her mean-mugging my baby with the same disdain she showed me. So for Mya's sake, I kneaded, combed, and brushed her hair until a silky shine arose on each spiraled strand.

Mya banged away on the colorful keys, drowning out the television. "Mommy, want to hear a song?"

"Absolutely."

She pounded away.

"Beautiful, sweetie. What's the name of that song?"

"It's called, 'Mya's Happy.'"

I leaned over and gave a soft nuzzle on the side of her face. "I'm happy, too." All too true. I really couldn't have been more thankful in spite of the losses of the past. Life had been on the upswing. When it all boiled down to what was left in the scalding pot of life, having my husband and daughter was my only real joy. I felt like the lucky one for a change.

"Okay, your turn. I'll make you a song." Mya's long four-and-a-half-year-old fingers covered every key as she commenced with a new creation.

Not more than a few seconds later, she asked, "Did you like it?"

I wish I could've answered, but I was too busy staring at the evening news on the television screen, my mouth gaped open. On the flat screen was Airic handcuffed, being placed into a police car like an episode of *Cops*. My hand fumbled for the remote. It slipped out of my grasp. The caption underneath read, TELEVANGELIST'S HUSBAND CHARGED WITH STATUTORY RAPE AND DOMESTIC BATTERY.

"Mommy, did you like it?" She twisted around to face me.

"Yes. I loved it, play it again, sweetie." My hands were gummed with the banana hibiscus cream I'd used on Mya's hair. This time I got both hands around the remote, but not soon enough.

Mya stopped playing when she caught the image on the plasma screen. Of course, she recognized Mr. Entertainment. That's what

Jake and I called him because that's all he was good for while we did the hard work, the real work. Late-night shifts, cleanup on aisle two after she'd been fed too much ice cream and cotton candy from their trips to amusement parks and movie theaters. Airic had never had to sit up all night monitoring a 102-degree fever, cough, or monsters under the bed.

Surely Mya recognized him, whether he was carrying bags of theater popcorn or amusement park cotton candy—or in this case, wearing handcuffs.

I finally managed to turn the television off.

The colorful keys started playing once again. I breathed a sigh of relief. She didn't ask any questions. Though there was a bit more urgency in her song, a few keys pounded hard for good measure. I went back to concentrating on Mya's hair, then stopped suddenly staring at the goo all over my hands. I wiped them on a towel then pulled the tight bands loose. I guessed Airic wasn't coming. The image of him in handcuffs, his head pressed down into a squad car played over with the pertinent questions: What? When? Where?

"Okay, sweetie, all done." I scooped her up from her armpits, helping her to her feet.

"You didn't finish my hair, Mommy."

"I know, sweetie, but I think it looks prettier this way." I fluffed it out and let the spirals move out of control.

I didn't wish Airic any ill will; however, I couldn't help but feel a little reprieve. After what I'd just seen on the news, I figured this would be a weekend he'd probably skip. The relief of not having to deal with Jake's dissension and Mya being caught in the middle of it all gave me a minute of peace. "Give me a kiss," I said, puckering up.

Mya stuck out her lips and closed her eyes.

The doorbell interrupted our lovefest. *No . . . it can't be.* I tiptoed through the foyer and pressed my eye against the peephole. Standing at the door was Airic. His usually pale skin was flushed, since the temperature outside was wintry cool. His hands rested in his jacket pockets, posed for nonchalance—but from the way his jaw clenched, he was the picture of annoyance. He knocked hard, startling me because my face had been pressed too close.

I opened the door. "I thought . . . I thought you might be detained." Shoot, I meant to say held up, or freakishly late, not sure what to say next. "Did someone post bail?" Darn it, that hadn't come out right.

"Can I come in?" he asked.

I was envisioning Jake coming down the stairs, turning the corner, seeing Airic sitting on his couch and not being happy about it. I was thinking *not a good idea*, but I pushed the door wide for his entrance.

"You saw the news." He cut his eyes from me to Mya, then back in my direction. "It's not what it looks like."

"I saw you." Mya held my hand slightly tighter than usual. "Why'd-day-take-you-away?"

"How's my girl?" Airic kneeled down, offering a kiss. Mya pulled back. "We're going to have a great time this weekend."

Mya skirted behind my leg, knowing the okeydoke when she saw it. She'd started school six weeks ago, boldly claiming her brave new world. She was hardly shy. Every day was an adventure as she tested the waters of independence. This was the most reserved I'd seen her in some time.

"I guess that's a good question. What happened? Is it true?" I finally chimed in. No need to let a preschooler do all the investigating.

"I don't think it's something we should talk about in front of Mya."

"Little too late for that," I said before hearing footsteps coming down the stairs and then Jake's voice before he saw us.

"Babe, did you see the news? Oh man, you'll never believe this." Jake stopped in his tracks. One side of his face still had shaving foam. The other side smooth and dewy. He used the towel thrown over his shoulder to wipe himself completely clean. Another towel was wrapped around his hips. Tonight was actually date night. Legend was being babysat by a new conquest he'd met in Atlanta. So it was going to be just Jake and me.

Certainly we took advantage of the visitation weekends. As much as we didn't want her gone, we made the best of it, forcing ourselves out for dinner and drinks. Come Saturday morning, we usually lay in bed till noon, pretending to enjoy the peace and silence. By Sunday we shared awkward silence and sparse conversation, anticipating Mya's safe return.

"Okay, listen, honey, I was just about to talk to Airic. Maybe you can take Mya upstairs." Silence was supposed to be golden. Here in the Johnston-Parson household, it was an indication of disharmony, most times the precursor to a brooding war. Like now, the words unspoken between Jake and Airic was like a stream of flammable liquid. I stepped between the two before someone struck a match.

"Nah, whatever he has to say, he can say in front of all of us. You know, one big happy family." Jake folded his arms over his bare chest. His muscular arms gleamed from the fresh shower.

"Jake . . ."

"Go ahead, let's hear your version," he said. "I just saw your face plastered on the news with the words *statutory rape charge*. Not good company for my daughter."

"Your daughter?"

"I didn't stutter, and don't ever doubt it." Jake stood firm, adjusting the towel snug around his waist. Still he was in no position to be picking fights. Naked wrestling would definitely be considered a demerit, since everyone was keeping score.

"Stop it, please. Let's not forget Mya is here. We're the adults," I half whispered. "Let's act like it."

"Yes, I think that's wise," Airic said, extending his hand toward Mya. "I'll have her back early Saturday. I have to leave town on Sunday."

Jake pushed his hand back. "Nah, man, I don't think so. We're going to have to put a stall on the visits until . . . well, until whenever." He rested his case.

I could see the anger rising. Airic's earlobes turning a bright pink. Jake simply puffed up like he was ready and definitely waiting.

"You don't know any of the facts, and frankly it's none of your business. I have visitation, regardless of your opinion. You don't have that authority. I have a court order that says I have every other weekend. This is my weekend."

"Oh, so my run-in with the law had nothing to do with you trying to get custody? And you didn't try to use everything you could against us? Now those little details don't matter?" Jake slapped his hand into his palm. "You are charged with rape? Wait, I forgot about the domestic battery. You're a bona fide criminal. If you think you're taking my daughter out of here, you're crazy."

"Okay, enough," I said.

"I'm not leaving here without Mya," Airic said flatly.

"Oh, you're leaving. Either walking out or carried. Your choice."

Mya rushed behind Jake. It was pretty clear her decision was not to leave, and I knew Jake would do whatever was necessary to honor it. More important, that towel wasn't very secure. It was time to intervene.

"No." I held up my hands, one for each of them. "Airic, please, Mya doesn't want to go. Please, outside." I opened the door. "Go!" I ordered.

"Don't let the doorknob . . . Well, you know the rest," Jake said with a smirk only to add more gasoline to the flame.

I closed the door, grateful for the wood-and-glass separation, even though I knew Jake was still hovering by the door, listening.

"Look, I'm sorry about everything that's happened to you. But Jake is right. We don't know the details. I think it's best until you're cleared of wrongdoing to suspend visitation." I was starting to sound like a lawyer. A bad sign that I'd spent way too much time in too many courtrooms.

"I didn't rape anyone. The young woman in the tape was Trevelle's assistant. She seduced me. I only found out she was three days shy of her eighteenth birthday when the authorities came knocking on my door. She gave the tape to authorities because Trevelle and I had reconciled. She was jealous." He dropped his head. "I should've known better, but I was so hurt over everything Trevelle had done. I was a fool. . . ." He seemed to be babbling now, and I had no idea what he was talking about.

I touched his sleeve. "I'm sure it will be okay. All right?" My neck craned upward to get a feel for his guilt or innocence. Not much about Airic had changed over the years. Grayish-brown hair with no delineation as to which was gray and which was sandy brown. He was close to fifty by now or already there. I'd lost count of his exact age, as I'd lost count of how many things about him irked me to no end. Like his air of superiority or the way his Adam's apple bobbed incessantly before he spoke, or his need to enunciate the more the other person didn't.

"As far as me being arrested for domestic battery, it's not true. Trevelle told the officers it was an accident. I was defending myself from her knife-wielding, and those asinine idiots still arrested me."

"She tried to stab you?" I swallowed the information, making more of a case for Mya not to be around the craziness.

"She did, but it was a butter knife. Things just got out of control. I said some things she didn't deserve. Trevelle doesn't deserve this," he said quietly.

Oh right, like she's an innocent lamb. Hey, did you hear the one about her having her baby in the back of her pimp's car then leaving it for dead?

He looked so dejected, I couldn't add insult to injury. I shrugged my shoulders. "I'm sure Trevelle will find peace with prayer," I said, and wondered if I was becoming a talking zombie. Lately nothing I said matched my thoughts. Always a quest to appease and avoid conflict. This kinder, gentler version was starting to wear thin.

"I'm really sorry you're going through this, Airic. Let's just say we postpone the visit this time and play it by ear. I think Mya's really shaken up. Next weekend she'll be good as new, but right now she seems a little rattled."

"You're right. I shouldn't have come here in this mood, but seeing my daughter is the only happiness I have left right now."

Now that was funny. The old me would've fallen down laughing. After all, it was outright funny, coming from the same man who didn't even want to hold Mya when she was born. Did I dare remind him how he'd refused to see her if he couldn't have me as part of the package. But instead I nodded. "I know the feeling. She's my joy, too."

The overcast sky broke slowly to reveal a full, bright moon. Airic squinted toward the light as if looking for his own break, a minute to take in a breath. "I'll give it till next weekend," he said. "Should I go in and apologize to Mya, for upsetting her?"

"No . . . no. No need. I'll explain." I heard Jake move away from the door, finally satisfied.

Jake

He'd settled Mya in the kitchen with a hastily poured glass of milk and a couple of errant Oreo cookies. He planned on cleaning up the spill later. Eavesdropping on Airic had been far more important. Eavesdropping, listening against the door best he could without casting a shadow. He then tiptoed away before Venus headed back inside.

Airic Fisher had become a thorn in his side since the day he showed up demanding parental rights to the child he'd abandoned at birth. Jake had been there from day one and still legally had no foothold. His name wasn't on the birth certificate, simple as that. During their court battle, he'd desperately hoped the DNA test came back with him being the father. His wish had been granted—only to find out someone had falsified the results. They'd yet to find out who. That's when he knew for sure he couldn't care less about the biology of the situation.

He'd never known unconditional love until the moment he set

eyes on Mya. He was there the day she was born. He would never forget the way her tiny hand wrapped around his pinkie finger as if to say, *It's you and me, Pops.*

The laws of the world were archaic and bent on preserving the rights of those who didn't deserve them. He could've legally adopted Mya had he not been focused on saving his company and defending himself from a stint in prison for a murder he didn't commit. Let's just say things got out of hand. The window of opportunity closed tight, and next thing they knew, Airic was knocking on it with his face pressed against the glass every other weekend. Him arriving to pick up Mya was a constant reminder of Jake's past mistakes. How not being proactive, and resting on assumptions left everything to chance. This, too, he'd planned to fix. No more missed opportunities.

"What'd he say?" He wiped the puddle of milk from the tabletop. Mya had eaten her cookies and was long gone to play in her fairy-tale bedroom.

"I convinced him to give it a rest and come back next weekend."

"Why?" Jake shrugged his bare shoulders. "He's still going to be a rapist and wife abuser next weekend, and the next."

"Honey . . . enough. I don't want to talk about this anymore. This day has been long and crazy enough."

It dawned on Jake. "Did he ever raise his hand to you? Try anything crazy?"

Silence.

"No, right, I guess I know better than that."

She eventually spoke, taking the sponge out of his hand. "Airic blames the leak of the tape on the jilted lover. Sounds more like something Trevelle would do to me. That woman . . ." She shook her head. "Treacherous."

"Hey, I don't give a damn about Trevelle or whatever she did to drive him into somebody else's arms. The fact remains, he slept with an underage girl. He's a criminal."

"I wasn't trying to make excuses."

"Yes, you were."

She dropped the sponge into the sink and put the milk back in the refrigerator. "Good night."

"Okay, wait. I'm sorry. I just hate when you defend him."

"I don't defend him."

"You don't realize it, but you do. A lot."

"Sometimes I just feel sorry for him."

He threw up his hands to say *exhibit A.*

"Because he's so pitiful. I mean, really. He's fifty years old and still can't get it right. This is his third marriage."

"Well, maybe he'll let you be the maid of honor at his fourth." Jake left her standing in the kitchen.

Not more than a few seconds later, he was back. "Observe this, understand it, take a picture—I don't give a—" Her raised brow slowed his pitch. "All I'm saying is this: I don't trust a man who has to be manipulated into loving his daughter. He has no spine. The only reason he's showing up now is because Trevelle thought it would be a good idea to have a picture-perfect family. I never did like that punk. I don't trust him, and he's not going to spend a minute alone with Mya until he's cleared of these charges. I don't care if his wife is a manipulative scheming liar. I don't care if he's innocent as a newborn. His ass is cut off."

This time he left for real, taking the stairs two at a time. He was still dressed in nothing but a towel. That was about to change because he was out of there.

"I have to go out," was all he said as he came out of the bathroom fully dressed, shaved, and smelling as good as he looked.

"Where're you going?"

"I'm meeting Legend in the District. We're going to talk and have drinks." He pulled out his Brunos and slid his feet into the expensive shoes.

"And this was planned when—considering this is our official date night?"

"Not much of a date."

"Please stay home with me." She blinked slowly, then rested her hand on his chest. Asking nicely was a ploy. It wasn't her style.

"Is this a trap?" He pulled her down on his lap.

"Is it working?" Her hands slipped under his linen shirt. She kissed the opening where a silver cross lay on his chest, then ran her tongue up to his neck.

He wrapped his arms around her waist and pressed his face into her hair. The products she used made her smell like freshly baked sugar cookies.

"Yes, I'd say it's working." Like a moth to a flame, he met her lips. He loved the soft wetness of her mouth as it rose to full bloom against his own. He held her head, caressed the base of her neck like there was no time limit.

He eased her T-shirt over her head, exposing her nipples to the cool air. He licked and nibbled on her chest then moved to the flatness of her belly where only a year earlier she'd carried his son. He pressed his face deep and inhaled. He tried not to think about getting her pregnant, though that was his wish. He traced the thin scar above her pubic line and lingered too long.

"Just make love to me, babe," she whispered.

She knew what he was thinking, reading his thoughts. She knew how badly he wanted a second try. She cupped his face with her hands, bringing him up toward her. "Fuck me," she breathed out near his ear. Meaning for him to shut out the rest of the noise. Giving him permission to take and receive.

A reckless flow surged as if he were being granted access for the first time. Greedy impatience took over. He lifted her, straddling her legs around his waist. She thought he was carrying her to the bed, but went in the opposite direction, up against the wall. She panted with anticipation. He pushed every inch of himself inside her. She held on for dear life while he delved deep into the warmth of her skin.

"Promise me," he moaned, elevating her with each upward stroke. His voice cracked from the ache and pleasure at the same time.

"I promise," she whispered. "I . . . to love you forever," she managed to finish against the crush of his weight. That's all he needed to hear. He poured his soul into her body until there was nothing left.

Somehow they'd made it to the bed. Jake stirred when he felt her hand stroke his shoulder. Post-sex pillow talk was the most revealing, the most honest. The goal of getting the prize was all out of the way.

Her perfect time to ask, "Is there something on your mind, baby? I mean, besides Airic . . . this whole thing with Legend being here seems a little strange."

He touched her face and leaned in for a kiss. Before she knew it, the moistness of his mouth had her breasts. Sucking and licking one at a time like they were his favorite flavor of ice cream. She scooted down into the softness of the sheets.

He teased and tantalized every hot zone she had until she was delirious with heat. The friction of his fingers and skillful tongue pushed her right to the edge until she was begging. She clamped her eyes shut. The climax came so hard, tears sprang from her eyes.

Jake rolled over and pulled her trembling body close underneath his arm. "You still feel like talking?" he asked. No answer. He didn't think so.

Till Death Do Us Part
Trevelle

I picked up the receiver after confirming the caller ID listed someone I could trust. Thank God it was Keisha calling. She was the only
person who truly cared about me. My daughter was a guiding light
who kept me from falling into the dark places in my mind. Everyone
believed that if you were a professor of faith, there were no demons.
When, in fact, the demons I faced were the strongest demons of
all—the ones that challenged God's children to prove Him wrong.

"Sweetie, I'm fine," I answered before she had a chance to voice
her concern.

"It's all everyone is talking about. Why didn't you call me? I
have to hear about it on the news."

"I'll tell you everything. Do you think you could come over?" I
stood in front of the mirror and leaned closer. The swelling was already going down. The hospital released me the next morning, sur-
mising that I had a very mild concussion. The doctor said the only
answer was plenty of rest. The bruises around my right temple deepened slightly but wouldn't last long.

Keisha had a heart of gold to forgive all my past mistakes. I'd
given birth to her and thought she'd died right there in my arms.
Delma Hawkins, an assistant district attorney at the time, found us.
She used her position to kidnap my child without a trace. She let me
believe the infant had died then erased her existence and raised

Keisha as her own. I'd never forgive her for trying to keep Keisha for herself, for being selfish and coldhearted.

I got settled to wait for my daughter's arrival on the damask high-back couch and flipped the remote. The news was hard to avoid, since it was on nearly every channel. The video of Airic being driven away in the squad car made me sad but relieved. Especially after Eddie Ray played the newest tapes. Airic had been planning to meet Chandra the entire time, even after I'd forgiven him and invited him back in. So maybe his being arrested was what he needed to have sense slapped into him—all for his own good.

That would teach him. Maybe on our next go-round he would understand I was not one to be fooled with. I'd canceled all his credit cards, removed his name from the accounts, and gone forward with the changed locks on both our homes. I'd have to take a real stand on these issues publicly. I'd already had to turn down four network news interview requests. Before I was ready to speak, I wanted all my ducks in a row.

The light tap at my bedroom door was Marcella. "Missus?" She let herself in without waiting for my reply. "Can I get you anything before I leave?" She fluffed the pillows, then paused in the midst of motion. I knew she was staring at the television. She continued on with a smooth hand over the linens. "Your bed is ready, missus."

Marcella left, gently closing the door behind her. I didn't want to fall asleep now with Keisha on her way, but the sedative the doctor had prescribed was setting in. I feared falling asleep, the very reason I slept alone. Even after being married to Airic for two years, I couldn't let him sleep in the bed with me. Our arrangement made sense. If I had the need for him, I went to his room a few doors down.

The nightmares had never ceased, my own gagging screams waking me in the middle of the night. Even after years had passed, I couldn't shake the horrible dreams of the men who violated and mistreated me, the times I had to push them off and fight for my life when a trick went bad. The one episode that I can't shake happened when I was six months pregnant with Keisha. I told Cain that I couldn't do any more tricks. I told him it was doctor's orders.

"Something must've crawled inside of me." I faked a fever and told him I needed antibiotics. I knew I wouldn't get away with it for long, but I had another life to look after, and I wasn't about to sacrifice my baby. I found the strength for Keisha that I never had for myself to say one simple word: no. Cain set me up, told me to go to a room and lie down because I was tired. How stupid was I to ever think that he cared whether I was sick or not? Within minutes, I could hear the sound of keys locking the door. Which meant only one thing; He planned to send someone up later and wanted to make sure I didn't leave.

The room was completely dark when the door finally opened later that night. A shadow was cast, and I couldn't see his face. "What is this? Who are you?"

"Don't worry, pretty young thang. Cain said you wouldn't mind a little company."

"I can't—I'm sick and I'm on my period."

"Cain said you would say that. Don't worry, I got all kinds of creative thangs in mind."

"No, please. I got a disease," I lied. "You don't want to do this." I knew the truth wouldn't have been enough to stop him. He wouldn't have cared if I was six months pregnant and that he could hurt my baby. I was so scared, my head felt like it was about to explode from the stress of trying to think of an escape.

"Just take it easy. This won't take long."

My eyes scanned the room trying to find something to grab. What would be big and hard enough to strike him down with one blow? The room was filled with dirty clothes and old take-out-food boxes. There was nothing. Before I knew it, my legs were moving toward the door, just trying to get the hell out. How silly was that—a six-months-pregnant teenage girl trying to out maneuver a horny grown man. He grabbed me and threw me clear across the room.

I may have messed up my own life, but there was no way I was going to allow anyone to hurt my baby.

"Looks like I'm gonna have to soften you up—you know, take the fight outta ya." He rushed me and hit my jaw so hard, I thought all my teeth had shattered. I was completely dazed.

Lucky for me, he thought I was knocked out entirely, so he started to pull his pants down. On the ground where I lay, I saw one of those cake cutters used to pick out 'fros, then grabbed it and jammed it into his leg. He screamed so loud, I thought the whole neighborhood might come to my rescue. Blood was gushing everywhere. I tried to make my way to the door again, and he kicked my legs from under me and I fell forward, right on my stomach. I screamed in pain. *My baby.*

"Bitch. Look at my leg! Look what you did to me," he wailed, holding his leg while blood seeped from his wound.

He pulled off his belt. He was trying to stop the bleeding by wrapping it around his leg. I knew once he got that belt on, he was going to kill me for sure.

Blood was streaming down my head from a deep gash. My body throbbed with pain, but all the while I could still feel my baby moving in my stomach. He pulled a switchblade from his back pocket and all I could think of was how determined I was not to die like this, in this rat hole. My life was going to be more than this, at least for my baby.

All I remember was closing my eyes when I saw the shine of the blade. He bent over me, and I rolled back as if to accept death. Then I raised my foot and jammed it in his crotch. I'd never forgotten what an older woman told me on the street: "Listen, baby, if you ever get in trouble—I mean real trouble—there is only one chance for you, no matter how big a fool it is, hit him in the groin as hard as you can and get the hell outta there!"

I took that advice, and thank the Lord, it worked. I got to the door and left him curled up in a ball, screaming about how he was going to find me and kill me. I ran out of that room. I ran as fast as my legs would carry me. I lied and told Cain that the man was a sadistic freak who'd tried to strangle me. I had to defend myself. He went back and found the man and, from what I understood, finished him off.

No one knows how hard I've had to fight in my life. No one knows how hard I fought to keep my baby, and I wasn't going to let anyone take her away from me now.

❧

A knock at the door awakened me from the partial sleep. I waited a few seconds before I called out. "Who is it?" I reached for the drawer at my bedside, where I kept a small-caliber gun.

"It's me." Keisha's gentle voice was music to my ears. She entered. "Marcella let me in as she was going out."

Keisha took off her Burberry trench and sat on the couch. Her white blouse tucked in to a high-waist skirt showed off her fabulous figure. She was definitely my daughter.

"Your face." She noticed right away before we hugged. "I'm so sorry he did this to you."

"It's nothing. I will make sure he doesn't get away with this. I gave him everything, and this is how he repays me. I will never fall in love again. Never. All men are liars and will discard you the minute someone better comes along."

"You're just saying that right now. You'll meet someone. You'll fall in love again. All men aren't horrible." Keisha slowly raised her large engagement ring and stared at it momentarily. "I just wanted to make sure you were going to be okay for the wedding."

I took her hand and peered closer at the ring. At least two carats. The clarity was all wrong—dull, unimpressive. "I can't believe Gray Hillman didn't have the respect to come to me first. I'm the one who introduced you to him and asked him to hire you, remember? Then suddenly you're engaged—"

"We didn't mean for this to happen. He's only five years older than me. Is that your concern?"

I tried not to tremble when I hugged her. "No. It's just such a shock. Gray and I have had an established lawyer–client relationship for years, and he didn't have the decency to ask me, your own mother, for your hand in marriage?"

"He did—I mean, he did ask my mother."

The salt she'd just poured in a far-from-mended wound burned. I touched my temples. The room felt like it was spinning, with me at the center. "He knows the situation. He knows I am your mother, plain and simple. I trusted him."

"I'm sorry," she said with genuine sympathy.

I'm sorry. Keisha's warm naïveté sometimes made her look brainless. This was a clear sign of disrespect, and she ignored it. This was Delma Hawkins's fault, never having instilled a sense of caution in the child. No ability to distinguish charm from danger. Gray Hillman was only concerned with one thing: how to get deals closed. Seemed he was about to close his biggest deal yet.

Barring any financial missteps on my part, if anything ever happened to me, Keisha would be worth millions. A very wealthy woman. I'd made sure everything was left to her. Gray Hillman knew this, of course, since he was the one who drew up the living trust just six short months ago—around the same time his interest in Keisha was piqued.

"I received this invitation like I'm some common guest. My goodness, can't you see how I could feel hurt and slighted by this entire situation? Who's in charge of the ceremony? I'd like to be involved. . . . Sweetie, I'm your mother."

"I know. I know . . . and I just wish—"

"You know, you're right. I don't think I'm going to be well enough. Certainly Gray would understand if you postponed the ceremony. It's not enough time to plan a decent event anyway. Don't you think you should give it at least a year? I won't have as much going on. Then I can help. I know everyone who is anyone."

"He's ready now. He even suggested we get married at the courthouse and then plan a ceremony later." Keisha stood up. "I really hope you can attend the celebration." She slipped her coat on. "I just wanted to come over and check on you." She stretched her long torso toward me for a kiss. She'd gotten her height from her father, Kellogg Lewis, now Judge Lewis.

"Do you plan to include your father in the ceremony?"

"There's still a lot of tension between he and my mom—I'm not sure."

I flipped a hand. "I'm sure they'd put that tension aside for you, for your special day."

"Could you do the same?" Keisha said, getting to the something she'd seemed to be holding on to from the start. "Do you think you and my mom can get along, for the ceremony?"

I steadied myself. "Delma and I have been extremely cordial. Why would you even have to ask? I am not some drama queen making trouble for the thrill of it. If someone is maligning me, I make sure they are corrected. That's all. What . . . now, do you think I brought this on to myself?" I pointed to the bruise I hoped was still prominent on my face. "Did I ask for this, too?"

Keisha's soft shoulders rose and fell. "No. I didn't mean that at all. I know what a good person you are." She took my hands and brought them close to her chest.

"I won't get in the way. You are going to be a beautiful bride." I kissed her cheek and hugged her tight. Someday, of course. *But now is not the time.*

Mother, May I?

"Mommy, did you love Daddy when he was a little boy?"

I backed the Range Rover out of the garage and glanced at Mya in the rearview mirror. Her inquiring eyes met mine. "I didn't know Daddy when he was a little boy. But I'm sure I would've loved him immediately." It took me a few seconds to realize where this was going. We were on our way to the preschool. I'd given thought to taking Mya out and finding somewhere else for her to go, but my dumb luck, Jory's mom would have the same idea. Having met Holly Stanton after Jory dragged her over to meet us—and watching her nervous twitch—I knew she wasn't happy about Jory's selection for a new best friend. She and I had run in to each other a few times before we knew who the other was. She was the dark-skinned sister who always made it a point to not look me in the eye, avoiding me entirely if possible.

Something about the hair wars I would never understand. Anytime a woman decided not to straighten her hair anymore she was ostracized by the group, frowned upon as an embarrassment to the entire black race. Holly Stanton was the epitome of once-a-week visits to the salon to keep her shiny extensions from frizzing up. I was everything she'd fought to renounce, and now here little Jory was dragging us together. While Jory and Mya stood locked in a good-bye embrace, she and I forced handshakes, small talk, exchanging "nice meeting you's," and kid's-are such-a-joy smiles. I'd quickly assumed Mr. Stanton was white. She hardly carried the blond-hair gene.

"Then you would've married him?" she asked with passion then surety. "I would've married Daddy."

"I'm sure I would've loved him no matter his age. But you can't love one another until you're all grown up."

"Miss Tess says I'm grown up, Mommy."

I pulled out of the driveport, trying to think of what to say next that wouldn't make her teacher sound like an idiot yet could quickly put an end to the analogy. As I was backing out, I saw a dark gray Ford parked right outside our estate. The only reason it caught my attention was that our nearest neighbor was nearly a quarter mile away. Not to mention our community was called the Briar Estates, an exclusive club of Range Rovers and latte drinkers. Not one member would be caught dead in a Ford sedan. I once scoffed at people who used that word, *estate*. I'd giggle at the garage sale signs posted in my neighborhood when I was a child that said ESTATE SALE, as if we all lived in the Hamptons instead of our little bungalows. Now, living in a house bigger than ten of the size I'd grown up in, how else could I describe it?

I couldn't see past the car's dark tinted windows. I drove slowly, noticing there were no license plates. I continued to stare in the rearview mirror. The Ford stayed put. It took me a minute to revisit our conversation. "She means you're smart for a little girl. Little girls can't get married, sweetie. That's the end of it."

Having given it a good deal of thought while on my way to the preschool to drop off Mya, then on to my floral shop, it hit me how deep down inside we were all little girls. The little girl buried underneath expectations, loss, and disappointment was probably the only completely honest part of our psyche. *We just want to grow up*

and get married. What if the secret got out? The education and career stuff was only a distraction until Mr. Guaranteed Future came along. Only sometimes Mr. Future didn't show up. And even when he did, he wasn't all the fairy tale promised. No horse, no castle, and sometimes a tiny inadequate sword. So the little girl pouted and raged on the inside, but the big girl on the outside had no choice but to smile and keep stepping.

For a few minutes I drove, feeling sorry for Mya. Let the games begin. The mating game—who knew it started so early and lasted forever?

"Hey, Vin."

"You're late, again. You're looking at probation, lil' lady." His New York or New Jersey accent or wherever he was from where people wore black every day of the year came through whenever he ended a sentence with *lil' lady*.

"Yay, does that include a couple days off?" I pulled the orders and started separating them by delivery date and time.

"What would you do with a couple of days off?"

I thought for a second. "Nothing. I'd curl up in bed with a good book and probably starve, since if I didn't cook, no one would get a meal in my household."

"One day I'm going to cook for you."

"A girl can dream," I said before we both turned our attention to the entrance. The door chime had announced a visitor. I handed Vince the stack of tear sheets. "All yours."

"Hello," I sang out. "Welcome to In Bloom."

The woman's silhouette was sleek and sophisticated. She wore a smooth bun at the base of her long neck. Her high-heel pointed-toe boots made soft taps while she strolled gently from one sample arrangement to another. She took her time turning to the sound of my welcome.

"Charming little place you have here." Trevelle's rich melodic voice was hardly music to my ears. When she finally faced me while taking off her sunglasses, she gripped her chest as if she'd seen a ghost. "Venus?"

"Trevelle, nice to see you," I said calmly, and for no other reason than to let her know I was expecting her.

She did the unthinkable and snatched me up for a rapturous hug. I gave a gentle touch on the back until she finally released me. "How are you? Lord knows I've wanted to call. All this scandal with Airic has made me realize you were right all along. He didn't deserve to be in Mya's life. He didn't deserve to know the precious love of that child." She took a long steady breath. "So this is your place. I had no idea." I didn't believe her. She'd rehearsed her mild surprise.

She continued surveying the store and me. "I know now what you experienced having a relationship with Airic. I now understand your bitterness. I wish I'd never put you through all of that nastiness. But here we are. Proof that prayer works, because I was just thinking about you and how I wished I could apologize for my error in judgment. All that you suffered defending your name. And your rapper—"

"My husband. Jake."

"Yes, how are you two doing?"

Before I could say *fabulous* or some other exaggerated term, she cut me off. "As they say, time heals all wounds."

Speaking of wound, her matte-finish makeup was flawless. There was no proof Airic was a wife-beating scoundrel who slept with underage girls. Her smooth brown skin showed no mark or bruise. There was nothing beaten or broken about Trevelle Doval.

She surmised my confusion and raised a weak hand to her face as if she were parched and needed the kindness of strangers. "Indeed, I've got a lifetime of healed hurts. I'm a survivor. But this . . . this time I don't know." She found her way to a chair without looking and sat down. "I still have dizzy spells from when he hit me."

"I'll get you some water." I was hoping it was my chance to escape.

"No, that's not necessary. I'm not staying long."

I took the seat across from her, and peeked out the window to make sure she had a car outside. If it was a taxi trip, I'd need to call ahead, and now wouldn't be too soon. To my relief, there was an escorted town car waiting in the red zone.

"Is it a coincidence that you are in charge of my daughter's wedding? I think not. I think God has a way of delivering us to just the right place of passage."

"I'm not in charge, Trevelle. I'm the coordinator."

"This is God's deliverance, bringing me to your door. For every right reason we are here before one another. I have to tell you—you are the last person I expected to see. I mean, that woman, Judge Delma Hawkins, dealt you the same underhandedness she dealt me. She was on that bench passing judgment on a case when she had no business, no possible way of rendering an unbiased decision. Yet she sat there, pretending not to know me, not to know she had kidnapped my daughter."

I took the quick few seconds I had while she gathered another long breath. "That's all in the past. Keisha is going to be a beautiful bride. And just for the record, all decisions are made through Keisha and her moth . . . er." I could see the damage was done before adding the *er* on the end, but I tried to clean it up anyway. "I mean, Delma is really the decision maker. I'm basically carrying out what she's asked for."

"Of course. I just thought—" Her voice lowered. "—I just thought maybe an arrangement could be worked out." She lifted a white envelope out of her purse. "There's five thousand dollars in here."

"No, I couldn't take your money. Everything is already taken care of."

"Well, this is if you can un-take care of it. Maybe inform Keisha and *her mother*," she said with enough scorn, "that you couldn't secure the necessary details. That maybe the wedding needs to be postponed."

My mouth fell open in shock. A bribe? Five thousand dollars.

The collar around my In Bloom T-shirt seemed tighter. My throat and mouth turned dry. I still managed to eke out, "My God."

"What? Oh . . . no. I'm not trying to bribe you. Delma's style is a bit thrift store, if you know what I mean. I just need to buy some time. Really think about if it was your only daughter about to take the biggest step of her life and you were completely excluded. What would you do?"

"Put your money away." As much as I liked hard untaxed cash, I couldn't do it. And basically, five thousand wasn't enough to betray my good sense. Now if she'd multiplied that number by ten, we could've at least had a conversation.

"I would love to chat, but I have an huge stack of orders. Flower deliveries," I said to clarify. "Time is a huge factor in this business."

As I attempted to make my mad dash away from the scene to the back of the store, Trevelle followed close behind, "Just promise me her colors aren't red and white. . . . That's about as tacky as it can be. . . . No, wait a minute, turquoise, cobalt blue, any blue! Why our people know nothing about anything but primary colors is a wonder. This is going to be a tacky disaster—I can already feel it. I've graciously tried to accept what she did to me, stealing my child, but this is the kind of thing that makes me wish—"

She'd continued to follow me but stopped abruptly when she saw Vince blocking her entrance to the work area. I opened my hands and shrugged my shoulders at Vince, who was now a witness to Trevelle's craziness. "How ya doin?" he said to Trevelle, extending a hand after wiping them both with a towel.

Trevelle stared at his hand with disdain. "Tell me you have a secret staff of elves back there. Are you a floral artist? Is this your profession, because you will need professionals for my daughter's wedding."

Vince put on his best smile, "We love what we do here, ma'am. That's why we need to get to work." Vince's thick arms folded over his chest while he spread his feet apart, not very floral-like. His first career must've included a *B*—bouncer, bodyguard, brute enforcer.

"Trevelle, I wish I could involve you, but it's not my choice." I offered as truthfully as I could, feeling somewhat empowered with Vince at my side. "If you want to come back with Keisha, and she wants to make any changes, I would be happy to oblige. But we're in a time crunch, so I doubt if that's even going to happen."

She waved a dismissive hand. "Nonsense. You call her and tell her what she picked isn't in season. Steer her professionally. Don't you know anything?"

"Okay, that's it. Time to say good-bye." I did a baby wave. "See you at the wedding." I turned and walked away before I said something totally mean-spirited. I had a list a mile long.

Vince seemed to be having too much fun to walk away. He basked in her berating. When she called him a moron, he laughed out loud. "You're the famous televangelist, right? You're even prettier in person, younger-looking, too."

I thought I'd fall over. I peeked out to see if his snake charm was working. Trevelle looked confused, not sure if the compliment was sincere.

"Yeah, I spend too much time up late. But I've landed on you a few times. You've always got the right inspiring message. Persevere. Manifest. Trust."

"Thank you." Trevelle nodded acceptance, deciding to calm down.

"I didn't see the inside of a church too often in my lifetime, unless I was burying a friend or relative. I'd probably gone more often if there was someone like you teaching."

Trevelle was falling for Vince's fake admiration. So much so, I felt sorry for her.

"Do you have time for a cup of coffee, or tea? I'd love to talk to you some more."

She fumbled for her car keys. "I have an appointment."

This time when Vince put out his hand, she took hold. He folded both hands over hers, a double grab.

"Okay, then, feel free to stop by anytime," Vince said as she rushed out.

I clapped for him when he stepped into the back room. "Award winning." I grinned.

"Who said I was acting?"

I put my hand to my mouth like I was about to throw up. "Please."

"Televangelists need love too, boo." Vin pushed his lips out to emphasize his meaning.

I put up a hand. "Please, not another word. I might hurl my lunch."

"So that means you don't want the money." He tried to hand me the envelope that he'd picked up off the floor.

"Absolutely not. I don't want anything to do with that woman and her bribe."

I had no choice but to report Trevelle to the high court. Delma Hawkins would not be pleased. Nor would she be shocked. I felt like I was caught in the middle of a catfight, only they were tigers with fangs and fingernails that could rip your heart out.

"Did you tell her to pound sand?" Delma asked as soon as I finished telling her the details.

"Absolutely. I mean, really, five thousand dollars? Not that I would've taken any amount." I quickly tried to clean it up.

"Looks like you have your work cut out for you. How about I add a bit more to our agreement?"

"No, really, you don't have to." I weakly exclaimed. No doubt I could use the money. Jake liked to mention how much my business was costing us just about every other day.

"I can drop by early tomorrow with a check."

"Okay, if you think you should." I felt like double-sided tape, sticking to everything I came into contact with. There was a small part of me that felt sorry for Trevelle, an even smaller part that felt bad for Delma. Yet both women had put my family in jeopardy without a second thought to what it would do to us. I hung up the phone and saw the envelope where Vince had set it in front of me. "You can always donate it to charity."

"I am the charity. Both these women cost me a mint in legal fees."

I pushed the envelope around, still scared to touch it, when in fact, this little four-digit contribution wouldn't put a dent in the amount Jake and I spent fending off the custody lawyer Trevelle had hired for Airic. And even after it was over, we kept a local lawyer on retainer to protect us if someone accused us of fixing the first DNA results.

I took the envelope and shoved it into my bag.

"That a girl," Vince said. This time he clapped for me. I took a bow and did a little belly dance before heading out the door.

Who's Zoomin' Who?

Venus

"She's using you, you realize that, don't you?" Jake poured himself a cup of coffee and pulled up a stool next to mine at the granite breakfast counter. I'd been so excited to tell him about Trevelle's visit to In Bloom. I even gave him the dirty details of Vince flirting with Trevelle right in front of me, and this was the thanks I got.

"I could say the same to you, except replace the *she* with a *he*." I narrowed my eyes. "Why is Legend still here?" I scooped out a chunk of grapefruit and slipped it in his mouth. Habit. I needed to feed someone, and Mya refused to be my baby anymore.

"Let's stay on the subject of you for a minute. The judge, she's up to no good." He grimaced then spit the bitter fruit into a napkin. "How do you eat this stuff?" He drank coffee, looking for relief, then made a sour face. "Great, now my coffee tastes like skunk piss."

I nudged him. *"Pobrecito."* Followed up with a peck on the cheek. It was barely light out, six forty-five in the morning, but it was our morning ritual to try to wake up before Mya, to have strictly alone time that didn't end in panting and pressed flesh. It was time to clear grievances and speak one on one.

"Miss So-sorry-I-was-going-to-give-custody-of-your-child-to-a-fool wants you to be the heavy. When Hurricane Trevelle whips through town trying to bully her way into that ceremony, she wants you to be the bad guy." He dumped three consecutive spoonfuls of sugar into his already sweetened coffee.

"Hon, your taste buds will return—give it a minute."

"I'm a busy man."

"Doing what? Palling around with Legend, that's what. What have you two been up to? Really, I'm ready for him to be gone."

"Stay on the subject."

"The subject should be what time you're driving Legend to the airport."

"We're still working things out."

I stayed quiet, waiting for the rest. He stayed quiet, too, obviously needing a push in the right direction. "I heard you guys last night, something about double jeopardy. He was talking about Byron Steeple. Why would he be talking about you being tried for a murder you didn't commit?" I was fishing, but from the way his shoulders tensed, I'd hit the nail on the head.

"He might know who was behind it. The reason he doesn't want to operate the clothing company anymore is because he's afraid the same guys are going to come after him."

"Oh, bullshit," I said. "Don't trust him."

"Legend wouldn't make something like this up."

I rolled my eyes. "Please."

"Okay, next order of business. Is that fool still thinking he's picking up Mya this weekend? Because you know what I said. I haven't changed my mind."

"It's not something we can decide. It's a court order. If we want visitation changed, we have to see a judge."

"Don't start defending him, V." He stood up and dumped his coffee down the sink. His back was facing me, but I could still see the hurt.

The hum of the refrigerator, the only sound, indicated we'd come to the close of our adult discussion hour. No one spoke.

"I'm sorry. I wasn't defending Airic. I'm stating facts." I rose up and slipped my arms around his waist. I knew the rule, though I couldn't help pressing my hips against his backside.

The good thing about Jake and me was that sex could usually solve any disagreement. I'd read somewhere in a women's magazine that this was no way to conduct a long-term relationship. Five years and counting, I was okay with our way of resolving difficulties. We'd been through just about every trial and tribulation a marriage could offer. To call it a rough patch couldn't adequately define the dips and dives our marriage had been through, from his relationship with a female coworker to the loss of our son.

I turned him around and pulled his face to meet mine. His bottom lip was sticky sweet from all the sugar he'd tried to put in his coffee. He may not have been able to, but I could taste it. I pushed my hands up his shirt and ran the smooth line of his strong wide chest. His body was a work of art—simple, elegant, and subtly sculpted. No hard ridges, only smooth tightness.

"What happened to the rule?" He said into the air, his head lolled back. "We're supposed to be hands off, all communication."

My mouth was trailing the center of his chest. "I'm communicating, and I'm not using my hands."

"Very well said," he moaned, letting his head fall back.

"Dayum." Legend let out a little chuckle. "Honeymoon isn't over, I see." Legend opened the cabinet and grabbed a cup for coffee.

We straightened up with shock and hurry. Jake pulled his shirt back over his head, and I shut down like a teen caught in the high school bathroom with her boyfriend. Really, I shouldn't have felt anything near shame, but Legend had that effect on me. All women were whores unless they could prove otherwise. He'd even seduced and slept with my best friend, who was married with children, just to prove his point.

"Babe, I love you. I'll talk to you later." Jake kissed the top of my head, my cue to leave.

I moseyed over to the coffeemaker and poured myself a second cup, then leaned against the counter and took a sip.

Jake gave me a pleading look. He was lucky he was fine. Even luckier I was a loving and respectful wife. I didn't want to embarrass him by appearing unruly. I took my cup of java and headed past Legend.

"No breakfast?" he mocked.

"Feel free to help yourself to whatever's in the fridge." I said. "We already ate."

"I saw that," Legend said. "Delicious."

Jake reached out and squeezed my hand to hold me back. My kinder, gentler façade was cracking with every moment our house-guest remained. I bit the inside of my jaw and left quietly.

Loose Ties and Alibi

Dying with regrets is the worst way to die. How could I have been so blind? I knew better than to be so trusting. I knew better than to turn my back on him. My instinct rose like a mother bear protecting her cub, and I ignored it. Now it was all so crystal clear. He had been playing right into his hands the entire time.

I dreaded the idea of going home, knowing my houseguest from hell would still be lurking around every corner. Legend's proposed exit date had come and gone. We were now on day five, with no signs of him leaving. Never knowing if he was sipping on cognac on the custom Italian leather sofa or dripping sauce from his latest fast food expedition on the dining room silk brocade chairs I had sewn and covered myself. No matter where I stumbled upon him, it was always to my horror. We kept our word exchange to a minimum. The tension spoke loud and clear.

"So what is it? You've never been this quiet thirty minutes straight." Vince pulled open the tab of his Monster Energy drink. He downed about four a day, spaced far enough apart to avoid cardiac arrest.

"I didn't know I talked that much so when I'm quiet it actually concerned you."

Vince made a face similar to the one Jake made when he didn't want to be too offensive and the truth would sting. "Tell Daddy what hurts."

I rolled my eyes. "I got enough daddies in my world, thank you."

"Okay, Brother Vin. How's that?"

"We have a houseguest, my husband's business partner, Legend Hill. Saying his name makes my teeth hurt."

"Obnoxious?"

"Just mean-spirited, cocky, and bitter."

"What's his ETD?"

I looked perplexed. I'd been out of the loop for a while.

"Estimated time of departure."

"None. He's quite happy eating my food and critiquing every bite."

"You cook?"

"Vin, you know I'm a domestic goddess. Hence the peanut butter cookies you've been eating once a week. Hey, as a matter of fact, why don't you come for dinner tomorrow night? You can taste my exquisite cuisine for yourself and see my houseguest. He really is the type you have to see to believe."

"I don't know . . . that's a lot of ego in one room. You, me, Jake." He grinned. "Be there at seven."

Vince walked me out though he was going back inside to finish a couple of orders. No matter how much I pried, he insisted this was the best time of his life, which meant he'd erased the previous one from his memory. Or he'd spent his prime in solitary confinement. There was no other way to explain his thrill with working for me in daisy land.

"If Jake knows how much this guy is getting on your nerves, why's he let him stay?" Vin rested his sturdy hands on my car door.

"He's a bleeding heart, always has been. Why do you think he puts up with me?"

"Ah, you're not so bad." His crooked smile showed a missing tooth on the upper right side. Teeth had a way of telling the story of one's travels. There'd been a rough patch for Vince.

I pulled out of the lot and realized I would be late picking up Mya. The more time I took to get home, the less I'd have to spend worrying about Legend.

I hadn't noticed the light had turned green. I checked my rearview mirror and wondered why the car behind me hadn't honked. I stepped on the gas pedal but not until the light had already turned yellow. The car behind followed, ignoring what was now a red light. Only when I gained a little distance did it dawn on me. It looked like the same car from earlier, the one sitting in front of my house. I eased on my speed and switched lanes. *Calm down, who would be following you?*

I hadn't found myself in any precarious situations in quite some time. In fact, I'd prided myself on the drama-free existence I'd led over the past year. No run-ins with the police, as seen on TV by the local gentry when Jake was held hostage in a sound studio by a gunman. I'd nearly run over Atlanta's finest with my car to get to him. Let the record show there was nothing I wouldn't do for my husband, including mowing down a few good men. Luckily no one got hurt.

The only consequence was being on the authorities' radar screen. Jake believed once you were in the system for anything at all—regardless of guilt or innocence—you were first on the list of suspects for the smallest to the biggest crime. Maybe even under constant surveillance.

I drove slow enough for the other car to pass me. No such luck. The car merely stayed on my right bumper, matching my turtle speed.

At the light, they pulled up behind me. For the second time, I let the light go from red to green then back to red. I sat there staring in horror through my rearview mirror as the two shadows simply sat, too, with nowhere to go.

Oh God, this is really happening.

I stepped on the gas full force. My wheels spun faster than I could move, sending up a puff of smoke from the rubber tread. I pushed the steering wheel button to get an open phone line.

The phone hadn't rang yet and I was already talking. "Someone's following me. Someone . . ."

Jake answered. "Baby . . . wassup?" His voice was sweet relief and music to my ears.

". . . I'm not imagining it. I already know what you're going to say. I'm telling you. They're right behind me."

"Wait," he said calmly. "Tell me where you are."

I checked the rearview mirror, anticipating the flashing color from the unmarked car, now that I'd actually been caught speeding and running lights. When I looked up, there was no one there. No gray car with two dark mysterious figures. I slowed down.

"I'm on Peachtree. But they're gone." I released a breath that turned into a cry.

"Babe, relax, take a deep breath. Where's Mya?"

"At school." I fought the shakiness in my voice. "I was on my way to pick her up when I saw this car. The same car I saw outside our house yesterday morning."

"You saw someone outside our house yesterday morning? Why didn't you say something?"

"I don't know. It didn't seem so strange then; now it adds up. They were definitely following me."

"Come home."

"But I have to get Mya."

"Come home. I'll get Mya. Come home," he said again, with no room for negotiation. "Now."

I wiped my eyes and began to drive again, watching the rearview every few seconds. I simply had to calm down. Whoever they were already knew where we lived. They already knew where I'd dropped Mya off yesterday morning, so evidently they'd know exactly where I was heading now. I was a sitting duck whether I was moving, speeding, running lights or not.

Knowing this didn't stop me from hitting the gas hard. I wanted to get home and find out what Jake knew. I could hear it in his voice. He hated uncertainty, he hated not knowing every detail of a story, yet he asked me nothing. *Come home*, was all he said. I slammed my fist on the steering wheel. Everything had been going so well. He promised. Was there some law in the universe that said, Thou shalt never be happy?

I'd worked too hard and sucked up too much dust in my life to let it all be destroyed now.

Shallow Past

Behind those clear thoughtful eyes and intellect was the scary truth that if you couldn't do anything for him, you were wasting his time. No one held this honesty against him. He couldn't help the internal clock as it ticked time down to the smallest unit, wondering how much longer was needed to get the deal signed. Wasn't that what life boiled down to—agreements and contracts, verbal, written, or otherwise implied?

He was about to enter the most important contract of his lifetime: marriage. He hadn't planned to act on the attraction between Keisha and himself, but there was no denying its existence. And then less than seven days after he'd taken her to his bed, he found himself on bended knee. "Will you marry me and make me the happiest man in the world?" Her sweet lips had answered, yes. She had cried. All his life he was brought up to be hard, stoic, stern, and cold. If you want something, you must go after it—holding nothing back.

His heart was softened the minute he was touched by Keisha's love and affection. Knowing that she was worth potential millions didn't hurt either. After his own family had lost their fortune, he'd kicked into full gear, working his ass off. Was there anything wrong with choosing a woman based on her worth? Women did it all the time. Pretty young women married the older, less attractive men because of money and status. He was just being shrewd, combining both love and security. And by God, Keisha was beautiful, so he'd essentially hit the bull's-eye.

He paced as he watched the digital clock move to ten past the hour. He opened his office door. The solid gold letters SHARK BOYD & ASSOC greeted him from across the hall. The law firm specialized in sports and entertainment management, and had recently been covered on *20/20* for winning a scandalous battle for a baseball player who'd used illegal steroids.

Nikki, the thick island beauty, sat in an oval station of deep cherrywood. She pushed her accent harder these days, curling her thick glossy lips around the *L*'s and sharpening her *I*'s. "No sign of her, Mr. Hillman."

"Call her again." He hated tardiness. He hated wasting precious time. Though Trevelle was one of his biggest clients and soon to be his mother-in-law, it didn't give her the right to waste his time.

"I've already dialed three times. I left messages each time," Nikki countered, as if defending her ability to do her job. She checked her watch. "I have to go. I'm meeting Keisha for her gown fitting."

"Really?"

"Yes, Mr. Hillman, you mean your new fiancée doesn't tell you of her every move?" She sneered.

"Don't leave until Trevelle shows up."

He closed the double doors of his office. Nikki was getting out of hand lately. He'd grilled her about the so-called prince. She claimed there was no man in her life, expect him.

He sat on the edge of his desk. Women quickly got out of control if you didn't keep a close rein. He would deal with Nikki. Right now he had to concentrate on Trevelle. He knew what *she* was doing, making him wait—think too hard, contemplate, and come to his own conclusion. Trevelle wanted him to fear her, but why should he? He was genuine in his heart and emotion. Keisha was the type of woman he'd dreamed about as a boy, the kind you cut out of the *Jet* magazine and glued to the wall. The sexiest of them all, with a smile that could light up the world and a body that could shut it down.

"Ms. Doval is here. Shall I show her in?" Nikki's voice sailed over the intercom.

"Please do." Gray stood up and smoothed his hand down his tie. He adjusted his slacks and took a comfortable seat behind his desk as if he hadn't been pacing the floor.

"Can I get you coffee, or anything to drink?" Nikki offered as she led Trevelle in.

"Thank you. No. I'm good." His future mother-in-law was flawless as usual. Her ocean blue suit fit with class but still showed off healthy curves and the long firm legs she used to strut across the stage during her ministries.

"I could use a double espresso." Gray's lilted voice was soft compared with his male counterparts. He never tried to deepen it. The kind of voice that offered to keep their secrets and promises. Lately he'd noticed it had lost its effect on Nikki. She gave him a look that said she wasn't asking him, but she'd bring it anyway.

"Always a pleasure, Trevelle. So glad you could grace us with your presence."

"Wish I could say the same." She took a seat, crossed her legs so her fitted skirt slid upward to the highest part of her thigh. One more inch to glory.

"Uh-oh, what did I do?" His eyes feigned cluelessness.

She bellowed a haughty laugh then stopped abruptly. "You're a piece of work. First you decide to marry my daughter like some thief in the night, then you don't do your job."

"I'll ignore the first part. The second accusation needs some clarification."

"With all of this going on with Airic and his public atrocities, you didn't bother to call."

"I'm your lawyer, not his."

"Well, if you'd focused on your work, instead of rushing my daughter to the altar, you'd know this mess needs to be handled. On top of that my book tour was canceled."

Gray's honey-colored eyes closed slightly under the weight of his smile. "Look, this is not the end of the world. You're so much stronger than what a little book tour and promotion could offer."

"So you did know."

For a minute there, he thought she was going to get up and slap him. If looks could kill.

"What's important is defining a new strategy. You've told me time and time again, 'Define yourself or someone else will.' Well, here is a perfect opportunity. Trust me, this is small in the grand scheme of things." He was prepared for her anger. He had his own issues with the way things were handled by the publisher. But more important, he needed to get her on his side. "So let's talk strategy."

"I already have one, you need to postpone this wedding and focus on the job at hand. Obviously, you can't do two things at once."

He shook his head. "Not going to happen."

"I need time to take care of all the drama in my life. Right now I don't stand a chance in being a part of my only daughter's ceremony while trying to put out all these fires that you should've been handling."

His laughter was more a defense mechanism. "Oh, I tell you. You missed your calling. Trevelle, you should've been a comedienne."

"You think that was funny. I have another one for you: If you don't postpone this ceremony, I will."

His perfect lips surrounding perfect teeth quickly met in a line. No more smiling for effect. He was angry. "Every week there's a new story about you and Airic fighting in public, making a spectacle of yourselves. Ford Motor Company sent a memo regarding your spokesperson deal. The one you were supposed to get one point two million dollars for to pose in front of a couple of SUVs for all of an hour. Well, guess what . . . they're currently putting a hold on all diversity marketing. Translation, they don't like the publicity your domestic spat has been getting." He leaned back in his chair. "I worked hard on that deal and you blow it up in a matter of seconds. Now you want me to drop everything and focus on you. I find that very ironic."

"I don't give a damn about sponsorship deals." Her hand tossed the notion aside. "Don't try to throw me off with that mess."

Gray tapped the pen he was holding. He knew the sound annoyed the hell out of her. "Okay, here it is. I suggest you clean up your act. For the good of you and your well-being, take the high ground and stop marching around town with your emotions on your sleeve." He was winning the war. He could see her crumpling under his admonishment. She may have thought she was coming here to give him an earful, but it was he who was pissed. He hated cleaning up messes. What he hated even more was giving back money.

The Ford deal had a nice clause in small print that gave them the right to cancel the contract for any negative public standing. Trevelle was a money train he hated to see derailed for more reasons than he could count. If no one else would tell her, it was up to him. "So, like I said, we need to be discussing strategy. When you're ready to stick to business, let me know. Right now I need to meet my lovely fiancée and hopefully catch her final bridal gown fitting."

She shook her head. "I thought we had an agreement." Her voice went low and unsettling. This is what he'd been waiting for. Her gaze was almost past him or straight through him, he couldn't tell.

"I'm the one who brought Keisha to you. Had I known I was delivering my daughter to the devil's door—what did I do to deserve your wrath?"

"Wrath? Isn't that one of those damning phrases like 'seeking to destroy.' Baby, it's not that deep. You weren't even on my mind when I got on my knees and asked Keisha to marry me."

"What would Keisha say if she knew?"

It had been two years since their last encounter, but time didn't make past actions go away or disappear. Even now, being in her presence—just the closeness—caused a swelling between his legs. Part thrill, part fear. She had a primal skill he remembered very clearly as her distinct gift, a natural. The woman knew how to work her magic. So it was a lie when he said, "Thankfully she doesn't remind me of you at all."

They'd been working too closely, too much sniffing distance. A relationship was not what he would've called it. More like a distribution of benefits equal and fair. No one got the best of the other. When the transactions stopped, there was no discussion.

"We're all adults here." He pushed away from his desk. "This little charade is taking up way too much time. I've got to tell you, this is a shock. You coming in here talking about us as if—" He shook his head. "Look, right now it's all about damage control. Trevelle Doval, the priestess of gospel, must put herself back together again. Your image has to be one of a strong black woman who is holding her head up during adversity. So let's concentrate on that for now. Shark and Boyd only manages top clients, and right now, you mean a great deal to this firm."

"I know who you really are, Gray. The more I think about it, the more determined I am to stop this wedding. You're not marrying my child. It's not going to happen."

"The wedding will happen. You will be there, and you will be happy for us."

"Don't do this. Let her find a man who really loves her, who adores her. Keisha deserves that."

"Okay, we're through here." He had a look of indignation. The alarm had sounded in his head. *Time's up.* He was tired of playing with this woman. "You know what, you're right. I'll tell her tonight, explain that we rushed in to things, that her dear sweet mother she's known all of fifteen minutes seems to know what's best."

"I'm going to be the one doing the telling. Trust me, you will lose." She stood up.

He opened his arms. "If that's the way you want to play it, I'll tell her you want to keep me for yourself. Our brief and not-so-wondrous affair made you delirious with jealousy, and you came in here and threatened to tell her everything. So I decided to tell first." He paused. "What do you think, how does that sound? Good enough?"

"Stop it. Listen to me. You are messing with the wrong person. Do you hear me?"

"Why don't we reconvene next week, after nerves have soothed a bit? Then we can discuss real issues, like the sponsors." He walked the length of his expansive office and opened the door. "Nikki, make an appointment for Ms. Doval for next Friday." He held up a hand to beckon to Trevelle. "Good to see you as always, *Mom*." He leaned in to kiss her cheek, knowing he wouldn't get far.

"That won't be necessary, Nikki. I won't be back. You'll receive your discontinued service via messenger." She said to Gray. "We'll see if you're still in consideration as partner when they learn you lost them their biggest client."

A smirk of laughter left his lips, though he was uncomfortable with the damage she could inflict. "Right." He managed to say, "You have a great day, Ms. Doval. See you at the wedding."

"Over my dead body."

If I could be so lucky.

"So can I go now?" Nikki asked with almost as much disdain after Trevelle had gone.

"Yeah, get the fuck out of here."

House Arrest

After putting Mya to bed, I'd showered for nearly an hour, scrubbing and sudsing from head to toe. All I wanted to do was wash away the memory, the fear I'd experienced. "Do you think it was the police?" I came out of the bathroom with the towel wrapped around my body and another drying my hair.

"First of all, it could've been a coincidence." Jake fell back in the lounge chair in our bedroom. He rubbed his chin and shook his head. "You need to stay home for a few days until I can figure out what's going on."

"I have a business to run. I have that huge wedding of Judge Hawkins's daughter. Not to mention everyday orders that have to be filled. I can't do it from home."

"Vince has got you covered, right? Your big boy likes making things pretty over there. He'll be cool."

"Don't you talk about Vince, not even a little bit, do you hear me? I can't stay home—that's all there is to it. I'm not going to be a freakin' prisoner." I pulled the wet towel off my head. I felt as out of control as my hair. "I'd rather take my chances out in the mean streets of Atlanta before staying in the same house all day with Legend." Either one was a high-risk situation. Someone was bound to get hurt.

He leaned forward on his elbows, his manicured nails resting on his knees. "It's just for a few days. In Bloom will survive. You're staying home. That's it. Please don't argue with me about this." He stood up to leave the bedroom.

I went into the bathroom and slammed the door. I pushed the hair away from my face and leaned into the mirror and took in the reality of the situation. I was too grown for car chases and husbands who wanted to lock me up at home while he figured out who was doing the chasing. Being married to Jake, six years my junior, had never been dull—I could say that for sure.

The knock at the door gave my heart a good rattle to add more stress. "What?"

Jake stepped inside. He wrapped his arms around my waist and nuzzled my neck from behind, inhaling fresh lavender. "I'm sorry, okay? I don't want to fight."

"I'm not listening. You know exactly what's going on. You want to make sure I'm the last to know. What, you think I can't handle it?"

"Babe, I swear I don't know why someone would be following you. But I'm going to get to the bottom of it, I promise. I just want you to be safe. You and Mya are my only concern."

"You always say that. If it was true you wouldn't have let that man stay in this house." I gave him a tough love elbow. "Move. I'm not going to be brainwashed. You do your stroke routine and then I say, 'Yes, sir'. Not this time."

He kept his place behind me. His hands slid down to the center of my hips. "I know how to reduce your stress."

"Aha." I spun around. "See, this is what I'm talking about. If you were seriously worried, the last thing you'd want to do is have a quickie."

"Who said anything about a quickie?" He lowered himself, one knee at a time, pulling my robe apart. His face pressed into the scent of freshly showered nakedness. He slid his hands around and pulled me even closer before I could get away, not that I wanted to. His warm mouth licked and played with the skill of a man who'd been trained well.

As much I wanted to take the credit, the truth was Jake came to the game a well-seasoned player. From the first time we kissed and held each other in his home on the beach, the chemistry was hot and magnetic. His breath in my ear was enough to send warmth shuddering between my legs. But every girl knows desire has to be followed up by technique, or you're left wrapped in sheets of bitter frustration. I'd lived through enough of the self-fulfillment era, waiting for the lackluster performance to be over so I could be alone, me, myself, fingers, and I.

Those days were long over, with Jake in my life. Just the pure sight of his tight brown chest glistening after a shower, and my panties went flying.

Even when I was angry, like now, I was no match for his presence.

With each heated stroke from the tip of his tongue, I melted. He had to stand me back up, leaning me against the cool birch wood cabinets. No use. I crumpled, unable to stop my knees from buckling. He still held me up, pinned against the cabinet doors, burrowing into his target.

My moan echoed against the bathroom marble. Total and complete satisfaction rippled through my body. "Oh . . . God . . ."

He stood up and held me. "Babe, you all right?"

After a brief recovery kiss, I still couldn't speak. I still couldn't answer.

He gently pulled my robe closed, tying the knot to put me back together again. He smiled into my ear, happy with the work he'd done. "You all right, baby?"

I nodded, light-headed and still reeling from the orgasm that could be heard around the world, or at least our city block. A light, brief kiss and he was gone. He'd gotten away with telling me nothing. I scolded myself in between shudders of satisfaction. Once again, he'd shut me down with his magic.

Pay It Forward

He was royally pissed. He'd had an exceptionally bad day and couldn't go home to his fiancée like this. Keisha was everything good in his life, and he never wanted her to see his ugly side.

He pulled his car up to the security gate and pushed the code. The red light glowed in the darkness, telling him he'd put in the wrong number, so he tried it again. The gate didn't budge. He flipped out his phone and touched the initials *NB*, for Nikki Beech. It rang a few times before her Trinidadian accent announced she was unavailable but would get back to the caller shortly. This was his ninth call. Nikki hadn't returned to work after Keisha's fitting. She wasn't answering any of his calls or responding to his text messages.

He was at a loss for words. Surely the security gate was broken and she hadn't changed the code on the building that was in his name. He paid the fuckin' note on the loft. Surely she understood the rules hadn't changed. He tried the four-digit code again, refusing to believe he was locked out of his own building.

He backed his convertible away from the gate and parked near the entrance.

The manager's office was closed or he would've demanded to be let in. Instead he waited. The nice tranquil area was pitch dark and quiet. He checked his watch. Keisha thought he was at a business dinner, so he still had plenty of time.

"Ungrateful bitch," he whispered to the open sky. Thursday

nights were a ritual. She knew he would be here. So it had to be true. She was seeing somebody. After all he'd done for her. Her airy loft-style condo was something she'd seen only in magazines, until the day he took her for a little ride and gave her the keys. "Open it," he'd said. "It's all yours."

The key had turned. She entered and began to cry like she'd finally gotten her Barbie Dream House. The floor-to-vaulted-ceiling window offered a breathtaking city view. The lights twinkled against the black sky. It was for her birthday. She thought he was going to give her diamonds—or more specifically, a ring.

He couldn't explain without breaking her heart that he could never marry her. As much as he enjoyed getting inside her, she was not wife material. And what he did to Nikki, he could never do to his wife. Just the thought—flashes of Nikki's behind, her arched back and the sweetness waiting at his beck and call—made his thickness rise. He had to adjust himself, sitting in an open car. He didn't want security riding by, thinking he was some pervert. He checked his watch again. After all he'd done for her. In addition to her overpaying job, he'd footed the bill for her travel back home frequently to see grandmothers, aunties, nieces, and her two sisters, who barely left the town where they were born.

Another hour had passed. Finally headlights circled off a high-priced vehicle. Gray was glad he'd put up his top, scooting down ever so slightly in the leather seat, not wanting to look like a stalker. He watched as they parked. He was hardly shocked when he saw the man walk around to the passenger side and open the door for Nikki. She extended her hand like some kind of princess. He took it and kissed her hand like some kind of prince. *One man's trash is another man's treasure.*

Gray twisted his neck around to watch as Nikki and her friend walked to the well-lit building. A gentleman, he opened the door for her once again. They kissed lightly at the elevators before she sent him on his way. Perfect, 'cause Gray wasn't in the mood to have to shut this shit down himself. He gave it a few minutes then dialed her number.

"Hey?" She sounded like she was in a happy fog.

"Hey, yourself. Seems the code was changed."

"Oh, yes. The manager gave out new codes. I forgot to tell you." The gate slowly parted like the Red Sea.

"I'll be right up." Gray closed his phone and stepped on the gas, afraid they might close on him, and he still didn't have the access code.

"I guess the real question is, can he afford you?" Gray said as soon as he entered the loft. Nikki was wrapped tight in a robe as if he hadn't just seen her walk in with high heels and a sexy sleek dress that hugged her every curve. "Can he afford this place, the note, the car payment, those trips you need to make back home?" All the while he pressed the remote control to silence the television, which was giving off various shades of light on their faces. "Sounds to me like you need to make a choice." His smile, the perfect white teeth gleamed even brighter from the television light. "It's a simple choice. Job, condo—hell, even your car. You think you're going to keep everything I've given you while you fuck another man?"

It was what she'd wanted. Some sign that he cared. A flicker of disdain was better than nothing. She'd had enough pretending. "You want to evict me, go ahead. You want your key to the car, your office, you want, you want, but what do I get in return? You want me to die as your mistress? I will not. I will not." She was standing over him, heaving. She must've landed a few specks of spittle, because he smoothed a hand over his face. He clicked the television off. The room went dark, darker than her eyes anticipated. She could see the silhouette of him but not his face.

"Gray, please . . . I'm sorry. All I ever did was love you. I don't know where this marriage to Keisha will leave me. I deserve . . . I deserve to be loved."

He gripped her hand and pulled her downward. He grasped her head and kissed her gently first, then prodded hungrily for her tongue. Gray's kiss was powerful enough to wash away doubt and any good sense she still had left.

He pulled his lips away long enough to ask, "Do you really think I want leftovers? Do you think I can share you?" He held a handful of her hair so she didn't have any room to turn away.

There was fear in her eyes. To her surprise and dismay, he simply pushed his open mouth against hers. This time the kiss was deeper. "I love you, baby. Okay?" Sincerity oozed from his words and his touch as his hand slid underneath her robe. She shuddered and writhed against his fingers pushed inside her. Before long, every one of his fingers had a home. Just prep work, giving him all that he'd come for and more.

With Friends Like These

They pulled up in Jake's midnight blue Mercedes convertible, greeted by stares and looks from the shopping and lunch crowd, wondering who the two fine gentlemen were, assuming they were either professional ballers or entertainers. Especially in Atlanta, now considered the new Black Hollywood. They were welcomed in the upscale Bluepointe restaurant and escorted to a prime table while every woman turned and twisted to get an eyeful as they passed. Jake had to admit he liked the attention. He seldom left the walls of his palace unless he was with Venus, who had a way of making other women scared to take a peek let alone give a full-on stare. He and Legend were feeling themselves, for sure.

The stylish hostess seated them. "You gentlemen enjoy your lunch."

"Will do." Legend watched her walk away. "My goodness, my goodness. How do you stand it? This place is a cornucopia of sweet ass dying to be tasted. How do you live like this, my brotha?"

Jake lifted up his left hand. "Easy. I like being married. I want to stay married."

"How y'all doin'?" A young woman made it a point to pass their table with an extra sway in her hip.

"Hey, baby, how you doin'? I like the way that skirt is fitting, my goodness. Pilates? Yoga?" Legend pulled his hair back slightly as if to get a clear look.

"Thank you. I like your hair, it's sexy. How long it take you to grow that?"

"It's a constant work in progress. You wanna feel it?"

Just before Legend could cast his spell, the waitress showed up, just as beautiful as the hostess. She lingered on Jake for a few seconds. "Do I know you? You look familiar."

At one time Jake would've taken the opportunity to explain. His hit song "Fat Lips, Juicy Hips" had sold over two million copies and put him on the *Billboard* list twelve weeks straight. At one time he wouldn't have made it to the table without five or six women lined up for his autograph. She was about the right age to remember him very well.

However these days he'd accepted his anonymity. "Nah, nobody famous, sorry," he told her, mostly to keep her heart from going pitter-patter.

"All right, now. It'll come to me. Meanwhile, what are we drinking, gentlemen?"

"Grey Goose martini," Jake said without having to peruse the menu.

"How about you, Mr. Lova Lova?"

"Whiskey sour—" Legend fanned himself. "—extra ice, 'cause it's hot as hell up in here."

"I bet you two are up to no good."

"Not me, just him," Jake said, pointing a finger.

She smiled with shiny soft lips. "I'll be right back with your drinks."

"Ah damn, all right. All day long." Legend was a kid in a candy store. He hadn't gotten off the plane before he was getting the phone number of an airline attendant. "You know you wrong. How come you didn't tell me what was going on down here in the dirty South, baby?"

"Well, now you know."

"Now I know why you didn't want to have nothing to do with L.A. It may never rain in Southern California, but it's a whole lotta ice from those cold flossing bitches."

"C'mon, man." Jake looked around slightly over his shoulder. "You liable to get a beatdown using that word around here." After they'd sipped on their drinks uninterrupted for a straight five minutes, Jake finally felt safe to talk. "Two FBI agents come to my house. My house, brah, okay. Whatthafuck is goin' on?"

"The law has landed on your door. I duly apologize." He did a mock bow, opening his arms like an English gent. Legend knew Jake like the back of his hand. His tone let him know when it was time to stop playing. He also knew he'd have to tell him the truth. "The dudes who off'd Byron Steeple have been under our nose the entire time. They worked in the JP Wear warehouse. They weren't really just dayworkers. They more or less were on the job to make sure Byron did what he was supposed to do, which was run money clean through our company. When he stole from us, he was essentially stealing from them. JP Wear made money, but a lot of what you saw on paper was an illusion."

Jake's face fell hard. "You're saying the company was operating as a front. My company?" He shook his head. "Bullshit. I put my heart and soul into that company. Every retailer in this country had JP Wear sitting front and center. It's still one of the largest-grossing clothing lines." Jake shook his head. "Nah, I created that. It wasn't some illusion."

Legend took a long deep breath. "It's the truth. The sales were up all the time, but the money never changed. You remember? You saw it, you questioned it, but there was no way to explain."

"I remember," Jake said, going back in his mind to the year before he'd given JP Wear over to Legend.

"Now you're probably wondering how I know, and the answer is, they wanted me to know."

"Who is they?"

"Ronny Wilks—or Big Red, as he is so lovingly called in his circle of the uneducated and uncouth. Byron stole from him, and for whatever reason, he's turning over buildings and bodies looking for where he put it." Legend leaned back in his chair. "Put a gun to my head, right here, and made me piss my pants, all to hear me say three little words, 'I don't know.'"

Jake was about to ask the most important question: Was he next? Were they coming after him because they thought he knew or had the money?

The waitress broke in. "Here you go. Is there anything else I can get you?" She set the appetizer of sesame beef between them.

"Nothing right now, beautiful," Legend said with a bit of an edge. Not his usual relaxed self. He downed the last of his drink. "Wait a minute. Another one of these." He jiggled his ice.

Jake's brows were raised as if to say *get on with it*. "Are they coming after me or what, man?"

"It would make sense if gangsta law made any kind of sense. But I told him you and I were equally in the dark. Byron was an independent fuckup."

"So all I need to do is point these Feds in Ronny's direction. Plain and simple."

"Not plain nor simple. C'mon, man. You know the Feds know what's going on. They're not trying to solve Byron's murder. They don't give a damn about a gay black accountant. They're looking for the money just like everybody else." Legend leaned in to add gravity to his theory. "As a matter of fact, how do we know they're even real agents?"

Jake sort of rolled his eyes but then paused. He did his best *Godfather* impression. "I try to get out, and they just keep pulling me back in." For a second or two they both laughed. "This is jacked up, seriously. The first time in I don't know how long I'm comfortable in my own damn shoes, and all this stuff gets dredged up."

Suddenly Jake felt a hand smooth over his shoulder and squeeze. He turned around to see a bronze beauty with a bright smile.

"Jake Parson, don't even pretend you don't know who I am."

He was up on his feet, hugging her. "Sirena, damn, been a long time."

She cheesed ear to ear. "What you doin' in the ATL?"

"Obviously same thing you are. I moved here a year ago."

"And can't look a sista up." She nudged him with her bare shoulder. She wore a white strapless knit dress that left nothing to the imagination.

Jake looked over at Legend as if remembering he was there. "Legend Hill, this is—"

"Sirena Lassiter, you're even more beautiful in person," Legend said, almost stuttering. Jake had never seen Legend speechless.

"Thank you." She took her hand back as politely as possible. Her angel smile was humble and irresistibly sexy. Her music career had risen steadily, but it was her acting that had put her over the top. Jake would be lying if he said he wasn't smitten by her like every other man who'd seen her in countless movies, always portraying the naïve love interest. Her true personality was hardly shy or modest, but it was hard to separate the real from the image on the screen. He knew all too well.

"Hey, I'm having a private screening of my new movie tomorrow night. Only two hundred of my not-so-close-friends. It'd be nice to have someone there who I've actually known longer than a season." She spoke to both of them equally but landed on Jake for the final decision.

"I'm not sure. My boy here is only in town—"

"Miss a screening of the lovely Sirena Lassiter? Insane. We'll be there." Legend had a defiant glint in his eye. Jake was used to women falling goo-goo-gah over his friend. Nothing had changed since the days of high school, when Jake lured them in and Legend took care of the follow-through. Nothing wrong with teamwork.

"No promises," Jake whispered to Sirena as he hugged her goodbye. "Nice seeing you."

"Damn that." Legend received his fresh drink in the nick of time. He took a long swig. "You're married, my brotha. Not dead."

"Not yet anyway. Stay focused, man. If I don't figure out how to get clear and free of Byron Steeple's reach from the grave, I'm going to be right there buried next to him."

"Even more of a reason to taste the fruits of life. Tomorrow isn't promised to anyone." Legend held up his glass.

For whatever reason, Jake raised his, too. They clinked glasses. "Touché."

Come Out, Come Out, Wherever You Are

Patience was a virtue but also a curse. Jake realized two years of his life had been wasted in fear since Byron Steeple was beaten to death. He was only thirty-five years old, and he'd folded his cards and settled for a suburban existence in oblivion, doing his best to keep a low profile. He'd been waiting patiently for a knock on his door and his freedom to be taken away. Of course, he didn't have anything to do with Byron Steeple dying, but he had been there. It was one of those catch-22's. He always felt Byron's hands in his sleep, gripping his sleeve. Knowing he could've saved the man's life only added to his stress.

Legend was right, tomorrow wasn't promised. Exactly what he kept telling himself as they walked in to Sirena Lassiter's home for the movie screening's after-party. Jake couldn't have told anyone what the movie was about if his life depended on it. He sat in the dark theater, his mind swirling with scenarios of how he could end the constant fear he'd been living in over the last two years. *Byron Steeple.*

"There you are." Sirena's eyes were like lasers zeroing in on his. *Please don't ask, please.* "So how'd you like the film?"

"I'd say you have a very bright future." He quickly changed the subject. "How's your family doing, your dad?"

"Everybody's real good. As a matter of fact, I talked to him today, told him I saw you. He got so excited. He totally thought we

had a future together. You would've made the perfect son-in-law."
She gently gripped his chin. "Oh yeah, you're happily married now.
Looks good on you."

"Thank you." He wanted nothing more than to run out of there.
Admit he'd made a mistake by coming. Legend had pushed and
pressured, and now he was nowhere to be found. "You want to point
me to the restroom?" The music was loud. The air felt heavy. "The
bathroom," he repeated. Maybe if he got a chance not to breathe the
same air as her, he could stop visualizing her ass firmly in his grip.

"This way." She took his hand and wouldn't let go. Jake's legs followed like heavy weights wrapped around his ankles. They zigzagged through people. Sirena wasn't allowing anyone to stop her.
She simply nodded and smiled at her guests. She was amazingly
strong. Her arms amazing. Her back amazing. Her ass amazing. It
all came rushing back to him. Her body, amazing. They'd met shoot-
ing the video for his hit song. At nineteen, she was already a teen
household name from her debut album. Sexy as hell, she walked on
the set wearing black ankle boots and a pair of leather booty shorts.
He knew the second he laid eyes on her he was going to have her by
the end of the day. What he hadn't planned on was spending the
next six months, every day, noon and night, entrenched in the moistness of her body. They held hands everywhere they went, only to
fall into each other the minute they were behind closed doors. *Kind
of like now*, Jake was thinking.

The music grew more distant with the beat of his own blood
strumming against his temples. She led him up the spiral staircase.
The bathroom can't be this far, he meant to say out loud, but his lips
wouldn't move. *Somebody save me.*

Sirena didn't say a word. Her grip stayed tight. She pushed the
bedroom door open with her free hand. Once inside, she used him
to push it closed, his back up against the door and her body against
him. *Passion Run*, he was trying to remember the name of the movie,
at least if his wife asked he'd know the name of the movie. Maybe he
would even remember what the movie was about.

Her mouth was warm and sweet. She sucked on his bottom lip while slipping her hand in his pants. She found what she was looking for with little effort. The gasp of victory left her lips. "You are happy to see me." She pulled her dress over her shoulders then off completely. Every curve measured to perfection. Round and perky breasts, sizably larger than the last time he'd seen them, begged to be touched. "Tell me what you want." She slid down the length of his torso, lifting his shirt to the firm six-pack prize underneath. "Your ass is so fine. You are still the most beautiful man I have ever seen."

He was ram hard. "Sirena, damn." His mind was fighting hard, but losing the battle. Every muscle in his body tensed. He gripped her shoulders and pulled her up to face him. "C'mon now. You know me. I can't do things halfway."

"I do know you." Her tongue traced the arch of his top lip then slid gently all the way around. Her hand gripped and tugged with gentle precision. "All too well. And I don't want it halfway—I want it all." She shifted her body and deftly pushed him close to the point of no return.

He slipped his fingers inside, hoping to buy himself some time. He needed to talk to the hardwiring. The system that was built to take advantage of a situation such as this one had been put in place long before Jake entered the world, yet as old and established as it was, there had been no upgrade. A man was weak to the proposition of physical pleasure. Stupidly weak and subsequently in danger of ruining everything for even the smallest promise of satisfaction.

She whispered in his ear, "I have a condom." She moved with ease to her nightstand. In those few priceless seconds, Jake could breathe and think. If memory served him right, she didn't take rejection well. He knew how passionately she loved and lost. He'd seen her cry, laugh, and climax all at the same time. She bent over to open the drawer next to her luxurious bed. Her naked ass au naturel, bare and smooth individual mounds. Memory also told him he was giving up what most men would sacrifice everything for, even for one night of brilliance.

Fast. He had to make a decision. Sirena's lips were back on his with tongues swirling. His arms wrapped around her small waist, and he held her tight, summoning up the strength to do what he knew he had to.

"Why are you shaking? You're scared of . . . me?" she asked incredulously. "Don't worry—it won't hurt," she chided into his ear. "Well, maybe a little bit."

He thought about the things he'd want if he could have anything at all. Like a dying man's last wish. He knew Sirena Lassiter should've been on that list. She was beautiful, famous, and deliciously sexy. He'd watched her from a distance like everyone else, via tabloids or gossip media.

"I wish," he said, kissing her lightly on the forehead, "that you and I had better timing."

She realized instantly what he was saying. The heat off her body not so easily put out. She kissed him one last time. Inhaling his goodness. She tucked him back into his pants and zipped him up. Her large doe eyes blinked disappointment. "I've never stopped loving you."

"I know exactly how you feel." He leaned over and picked up her dress. She covered herself up with it. He couldn't help touching her bare shoulder.

"I'd love to meet the woman who owns your heart. She must be something." Her eyebrow rose with curiosity.

"We've been through a lot." What he didn't add was that he couldn't break his wife's heart, not ever again. Not even for one of the most beautiful women he'd ever known.

"Is she one of us? In the business?"

Jake shook his head and vowed not to get in to the discussion of who Venus was or how they'd met. He understood the process always started out innocent enough. Then the questions would turn inward and out, looking for weaknesses and cracks in the armor. Somehow she would find the right button to prove he needed more than he was getting.

"What about kids? Do you guys have kids?" And so it began.

"One daughter, four years old." Jake tried not to, but he did it anyway. He flipped out his wallet. "Mya, a total trip. Every day's an adventure."

Sirena hesitated. "She must look like her mother."

"Yeah." He shoved the wallet back in his pocket.

"I always wondered what our kids would've looked like." She snapped the buttons in the back of her halter dress. "Two, a girl and a boy . . . Remember we said we'd name them Gravity and Theory? Those are the kind of names destined for stardom." She adjusted her hair and made sure she had on both earrings. "So are you planning to have more kids?" Her shimmering turquoise dress skimmed barely past her upper thigh. Now that Jake knew she wasn't wearing any panties, it made him nervous when she bent to slip on her high heels.

"It would be nice." His face had betrayed him. He hoped she'd have enough tact to end the third degree.

"Nice? With all that artillery you're packing, you should have your own Little League team. You're only thirty-two. How old is your wife?" She zeroed in on the bull's-eye. "How old is your wife, Jake?"

"You better get back down to your guests. I'm sure they're looking for you."

"So you went for the older woman, huh?" She slipped in front of him before he could get the door open. "But surely she's able to give you a son. You always planned on having a son." She'd found a hole. The biggest one of them all.

"Sometimes planning's not enough."

"Can I ask you something?"

"Why not? Why stop now?"

"Why did you come up here with me? What made you follow me up those stairs and straight into my arms if you didn't want to be here? Then all of a sudden, I'm not worth the risk."

"I never said that."

"You did, too—loud and clear." She had him pinned against the door. "Now I'm not good enough for you? You're Mr. Holier Than Thou."

"I think—" He was looking for an easy way to say it. "You and I both know the possibility of things going very wrong here. This wouldn't be a one-time thing. You and I both know this wouldn't be a one-time thing."

"So let it not be a one-time thing." She cupped his face and kissed him deep and hard. He would go to hell for this, that much he knew for sure.

Jake left Sirena's bedroom first. She came out a few minutes later, fresh faced and retooled. There was still no sign of Legend. Jake decided he'd have to find a ride if his boy didn't make a showing in the next ten minutes. He had to get out of there. Unlike Legend's prediction, tomorrow may not be promised, but you damn well better be able to live with yourself if it came. Watching Sirena come down the stairs, he couldn't help but ache with regret.

"Jake." Sirena said his name, and he wasn't sure if it was the here and now or already the memory clouding his senses. She squeezed his arm. "I wanted to introduce you to my manager, in case you thought about using your good looks and charm for greater good than seducing old girlfriends." She linked wings with his and guided him through the crowd that had grown in the time they'd been upstairs.

"So I seduced you? Is that your story?"

"And I'm sticking to it." She tapped a sharply dressed man on the shoulder. "Mr. Gray Hillman, I'd like you to meet the multitalented Jake Parson." She watched as they shook hands like fighters in the ring before slipping off in another direction.

"I know exactly who you are. I was a fan." He tilted his head. "You segued into the fashion industry successfully. Very well done. So what's next, now that the hip-hop clothing industry has pretty much died a righteous death?"

"I've dabbled in producing," Jake said, still keeping his eye out for Legend. "Not really sure. I've been preoccupied."

Gray nodded. "I understand how that could be a problem." His eyes landed on Sirena. Jake didn't have the time or inclination to correct his assumption. "If you want to talk about your next career move, give me a call."

Jake took his card and resisted the urge to do a one-finger toss. "Yeah, see you around." He felt Sirena watching as he headed for the door. The great escape was thwarted by Legend as he rushed in front of him. "Where tha hell you been, man?"

"He's here," Legend huffed, out of breath with panic. "Ronny Wilks is here."

"Where is he?"

Legend double-nodded, and Jake took off in his direction. "Ah, shit." Legend moved behind him. "You don't want to do this." Jake took hold of his friend's arm. "You don't want to do this right now." Jake twisted around to see Gray Hillman and Ronny face-to-face. Ronny was a stubby short guy with a thick neck. He pressed his forehead into Gray's chest like a bull squaring off.

"Not here, uh-uh." Sirena had stepped between the two of them and grabbed Ronny's shoulder. "I paid too much damn money for this house. Y'all got to go outside."

Ronny's elbow connected with Sirena's jaw accidentally while he was shaking her loose.

Jake felt Legend's grip go even tighter. "Don't. She can handle it. Let's go."

If Jake remembered anything, it was not to get in the middle of a dogfight. But he also couldn't walk out the door after what he'd just seen. He moved swiftly, faster than Legend could stop him.

"C'mon." Jake grabbed Sirena around the waist, lifting her nearly off her feet.

"Wait a minute. I'm not going anywhere." She clawed at his arm. "I didn't even invite him. I'm not letting that thug tear up my house."

Jake let go of her once they'd gotten a good distance away. One of Sirena's girlfriends rushed to her side. "Are you all right?"

Sirena straightened her dress. "Call the police, I'm not letting fools destroy my house. I worked too damn hard."

"I have to go. Stay out of it, whatever they got goin', it's not worth getting hurt."

She frowned and pouted, crossing her arms over her chest. "Your people, your people." Something they used to say to each other. Their way of questioning what never made sense.

"See you later," Jake said, knowing it wasn't the time to say good-bye. He moved past the two men who'd already simmered down. Gray was doing all the talking. Maybe the man's card would come in handy after all.

Easy Like Sunday Morning

Jake had stumbled in the dark, coming to bed around three in the morning. He'd thrown his leg across mine, followed by his whole body. "You are the most beautiful woman in the whole world. I'm the luckiest man in the world to have you." Not that it wasn't a truthful statement, just that whenever he used the term *whole world,* he'd usually been faced with a come-to-Jesus moment after being tempted by long hair, sexy hips, and fat juicy lips. We made love like ravenous teenagers. Someone had lit his fire, and I was the lucky girl that got to put it out. He rolled over and fell into a deep loud snore.

So I'd expected him to sleep in until at least ten in the morning. I'd planned to make him a big breakfast. Then midway through, give him a warm succulent kiss and tell him there was more where that came from once the house was cleared of the unwanted guest. In other words, *Legend must go.* However, the clock read eight thirty, and Jake was already gone, so my plan was spoiled.

Sunday was the only day In Bloom was closed and I could relax. No weddings. No funerals. No bar mitzvahs. My cell phone blinked to let me know I had messages. The first message was Jake's, sweet and deep: "Babe, we hit the court this morning. See you around noon."

The second message was Vince. "I hate to be the messenger of bad news, little lady, but the shop was ransacked. Stuff turned over and broken everywhere. You probably should get down here."

Somehow, I thought I'd missed something. I replayed the message three more times before calling Vince back. I paced around the bedroom, determined not to panic. "Vin, are you kidding me? In Bloom was broken into?" I still couldn't believe it. "How? Is the window busted out, or the door kicked in?"

"Actually, the door was locked." Vince got quiet, as if it had hit him that someone could still be in the shop and he was a sitting duck. "I'll call you back."

"Vin . . . wait." The phone went silent. I dialed Jake's number, and no one answered. I wasn't about to drag Mya to a crime scene. I pushed the button to answer the vibration.

"All right, we're all clear." Vince said. "Looks like they broke the window."

"I can't handle this right now. I'd appreciate it if you could call the police and file a report."

"Nah, can't do it."

"Why not? I mean you're there, you're the one who saw the place first. You're the only one that will have any information." I paced back and forth.

"I don't have any information. Either one of us could've walked in here and seen this mess. I'm of no help."

"You're a help to me if you just call and at least get the police report filed. I'm probably going to need it for the insurance claim."

"Nah, can't do it."

"Okay . . . you're scaring me. Is there something you want to tell me?"

"Nope."

Frustration permeated my brain. "Fine. Fine. Whatever." I slammed the phone closed. Unbelievable. What next? This was unlike Vince. Had everyone gone mad? I dialed Jake's number. He didn't answer. He and Legend were out fondling balls while my life was being turned upside down. I thought about how angry Trevelle had been about me not accepting her bribe. Maybe she'd decided to give the money to some goons on the street to tear up my place. Racing through my mind was a list of people who had it in for me.

The lady I'd cut off getting on the freeway. She'd honked and given me the finger. My In Bloom van was slow getting up the ramp. Maybe she had remembered the name of my shop and exacted her own kind of road rage justice.

And then I thought about the people who'd been following me. Chill bumps covered my arms. Maybe this was their way of getting me to leave the house. Now I was angry. Bravo. Job well done, because I was going to see about my shop. My only hope was that whoever was responsible was somewhere nearby. I was so mad there was a good chance they would be the ones fearing for their lives.

⁙

I drove with Mya in the backseat. She reminded me at every stop sign that she had a birthday party to go to and I was going in the wrong direction. How a four-year-old knew direction better than me boggled the mind. On the days I promised the park and took a slight detour to the bank or store, she'd spring up from her booster seat, alarming me with a shriek. "Mommy, that's the wrong way." Gasoline stops were the only permitted route change—if I bought her a cherry Slurpee and a package of Cheez-Its.

"Sweetie, I told you: Right now we're going to Mommy's floral store. Jory's birthday party is at two. That's four hours from now. You'll be there on time, with bells on."

"I don't want to wear bells."

"Mya. Never mind, okay, you'll be at Jory's party." My heart was beating too quickly. I was scared of what I would see when I arrived at In Bloom. Angry because I had a feeling it was more I could blame Legend for. His fault—everything was his fault. If there was an earthquake two thousand miles away, I'd blame him for that, too.

My cell rang. I let out an exasperated sigh when I saw it was my mother. I thought about letting it go to voicemail. That meant she'd call back every thirty minutes with worry. I decided to get the conversation over with. "Hey, Mom," I answered lightly, so as not to show my usual panic over the slightest upset in my life . . . especially after she'd said how proud she was of me for being so grounded and responsible the past year. As if I were some problem child. I was a grown woman who'd been independent and successful in my career for the better half of my life, but somehow, all that mattered was my emotional state. If I was sad, I was a failure. Happiness meant job well done.

"I guess you didn't hear about the earthquake. You obviously didn't hear, since you didn't call to check up on us. Your daddy and me were shaken out of our beds. A five-point-four magnitude centered right up the way in Pasadena. All the pictures on the wall are crooked now."

"My goodness," was all I could muster. My mind was whirling. This was a call from the universe, confirming my assumption. One word: *earthquake*. The cause: Legend Hill. Something kept gnawing at me. Nothing had been right in the world since Legend had shown up on our doorstep. First Airic and his misstep with the law. Then Trevelle coming undone over her daughter's wedding. And here I was about to see my household turned upside down, all that I'd built torn apart overnight. He was a karmic disaster, carrying around destruction and dark clouds, and he'd landed in my house.

"I've been preoccupied. Sorry. Someone broke in the floral boutique and trashed the place."

"What'd they steal, a pocketful of posies?" She giggled at her own joke.

"Not funny."

"It's a flower shop," Pauletta said, still not getting the gravity of the situation. "What in the world could they want? You're not some front operation, are you? Jake hasn't gotten himself involved—"

"Mom, please. You know better than that."

"Well, he was a rapper. He may still have some of that thug life running in his veins."

"Are you serious?"

"Oh, yeah. I've been watching these young men. They're not just mimicking videos and sagging pants. It's a mentality. I've been volunteering in the teen ministry program at church, and these boys really think and act like prison inmates. Never even been to prison, but the mind can program your behavior. You are what you think," she said, with more proof coming. She took a breath, gunning up with examples.

"Jake is not a boy. He's a grown man who takes care of his family." I ran a red light, not paying attention, then automatically checked the rearview to see if it was about to cost me. Maybe if there were a police officer behind, I could lead them straight to In Bloom to solve some real crime. But instead of seeing a blue-and-black cruiser with patrol lights, there was the dark gray car, the same one that had been sitting in front of my house. The same one I thought I'd seen following me. "*Shit . . .*"

"What? What is it? You all right? Tell me what's going on."

"I have to go, Mom."

"Oh, no, you don't. Do you have my grandbaby with you? What-ever's going on—"

"Mom, I promise, I will call you back." I pushed the button on the steering wheel. "Jake, dial." I ordered, enunciating so I wouldn't have to repeat to the Bluetooth system. *Dialing Jake,* the computer voice re-peated. The phone rang only once before scooting into voice mail.

"Mommy?" Mya didn't have to say more than that to let me know I'd scared her. "I want to go to the party right now." She stuck out her bottom lip in preparation for a full-blown cry. Her arms crossed to show she meant business.

"Okay, sweetie, okay . . ." I tried to keep my panic hidden. After all my talk of wanting to see the culprits who'd damaged my store, now I was frightened out of my mind. "You know what? That's a good idea." I barely braked when I swung the car around, crossing over double yellow lines. I pressed the gas and heard the tires screech like Mario Andretti.

The car spun around to follow but didn't make as smooth a tran-sition. I watched in the rearview mirror as it got out of the way of an oncoming eighteen-wheeler. Once they got their bearings, they were back on the road and following me.

Oh God, oh God. I stepped harder on the gas. The car leaped when I hit a bump. I pulled into the Wal-Mart shopping center and swerved around the crowded parking lot until I was sure I'd lost them.

Mya wailed. "I want Jory."

"Stop it. I said that's where we're going—now, not another word, you hear me?" She buttoned it up quick, but the tears poured at an alarming rate. "Okay, no, I'm sorry, sweetie. Don't cry, okay. Don't cry." It was true I wasn't known for excellent decision-making skills in a time of crisis, but this made perfect sense.

If these guys already knew where I lived, there was no sense in running back home, where they could easily find me. Jory's dad was a state senator. Their house was in a private suburb called Hadley Park, where an armed guard stood at the gate and asked every man, woman, and child for ID before entry. Whether the leather encasement around the guard's waist was a cell phone or a gun, I stood a better chance of being protected and safe in Hadley Park than going home to an empty house.

I idled for a few minutes more and said a prayer before cautiously backing out and moving to the exit. Up and down the street I searched. When it was clear, I took off toward the highway. Exhilaration pumped through my veins. At ninety miles per hour, the trip came to a close pretty quickly.

The Company of Women

Delma and Hudson weren't regular members at Trinity. The church was young and growing. Bishop Talley couldn't have been more than thirty, but he spoke the Word like an old soul who'd lived multiple lives. Keisha waved Delma over. She wasn't a regular member either, but if she wanted the bishop to preside over her ceremony, she'd have to make a few solid appearances. Delma led the way for her and Hudson past feet and knees.

"You made it. How you doin', Hudson?" Keisha leaned in for a half hug, stretching best she could past her fiancé who was in the way. Gray stood erect, shoulders back in his exquisitely tailored suit, refusing to lean to the side. He had the nerve to pat Delma on the back.

She patted him right back. "Morning," she said, offering as much politeness as she could. They were in a house of worship, after all. She should at least be grateful the good Lord woke her up—or some nonsense that had nothing to do with how she really felt. She was plain annoyed. Unable to shake the dream she'd had last night. More like a premonition. Gray standing over a cowering Keisha while she hid her face and cried, slumped in a corner. Though Delma couldn't see her face, she knew it was her baby. She woke up seething, hot with revenge. Hudson told her to relax, it was only a dream. "Fears manifest themselves in dreams," he'd warned. "You don't want your imagination sending you to the hospital with heart palpitations."

He had a point. The mind could play terrible and powerful tricks, that much she knew. But what followed was no dream.

"I know I promised a dynamic speaker this Sunday. I know you all were expecting to be rid of me for at least one day." The congregation laughed at the bishop's jest. "You all have heard of the unfortunate events that have taken place with our beloved sister in Christ, Trevelle Doval. So I'm going to ask all of you to pray for her." He raised his hands and closed his eyes. "Father, we ask that you keep her in your heart, keep her with good thoughts for speedy resolution and recovery so that she may come back strong and ready to speak your holy name, Amen."

Bishop Talley turned his attention to the robed choir member approaching. She whispered something in his ear. He covered the clipped microphone on his robe and answered excitedly in favor of the request.

Meanwhile, Delma felt a slight burst of heat break out under her armpits—half relief, half anger for feeling set up. "Did you know about this?" She peered closely at Keisha.

"No." Her daughter shook her head for emphasis. "I would never invite you here, knowing Trevelle was speaking. Really."

Of course not. Delma calmed herself. She patted her forehead dry of moisture from perspiration. Keisha knew better. *She would never trap me into listening to that hypocritical nutcase.*

"Well, thank goodness she couldn't make it," Delma whispered to Hudson. "I would've walked right out of here."

"Let's just enjoy the moment. We're here. We're healthy. All is good." He took her hand and squeezed. Hudson knew her every thought, her every doubt and fear. Sometimes she wondered if she even deserved him, such a good man with a heart of gold. Most of the time she didn't feel like a good person. Deep down inside, she'd wrestled with her past. Forging Keisha's birth certificate and adoption papers. Deep in the crevice of Delma's soul, she knew she needed to ask for forgiveness, make amends, but then the tiny voice inside would say, *You did the right thing.* She did what she had to do to save a child from being put into foster care, or worse, in the arms of a child prostitute being subjected to drugs.

Music cued up, and the choir stood. Delma was relieved to end the loud clash of right and wrong battling in her mind, grateful to hear the sweet melodic voice as it sailed over the church. "He will find a way . . . hold on."

Delma craned her neck to see after everyone else had begun to stand. She should've known something was afoot when Keisha's black jewel eyes got big with apology.

There on the stage was the diva herself, Trevelle Doval. It was her voice sailing over the land. She walked slowly to the center with the microphone in her hand. Each exaggerated step of her high heels seemed to make the congregation clap harder.

"Sing. Tell it. Sing," the woman next to Delma yelled and clapped. Trevelle reached the center of the stage, and the bishop opened his angel-robe arms, wrapping her in a long hug. This act brought about a standing ovation. The dramatic entry left not a dry eye in the place. Delma looked over at Hudson for a companion smirk, and even he had moisture welling up behind his glasses. Did he think she wouldn't notice? She gave him an elbow near the rib to get his attention, then narrowed her glare.

Hudson put a comforting arm around her shoulders. He held her while he swayed gently to the beat of the music. Contagious was all. Crazy was contagious; she'd always known it. She had to fight off the urge of emotion not to be sucked into the fray herself.

The choir roared out, "Hold on, He's coming . . . Hold on . . ."

Delma closed her eyes, willing herself to go numb. She didn't want to be a part of this nonsense. That woman should've been holed up under a rock somewhere with embarrassment. Especially after the news and entertainment shows all ran the video showing her husband's naked body blurred on the screen with another woman. How convenient everyone felt sorry for her. She'd never fool Delma, who knew exactly what Trevelle was capable of. Delma had seen the truth with her very own eyes the night Trevelle Doval murdered a man and walked away without a shred of conscience. If anything, Trevelle made multiple copies of the disc her damn self and sent them out to the news channels.

"Hold on . . . He's coming. You don't have to stress. You don't have to worry . . ." The sweet melodic voice could have been that of an angel—if Delma hadn't known better.

Keisha reached out, tapping her on the shoulder. Tears pooled down her cheeks. Delma clasped her daughter's hand. *"Hold on" was right.* It was going to be a bumpy ride, indeed. Life was a one-shot deal, but the ups and downs were endless. For a moment, Delma choked up. She kept her eyes straight ahead and willed herself not to see anything or anyone but the life-size statue of Jesus hanging on the embossed gold cross. *Lord, have mercy. Protect my daughter from liars and false prophets, please, even if you don't give a cat's eye about me, protect my baby.* This time, Delma didn't fight it. She let the tears trickle down her nose, past her lips—and hoped her prayer made it to God's ears.

◌◌

The congregation filed out into the large lobby area that was as extravagant as a luxury hotel. The money spent on megachurches could have been used to feed a starving country. This, Delma knew, was not their goal. In fact, she'd been invited to sit on a new committee specifically commissioned to investigate the legitimacy of million-dollar preachers and their nonprofit status. She'd accepted with the hope Trevelle Doval and her phony-baloney ministries would be one of the first to be investigated.

"Keisha, darling, I thought that was you." Trevelle pushed her way past the crowd that had gathered around to praise her. "What a surprise. How wonderful of you to come here to support me."

"Yes, it was a lovely surprise." Keisha hugged her.

Delma stood off to the side, counting the beams in the ceiling, the lights in the grand chandelier, even noticing the hidden cameras that most didn't know existed. The bowl-shaped glass housed the type of security spyware that spun 360 degrees. Another useless expense. Had they really expected a midnight robbery? Then again, from the number of folks at capacity, there was probably a boatload of cash sitting in stacks.

"Delma, good to see you. Praise the Lord."

"You, too," was all Delma could say on her best behavior. "Sorry I haven't had time to return your calls."

"Five times," Trevelle said. "I've called five times. I only wanted to offer any help I could on the wedding plans. I know everyone who is anyone. I probably could get the best of what you need at half the cost, or even free. Who wouldn't want to help the daughter of Trevelle Doval?"

Delma felt her temperature rising. "We have everything covered. And I figured with everything on your plate—"

"It's going to be beautiful," Keisha interjected. "You really don't have to do a thing but show up and relax on the big day."

"Well, there she is—the woman of the hour." Gray arrived from his powwow with what looked like a professional basketball player. He leaned in and kissed Trevelle on the cheek. Her long lashes closed and fluttered, as if he'd breathed fire on her. Maybe Delma and she had one thing in common: a dislike and distrust of Gray Hillman. But it had been Trevelle who brought the two of them together. She who'd wanted Keisha to work for the famous law and entertainment firm that represented her. Obviously, the plan had backfired.

"One big happy family." Gray's bronze eyes homed in on Trevelle, almost daring her to make a wrong move. He didn't back away. "You're looking lovely as usual, Trevelle."

She ignored his compliment. Instead she took Keisha's hands. "Can I speak with you for a moment? I promise it will be quick and painless."

Delma gripped her purse in both hands, feeling something was being stolen right before her very eyes. She watched as Keisha was led by Trevelle to a shiny wooden door. They went inside, leaving Delma, Gray, and Hudson in their awkward silence.

"Don't worry, Mama D, she won't eat her. She'll be back in one piece," Gray said coolly, though his demeanor made him look more nervous than Delma felt.

Hudson took a hold of his wife's hand. "Let's go. We'll meet them at the restaurant." The engagement brunch was scheduled directly after church. He tugged, but Delma didn't budge. "Come on, woman. Don't make me carry you out of here."

"I wish you'd try." She'd had enough anger built up. If it had to be her loving husband who got the wrath of it, then so be it.

"Mama D, I'll wait for Keisha right here." Gray kissed her lightly on the cheek. "I promise we'll be at the restaurant shortly."

She reached and took Hudson's hand. "Fine. See you at the restaurant."

When they got outside, Delma turned to Hudson. "Did you see that? Did you notice the way Trevelle cringed around Gray? You see, it's not my imagination. She knows something about him, and she's not fessing up. I'm telling you—"

"I saw it," Hudson said apologetically, and left it at that.

Delma snatched the keys out of his hand. The car door remained locked. She wasn't letting him in until he gave her the satisfaction she was after. "Well . . ."

"Well, what? That doesn't prove the boy is an axe-murderer. Baby cakes, you're just scared 'cause you think you're losing your only child. She's always going to be your child, even when she has babies of her own. Even when she's fifty and you're a hundred."

"Watch it." Delma poked him. "Don't get hurt. I'm only fifty-four." When she'd found baby Keisha dehydrated and near dead, she was a young woman, barely thirty years old, and from that day forward, she'd lived every day for that child. Every single day.

Hudson drew her in for a long hug. He rested his narrow chin on her head. "I know it's scary. Nothing's going to change. She will always love you."

"It's not just that, Hudson. You know I'm not that selfish."

He chuckled. "Yes, I know. I say we give the boy a minute to prove himself. Give him the honor of being innocent until proven guilty. That's what we do. That's how we handle every man, woman, and child—with fairness and objectivity."

"We're not in a court of law, Hudson. This is my life, Keisha's life. No one is objective when it comes to their own child. You know that."

"I'll keep my eyes and ears open. You have my word on it. Keisha is important to me, too." He was so protective. Hudson was her knight in shining armor, even if Delma was the one who'd rescued him, giving him a job as her law clerk even after finding out he'd lied on his application about having a degree when he'd barely earned a GED. After growing up without a father or even a big brother, it was something that quickened the heart of a woman, when a man could wrap his arms around her and make everything all right. He cared for her when she was sick, softened her when she became too hard, and stopped anyone in their tracks who meant to cause her harm.

"Thank you, Hudson," Delma said, finally satisfied. All she'd wanted was to know she wasn't crazy. That it wasn't her imagination or fears making her lose sleep at night. Now that Hudson had noticed the strange behavior of Gray Hillman, she felt relieved.

Gray leaned against the door as if he needed a place to rest, but really he was listening, doing his best to eavesdrop on Trevelle and Keisha's conversation. There was no real cause for alarm. Trevelle had been bluffing—all bark and no bite. She wouldn't dare jeopardize her relationship with Keisha after it had only just begun to take off.

"Looks like someone found Jesus." Nikki's voice penetrated his eardrum. "What happened to you last night?"

He put his finger to his mouth to shush her. Then he put a gentle but firm hand around her waist, escorting her away from the door. "I got held up at the Sirena Lassiter screening."

"You could've called to tell me." Nikki folded her arms around herself. She was losing patience with his neglect. He'd made promises, but only to stall her from trying to get away. Gray planned to end their clandestine relationship, but it would be on his terms, not hers, and he damn well wasn't handing her over to another man so easily after he'd taught her every trick in the book. She was his till he said otherwise.

"Yes, you're right. I should've called." He pushed his lips out for a distance kiss.

She rolled her eyes toward the ceiling. "Whatever, Gray."

"What're you doing here anyway? You're supposed to be at the restaurant, organizing the engagement brunch."

She tilted her head like a punished puppy and batted her silken lashes. "I'm not at your beck and call. Tomorrow I fly to Trinidad for my mother's birthday. Remember that. Don't look for me to be waiting on you and yours hand and foot." She opened her purse and pulled out her cell phone, which was ringing. She silenced it before putting it back. "I'm not your housemaid while you treat your bride like a princess. When I get back, things are going to change."

"Who was that calling?" Gray felt like snatching the phone out of her hand, ignoring every single thing she'd said. The phone, like her, belonged to him, so he didn't really want to hear what she would and would not do. He would've hoped she'd learned her lesson the other night. As he reached toward her, "I told you—"

Keisha came out with Trevelle close behind. "Hey, girl." She hugged Nikki, who smiled over her shoulder.

"I enjoyed the service very much. And you, Miz Trevelle, you are a wonder, such a blessing. I feel so honored to have heard you sing."

Trevelle nodded. "Thank you, Nikki. It's always a pleasure to see you." She cut her eyes in Gray's direction. "If you ever need to move along from Shark and Boyd, I can use a good assistant."

"Miz Trevelle, I'd hoped you and Gray would resolve—"

Gray interrupted. "Nikki, you need to get to the restaurant and make sure everything is set up."

"Right." She pushed back her wild Tina Turner hair. Everything about her was the opposite of Keisha, and he liked it that way. She was short and thick. Keisha was long and lean. Her skin was berry chocolate, and Keisha's was warm mocha. He felt like a man who had everything, the perfect combo. He'd even fantasized about having them both in the bed with him at the same time. The ultimate wish. Though he'd experienced it a few times, he knew nothing could top having it with someone he loved.

He reached out and took Keisha's hand. "More important, your mother is waiting at the restaurant." He adjusted his cuff-linked sleeve to peek at his watch. "You know her better than I, but something tells me she doesn't like to wait."

Trevelle winced with the mention of Delma—just the reaction he was looking for.

"You're right, yes." Keisha leaned into Trevelle. "I can't wait for you to see the dress I picked out." They kissed and hugged.

"You know, I'd love to come to the engagement brunch. I realize you hadn't planned on one more, but I promise not to take up too much room."

Keisha looked to Gray for a confirmation. He had no choice but to agree. "I don't see why not."

"Great. I'll ride with you all."

"Probably be best if you met us there." Gray nearly shivered with the thought of her in his backseat. He'd never been stupid enough to turn his back on a enemy, and he wasn't about to start now.

"Fine, I'll meet you there."

"Nonsense, you can ride with me," Nikki offered.

"Ladies." Gray nodded at Nikki and Trevelle before they turned away. He looped Keisha's arm through his and said a small prayer. Having Trevelle in an intimate setting with Nikki wasn't that much better than having her in his car. He prayed they didn't exchange any stories. "Are you sure it's a good idea to have Trevelle at the engagement brunch?"

"Gray, that's why I asked you."

"You didn't ask me. What you did was put me on the spot."

"Well, it's time we stop dancing around the issue. My mother is going to have to accept Trevelle, and vice versa. I've had enough of being caught in this tug-of-war."

His phone started vibrating as soon as they hit the outside of the church. His heart raced. Sunday calls were never good. They were usually the result of one of his many clients who'd run into trouble the night before. Caught on camera doing something they wished they could take back. His only advantage was that most of his clients were African American, and brown skin didn't fetch as good a price as white skin in the tabloids, regardless of their status. So whatever was caught on tape stayed on tape and hardly ever made it to public viewing. He looked at the number and pushed the ignore button.

"Who is it?" Keisha was leaning on his shoulder as they walked.

"I don't know. They'll leave a message."

"I just wish everyone could get along." She picked up right where they'd left off before the interruption. Keisha could talk when she felt like it. Most got the impression that she was quiet and reserved. He knew better. She was funny, too. Not in a goofy kind of way, just sometimes the most ironic twist of words got him deep belly laughing. "We haven't even thrown your family into the mix. I think we should order a metal detector for the chapel door."

He found himself cracking up in spite of the mood the phone call had just put him in. "Yeah, I can already see it, all the little church ladies throwing their Gats in the security tray. You know what?" He tapped the unlock button on the sleek BMW 745. "We should just go ahead and call VH-1, see if they want to film this thing. *Hot Mess Wedding Drama,* ten P.M. on Wednesday nights."

Her smile was all he was after, but her sweet laugh sealed the deal. "You're too much."

"So I've been told." The buzz signaled that a message had been left on his voice mail.

He couldn't resist. He listened to the first few seconds. *"It's Ronny, don't make me call you before you call me, you know what I'm sayin?"*

Gray squeezed the button until the phone powered off. He knew exactly what Ronny was saying. *Criminals.* Dealing with the unsavory came with his profession. He was a lawyer who specialized in clients with too much time and money. With money came power, which nine times out of ten led to trouble.

Ronny was a music producer who financed his first label with drug money. Most liked to believe that a shiny new profession could turn the dirty clean, but Gray knew better. If you played in the mud, the dirt didn't wash off easy. Ronny needed someone like Gray, who could be the fresh clean face on a business deal.

"We're here," Gray said casually. "I'm going to let you out, then go park." He and Keisha kissed before she got out.

He wasted no time pulling out his phone and dialing before he'd found a parking spot.

"Yeah, it's me. Speak," Gray said with a deeper voice than most of his associates knew he was capable of.

"You speak, and you better start talking fast. I told you last night: I'm losing my patience."

"Look, nothing's changed since twelve hours ago. It's Sunday. What do you want me to do on a Sunday? Besides the fact that I don't know a damn thing about hidden bank accounts. I'm not involved. I've explained this to you."

"Then you better start speaking a language I can understand, 'cause I'm not getting it."

"The man is dead and buried. What am I supposed to do, dig him up and shake some answers out of him?"

"You know what, that's not a bad idea. Maybe you need to join Byron Steeple in the ground."

"Wait, wait a minute. Calm the hell down. Byron Steeple was working alone. I don't have any idea where your money is. How many ways do you want me to say it?"

"See, that's where I'm havin' the problem. You're the one who hooked me up with 'em. You said he could be trusted. Now you don't know nothin'. Now you aren't involved. I want my money. You owe me."

Gray leaned his head against the leather rest, then popped up.

"How many ways do I say I'm sorry?" He felt like laughing for sounding like a Hallmark card. Keisha would've got the joke. He pushed the air-conditioning up to its coolest temperature and cursed under his breath, feeling perspiration spreading to his expensive suit lining.

"Find my money. Find my damn money. If you don't, I'm going to start speaking a language we both can understand."

The dead air was all that remained between them. Gray powered down, this time tossing the phone in his glove box for safe measure. He didn't want to even see it again until Monday morning.

Tell My Story

"I'm a guest of the Stantons'," I told the guard. "The birthday party . . . ," I added, trying to keep my voice from cracking. The entire time, I couldn't take my eyes off the rearview mirror.

"The party is at two, ma'am. The Stantons aren't accepting guests until that time." He eyed Mya in the backseat. "Hey, pretty girl."

"Well, not in our case. My daughter is the birthday boy's best friend, so she has permission to come early."

"Your name?"

"Venus Parson, and this is Mya." I handed him my ID as I'd done a few weeks back when Jory and Mya had a playdate. Neither of his parents had been home, leaving me to chat with Greta, the German nanny, who couldn't keep her eyes or her hands off my hair. "You no afford to fix? Your employer no pay you enough money. I know a good family to work for." It took me the entire afternoon to convince her that my untamed 'fro was a choice, not a situation that needed rectifying. Making her understand I was Mya's mother and not interested in joining the union for disgruntled nannies was the least of my problems.

I watched him pick up the phone and face the opposite direction. He returned, holding my ID. "Two o'clock. If you'd like to park in the waiting area in the shade, you're more than welcome." I followed his eye to the shaded parking spots on the wrong side of the ten-foot-high gate.

"Please, can I just pull in? I won't go to their house until two P.M., but I really need to come inside. Isn't there like a park or something? She needs to go to the bathroom." I gave him my most endearing "Please."

"The clubhouse is open. She can use the restroom in there." He leaned his hands on his knees. "I don't see any harm long as you promise not to make any trouble." He winked.

"Trouble, me? No." The gate slowly rolled open. Relieved to finally feel safe. I checked my rearview mirror one last time.

Up ahead I saw the clubhouse but turned in the opposite direction. I didn't care if the party started hours from now. We were headed to the Stantons'. I had one goal: to get Mya and me to a safe place.

The palatial home flanked by pillars now had balloons billowing from each side over the front door. "Mya, sweetie, wait." She'd already taken off sprinting across the perfect lawn and cutting through the small boxwood hedge.

She could barely reach the doorbell, thank goodness. I got beside her in time to make sure she pressed it only once.

"Well, hello." Holly Stanton held on to the doorknob. One hard pink curler was rolled at the top of her head. The rest of her hair hung straight past her narrow shoulders. "I . . . thought I explained to the guard, the party starts at two." She looked us both thoroughly over.

"I know. But Mya really is anxious to see Jory. She wasn't going to let me go all the way back home. I got the time wrong."

"Someone's here." Jory must've heard the doorbell. He peeked his head underneath his mom's elbow. His face lit up when he saw Mya. "Come in," he welcomed, and then took her hand. He certainly didn't get his manners from his mother. The little picture-perfect duo was Benetton-advertisement ready, Mya with her wild mop of hair and Jory the spitting image of a baby Brad Pitt. They dipped underneath her arm, which still held fast to the door, and darted off inside.

While we stood in our awkward silence, the kids' glee and laughter receded as they raced down the marble-floored hallway. "I guess you'd like to come in," she finally offered.

"Yes, thank you."

"I'm still getting ready. You can wait out here. Help yourself to the snacks." She disappeared after leading me into the large enclosed veranda. The house was infinitely large. I could hide there, which was exactly what I'd planned to do. Snacks. I'd call it a full spread with shrimp kebabs and a cheese and fruit platter that rivaled any wedding I'd attended.

I popped a couple of grapes in my mouth and took a wedge of watermelon to the couch. I was famished. I dripped all over myself and kept looking at my cell phone, waiting for Jake to call me back.

"Well, hello there." Mr. Stanton stood in the doorway. Senator Robert Stanton was hardly your everyday-looking politician. His glossy bronze hair was tousled and hung long enough to push behind his ear. "Venus, right? How you doing?" He put out his hand.

"I'm good. I'm sorry I came so early. We were in the area." My fingers were sticky from the melon, so I gave him a pinkie.

"Are you kidding?" He took my hand in his, then brought it to his nose like a Southern gent. "We could shut this whole thing down right now since Jory's got Mya here. It's his day. Let 'em enjoy the hell out of it."

I was relieved. His easy spirit made up for his uptight wife. I'd learned most relationships were like good cop–bad cop scenarios. In my relationship, I would definitely be classified as the bad cop. Jake always gave at the office, the one with the open mind, offering the benefit of the doubt—except when it came to Airic. Every superhero had to have an archenemy, I guess, even the perfect ones.

My phone began to buzz. I was hoping it was Jake. But speak of the archenemy, I saw Airic's name pop up and couldn't help my disappointment.

Robert Stanton smiled. "You need to get that? I'll go round us up a sangria, perfect early-afternoon pick-me-up."

"Venus, I'm here at your house. Where is Mya?" Airic was irate, but what else was new. "We agreed on this Sunday. I'm not going to stand for this. I've already missed two of my visits."

"Listen, I completely forgot. I've got a lot going on. Not to mention Mya had a birthday party of her best friend from school that she was not going to miss." I shook my head like a petulant child, my best imitation of our daughter—or maybe she was constantly imitating me. I'd often caught her staring at me intensely with those big bold eyes, studying my inability to be reasonable. Then I remembered my promise of a kinder, gentler Venus. "I apologize, but I'm not going to bring her all the way back to the house. The party won't be over until four at the earliest."

Airic proceeded to yell in my ear. "I don't want to get the authorities involved, Venus, but I will if I have to."

"Don't you have enough on your plate? Why are you pushing this?"

"Tell me where you are, and I'll pick her up from there," he demanded.

Before I could scoff at the ridiculousness of Airic's attitude, Robert Stanton returned with two tall glasses filled with ice drowned in the punch. He set one down on a coaster in front of me. From his expression, I could tell he could hear Airic's loud bark over the phone. He sat directly across from me and gave a sympathetic raised brow.

"Okay, so I'll call you in about an hour." I smiled into the phone. "Yes, yes, absolutely, whatever you say. I will call you back, okay. Maybe we can work something out for later this evening." We hung up.

"Your ex-husband, I presume." He crossed his leg and draped his arms over the sides of the chair.

I took a sip and did my best not to keep going. I held up my glass and drank until the ice tumbled into my face. An instant buzz floated around my head. I took a deep breath and relaxed. "My ex, but not as in husband. I was engaged to be married when I got pregnant, but then we broke up." In one fell swoop, I'd painted myself as a slut. "I mean . . . engaged to him and pregnant by him, but then we broke up." I stared at the empty glass on the table and scolded myself. Let that be a lesson, boys and girls, don't drink wine on an empty stomach—even if someone calls it punch.

Feeling increasingly ridiculous for telling a stranger more about my life in thirty seconds than I had to anyone in the past year, I put a hand to my head.

"You all right? Is there anything I can do for you?"

It sounded like a high-pitch whistle that only dogs can hear. Code language. When a man says, *Is there anything I can do for you?* he's usually referring to only one thing.

"No, I'm fine. Just needed to take it slow."

He reached over and touched my knee. "You sure?"

"Yes, my ex is just giving me a hard time." *Aughh,* there I went again. The act of spilling one's guts is messy at first; then suddenly there's this veil lifted and you really don't care what anyone thinks. Releasing the burden of information is too good to pass up. "Only this past year Airic became interested in being a part of Mya's life. It's taken some time to get used to for me and my husband."

"I've heard of your husband, the hip-hop musician."

"What? Yes." I narrowed my eyes. "What have you heard?"

The creases around his mouth deepened. He laughed. "You're funny. It's part of the climate these days. Have to know who your friends are. Jory might want to run for president. Next thing you know, they'll say his best friend was a daughter of a terrorist."

"My husband?"

"No, I'm just saying I know who both of you are. Just routine . . ." He scratched his head. "Hey, you want to hear something? I just got this amazing sound system. I got hip-hop, rhythm and blues, jazz—you name it."

"Nice. So you listen to hip-hop?"

"Oh yeah," he said with a slight head tilt. "I bet you'd be surprised at my playlist."

"I bet I would, too."

"What's your preference?" he asked, and I suddenly felt a hot swirl from my head to my stomach. He was good-looking, no doubt about that. I'd been around the block and up the street a few times and I was in no mood to be seduced by a handsome, sweet-talking, worldly senator, regardless of my light-headed buzz. "Music, your music preference?"

Oh right, music.

I sat starry-eyed. "Um, old school R and B right up to all the new hits out now." Wine on an empty stomach plus my panic attack from being chased by henchmen had left me slightly off kilter. I would use that for an excuse later.

Meanwhile he stuck out his hand. "But you're definitely a rhythm and blues kind of lady, huh? Nice. C'mon." I grabbed it for a lift up from the couch and followed diligently.

I had a theory about life: Whatever you might be thinking and feeling, someone else was also thinking and feeling at the exact same time, possibly in the exact same situation. It helped to know this. To know you weren't alone, you weren't the only person doing the stupidest thing.

"Listen to this." We sat in the darkness of the garage. He turned the ignition so the lights of the dash came on. The music was like gliding on air. "I have over ten thousand songs loaded. I bet if you name a song, I've got it," he yelled over the mellow jazz.

I really couldn't think of anything. "Earth, Wind and Fire," I mumbled. My body fell into the feather-soft leather seats. I closed my eyes and was ten seconds from falling asleep. If I could hide there for a couple of weeks, I'd be good.

"Reasons" started playing.

For whatever reason, I laughed. He laughed, too.

My phone started vibrating against my body, where I held my purse. I could guess that it was still Airic not giving up without a fight. I was so sick of being in the middle between him and Jake.

I didn't know how long I could honor my husband's wish for Airic not to pick up Mya. My phone continued to ring in my purse.

Robert Stanton leaned back and started singing the words to the Earth, Wind & Fire song. "This is a good one," he said when it ended six minutes later. "Songs were long back then. Now, we were lucky to get three minutes of solid music."

I was hardly listening. The garage was dark except for the light coming off the stereo display.

"It's Sunday," he said, still making conversation. "Too bad we only get one a week. Saturdays are all right, but seem to have a honey-do requirement. Sundays are the best. You can just sit back and relax."

With that, for whatever reason, I welled up underneath my closed lids. He stuck his finger to my cheek and gathered the tear. Which meant his eyes weren't closed, and he'd been staring at me the entire time.

"Why are you sad?"

"I'm not. I swear. This is the happiest I've been in a long time. I'm tired. You can get tired and still be happy."

"Yeah, I guess you can."

"Thank you, for the minute of peace. It was nice." I pushed myself up from the incline of the seat.

"If you ever want to just talk, or relax, you know where to find me."

"Yep, I sure do." I said, grabbing for the door handle, which seemed to have disappeared. He reached over me, and I swear I nearly swooned. I inhaled the soft scent of expensive colonge. His cheek conveniently brushed against my chest, and my body jolted. He felt it, too—I saw the satisfaction on his face. I should've been flattered as well, but I knew he was only testing me. I'd failed miserably. He pushed the door open, and I staggered to my feet.

The bass and guitar of the current song sailed up and out of the car right along with the mood.

"There you are." Holly Stanton had removed her one roller. She was made up. Her eyes were visible now, with thick mascara and smoky brown liner. We were coming out of the garage, looking like the cats who'd ate the one damn canary. Equally guilty, though nothing concrete had happened. In a court of law, we'd both be found innocent. "I need you to fill the last of the balloons," she said. Then peeked at me close behind her husband. "You're still here."

"But leaving." I held up a hand to say good-bye.

"I thought we paid good money for balloons. You need more?" He didn't move, standing between us.

She folded her arms across her too-perfect chest. "Yes, you can never have too many balloons."

He raked a hand through his hair. "And there you go—a Sunday becomes a Saturday, just like that." He turned around in my direction, as if we shared a private joke. "I'll walk you out," he said with too much determination.

"Oh, no, I'm fine." I wanted to run as fast as my feet would allow. If there was one person I didn't need on my bad side, it was Holly Stanton. The woman oozed vengeance.

Her long legs began to lead the way. "I'll walk her out. You handle the balloons."

"Ay, ay, Captain." He was going to get us both in trouble.

She escorted me like a prison guard, marching with purpose. "You should take advantage of this beautiful day. The kids are playing. They'll be fine with Greta watching them."

"You're right. You know, I really haven't had a day all to myself in so long, I forgot what it was like. So around four is good?" I said, peeking out the long rectangular window next to the door, checking to see if there were any strange car-fellows.

"I expect this house to be cleared by five. I'm actually hosting a dinner party later this evening for a visiting senator, so please be on time."

"My, my, you're a busy girl."

She opened the door for me. "All right, then, four o'clock sharp."

I paused in the doorway and thought about telling Mya I was leaving. But I knew she was in good, solid hands. Greta, the nanny, didn't take any mess. She wouldn't let anything happen to my baby. "See you then." I held up four fingers. "At four." I rushed down the pathway, feeling her still watching—as if I planned to circle back and steal all her worldly goods, including her husband.

No thank you. I had one of my own, and they were far too much work. I certainly didn't need hers, too.

A Toast to the Bride

When I was a little girl, I believed in fairy tales. Snow White, Cinderella, Little Red Riding Hood, Hansel and Gretel—they were all saved by the prince, or the gallant father who loved them more than anything in the world. He would swoop down and slay whoever attempted harm. I believed in those fairy tales even after I'd been lied to, cheated on, bullied, and even physically hurt, all at the hands of the man who was supposed to save me. Yet I still believed.

My throat was closing. I hadn't anything to drink since the preceremony toast with the wedding party. Regardless of how I felt about the people involved, it had turned out wonderfully. I remember looking across the room at my daughter and seeing her dancing with her father and feeling overwhelming love. How many times in life do we feel the assured truth of love? I wanted her always to know that feeling. I wanted her to believe in fairy tales. I wished for her never to know shame, or doubt. So no matter what happened in the story, the ending would be happily ever after. All I'd wanted was to protect her from hurt. A chill swept through me. What if he'd taken my daughter, too? Ohmigod, my baby . . .

"Attention, everyone, I'd like to make a toast." Gray stood up with his glass of champagne. His eyes scanned the room. "I want to thank you, all of you, for being so gracious in helping us pull off one of the fastest weddings, planned in record time. I wish I could say it was a shotgun wedding, because I can't wait to have a baby with this woman." Keisha cast her eyes down and shook her head, mocking embarrassment.

I, on the other hand, started to choke on the full gulp of carbonated apple juice I'd requested instead of champagne. I dabbed at my mouth and eyes where involuntary moisture appeared. No one had bothered to ask if I was all right. I spot-dried the spittle drops on my chest and the wet blemishes on my blouse with the napkin, then turned my attention back to the lying scoundrel making the toast.

From the corner of my eye, I could see Delma beaming her evil eye into me, as if I were making a scene on purpose. On the other side of Gray was Keisha, also looking at me. Her eyes gently begging for me not to ruin everything. *Please, Trevelle, don't make a scene.* That's what she called me, no matter how many times I'd asked her to call me Mother.

I cleared my throat one last time, or at least I'd hoped. Gray continued, "Keisha is the woman of my dreams. I want to thank her for loving me as much as I love her. I want to thank you all for loving her, because without family, we are mere lost vessels floating in a huge ocean with no destination. To family."

He held up his glass while everyone else did the same, then in chorus repeated, "To family." Everyone seemed to be drinking the Kool-Aid of lies.

"I'd like to make a toast." I stood up. I could see Delma's *I told you so* expression with her lopsided frown. Hadn't the woman learned not to make those kinds of faces? One word: Restylane. I knew of a good dermatologist who could make the great Betty Ford look twenty-five again. Surely Delma wouldn't be so hard to fix. I gave her a half smile before beginning.

"I'd like to say a quick toast. Most of you know me as the famous

Trevelle Doval. But you don't know why I'm here. Keisha, you are a wonderful young woman, and I am proud to call you my daughter. I gave birth to you twenty-seven years ago." This time it was Delma who did the choking. She coughed and gagged, making exaggerated efforts to clear her throat. The only one louder than Delma was Gray's grandma Edna. She squinted and clucked every few seconds in between her story of how she'd spanked Gray almost every day for some mischief or other. She was hard of hearing, so hadn't realized she was interrupting.

"I've never really had a family until now, and I am so grateful to be a part of this beautiful union. May God bless them and turn their hearts toward one another for the duration of their lives."

"Attention, everyone, I'd like to make a toast." Delma stood up. She had the nerve to adjust her floral bow on a dress she'd probably owned before Keisha was even born.

"Sweetie, I think there've been enough toasts," her husband interjected. He stood up a foot taller than she, attempting to take the champagne glass out of her hand. She leaned away from his grasp. "First of all, I am Keisha's mother . . . the only one she's ever had from the day she was born. I may not have given her life, but I damn well saved her life from the likes of a junkie, prostitute, no-account teenage mama who was going to do nothing but bring her misery and pain."

"Well, damn," someone called out, followed by soft chuckles. "This is better than *The Young and the Restless*."

"All right, that's enough." Keisha stood and wrung her hands. Gray touched her shoulder to say he was handling things. "No." She refused his offer. "How dare they embarrass me this way. Both of them."

Delma called out, "I'm embarrassing you? She's the one coming in here talking about, *I'm Keisha's mother*. How dare you defend her?"

"She doesn't need to defend me. I have God on my side."

"Oh, stuff it—you have John, Dick, Harry, and Larry on your side, too. Don't forget I know who you really are. I know everything about that night. Don't you forget that," Delma growled.

"That makes two of us. Baby thief!" I yelled back.

Keisha shoved her chair back and snatched her purse. She was storming out of the restaurant.

"Darling, wait."

Gray caught up with Keisha before she was out the door and wrapped a comforting arm around her. With the other hand, he put out a warning. "Don't come any closer. I think what's best here is pretty obvious. Keisha doesn't deserve this. It's tearing her apart."

"How would you know what she deserves. You've known her, what, three months? Don't tell me what my child deserves. Someone better than you, I can say that much."

"Trevelle, you really don't want to go down this road."

"Oh, really, is that a threat?"

Gray continued, unfazed. "Guess what, Trevelle, I don't need to make threats. You're doing all the work yourself. You're sabotaging what little strides you've made in this relationship all on your own. As a matter of fact, you know what I think—?"

"No, let me say it," Keisha interrupted.

I crossed my dolman sleeves over my chest, bracing myself for what she was about to say. As God is my witness, I wasn't about to be nixed from my baby's life. Not over the likes of Gray Hillman or Delma Hawkins. "Don't make any rash decisions you will regret, sweetheart. We've come too far."

Keisha's pained expression said it all. "I don't want to be torn between the two of you. But I swear, there is no contest. I love my mother with all my heart. And I want to be in both your lives. But for this day, for this one moment, if this is any example of how you're going to act, I'm going to have to regretfully ask you to leave the wedding."

"Are you serious?"

"I just can't do it. I just want to get married. That's all. I can't be on pins and needles. Please, try to understand."

"I understand. But you are making the biggest mistake of your life—"

"No, I think this is the best decision for everyone."

Gray's eyes narrowed. He knew exactly what I had planned to say. "Now is not the time or place. Maybe we can all talk later. Come on, everyone, I'm sorry. We're going to be leaving. Please try to enjoy the rest of your meal."

"No, wait a minute." I followed closely on their heels. Gray escorted Keisha like she was some invalid. He helped her into his car, and then quickly moved to the driver's side. "This is your fault." I followed him around and scooted between him and the door. "You better fix this."

Gray lifted both his hands. "You were warned."

"You're the one whose been warned. Fix it, or I swear—"

"To God . . . I thought that was a no-no." He got into his car and turned a half smile into a sneer.

I watched as the car backed out then pulled away. Keisha didn't bother to meet my eyes, keeping her head down. She should be ashamed. Her behavior was unspeakable.

"Well, that was interesting." The accented voice came from a few feet away. Nikki clutched her bag in front of her. "And a little scary. I'm so sorry you had to go through that. Are you okay?"

"No, but it's not about falling down; it's about how long it takes to get back up. Gray Hillman has underestimated me for the last time."

Nikki touched my shoulder. "Let's go back inside. You sound like you need an ear. We can go somewhere and have a decent meal."

I hunched and jarred her hands off me. I had never gotten over feeling uncomfortable when touched unexpectedly. "Thank you, but I'm going home. You can do me a huge favor and grab my purse then drop me off to my car."

"Sure, no problem." Nikki waddled off in her high heels, too happy to oblige. She was Gray's little lapdog. I made a mental note to trust her only as far as I could throw her, which wasn't an inch.

Shattered Luck

"Hey, baby, where are you?"

"Better question is where are *you*? I've been calling all day."

"Legend and I—"

"Don't finish that sentence. Do you know what kind of day I've had? Someone broke into In Bloom. Then two men were following me in the car. On top of that, Airic calls, screaming that he's going to call the sheriff to enforce his visitation. So please, whatever you have to say better be good."

"Someone broke in?"

"Yes." I turned into the parking lot of the coffee shop. I parked and rested my head on the steering wheel.

"I'm sorry. I know that had to be a shocker."

"Not much shocks me anymore, Jake. I'm long over being surprised. All I want is for you and me to get back to our little suburban comfort zone and life. Is that too hard? I mean, am I asking for too much?"

"Where are you? We need to talk."

"I'm listening."

"The phone's not a good choice."

"Oh, so now what? Are we being bugged?" I gave it a moment of thought. "Okay, now I'm scared. Do you understand whatever game you're playing is putting me, your daughter in danger? There were men chasing me on the street. The kind of high-speed chase you see on *Cops*. Seriously, do you understand the words coming out of my mouth?"

"I do. That's why I'm telling you we have to talk."

I let out an exasperated sigh. "Please, the only thing I want to hear you say is that Legend is leaving."

"Babe," he said quietly. "This isn't Legend's fault. Okay?"

I wiped the tear rolling down my face. "Okay."

"We'll talk when we get home. Just go home."

"I can't. Mya's at Jory's birthday party. I'm going to In Bloom, then I have to go back and pick her up at four and then we'll be home."

"I can meet you there."

"No. Don't come. Not if you have to bring Legend." I wasn't trying to make it a point to stay mad. I simply couldn't help myself. No matter what Jake said, my instinct kept telling me Legend had started this hailstorm.

Silence followed.

"Oh, come on. Do you have to bring him?"

Jake was nearly whispering, which he wasn't good at. The tunnel sound made it obvious he'd cupped his hand over the phone to spare Legend's feelings—as if he had any. "Look, I'm already at the exit. I'm not going all the way cross town to drop him off then back just 'cause you don't want to see him. I'll tell him to stay in the car."

"Please, do that. I'm at my wit's end. I won't be able to handle his sarcasm today."

Pulling up to In Bloom, there was glass everywhere, like someone threw a brick through the window. Vince was nowhere to be seen. I dialed the police department, informing them that I'd like to report a burglary. When the police operator asked me what was taken, I had to answer honestly, "Nothing. I don't have a cash register. Seems everything is here. It's just smashed up. The place is turned upside down."

"What time did the break-in occur?"

"I'm not sure. I assume last night sometime." I kneeled down and picked up a floral catalog. The laminated pages had disassembled. I was glad it was only pictures of bouquets destroyed and not the real thing.

"Are there any witnesses?"

"Uh . . . I have no idea. Maybe if you send a police officer here, they can find out the answers to these burning questions."

"In this kind of case, we usually don't send out an officer. We take the report over the phone. You may use this report to file with your insurance company."

"*This kind of case,* what's that supposed to mean?"

"No robbery or bodily harm took place. It's considered vandalism, and unless you suspect or know who was involved, there's little or nothing we can do."

Jake walked in with Legend right behind him. My annoyance meter jumped to maximum. "Fine. When they come back and kill me, I'll give you a call."

The man chuckled. "Oxymoron. You can't call if you're already dead."

I hung up the phone. Jake was already wrapping his arms around me, giving me an apologetic kiss on top of my head before I could say something mean and regrettable.

"You two lovebirds stay there. I'll check the place out."

"Someone really doesn't like me, or us. They didn't take a thing, just wanted to tear the place up."

"Did you consider it might be random? Maybe some kids with nothing better to do?" He said quickly, "I don't want you to be scared to come to work. I know you love this place. In Bloom has made you the happiest you've been in a long time. And let's face it, when you're happy, we're all happy."

I poked his sides so he jerked. "If you cared about my happiness, he would've been on the first thing pulling into airspace." I darted my eyes in Legend's direction.

He was coming out of the back, stepping on broken glass. The crunching sound made me realize he was doing further damage to the hardwood floors.

"Could you watch your step?"

"I think where I step is the least of your worries." Legend kneeled down and picked up a cigarette butt. "Look at this—I bet this came from whoever did this."

I put my hand to my mouth and gasped exaggeratedly. "You think so?"

Jake opened his arms. "Please, can we all just get along?"

"See, right about now, I need a Baggie for the evidence. Some real *CSI* stuff right here." Legend stood up with the cigarette butt pinched between his fingers.

"Not funny, man."

"Who's joking? I wouldn't doubt if it belonged to Ronny or one of his boys. Better yet, those FBI agents looking for their payday."

"I knew it." I coughed with my *ah-ha* moment. "I knew you had something to do with this. So you know who the guys are who've been following me, too?"

Legend raised his hands. "I don't have anything to do with this. I'm merely your husband's right-hand man. Always have been." He glared in Jake's direction.

"I want some answers, and I want them right now." I looked between Huey and Duey. "Start talking."

⟡

"Wait, let me recap." I paced gently. "The FBI showed up on our doorstep and told you that you are still a suspect in Byron Steeple's murder. Not only that, but they think you have the millions of dollars he stole from not only yourself but America's Gangster."

Legend chuckled. Jake gave him the eye. "What? She hit the nail on the head. Getting bright in your old age."

I pushed up my middle finger. I wished Legend didn't make the ugly come out in me. "So, where does that leave you? Defending yourself against criminals and the FBI—is that what I'm hearing?"

Jake nodded. "Basically. I need to get some alone time with this Ronny guy."

Again Legend chuckled.

"What is with you? My God, are you on medication?"

"After this trip, I'm sure I'll need to borrow yours."

That was the last straw. I lunged toward Legend. I caught the end of a handful of locks. He squealed like a girl. Fortunately for him, I was afraid to slip and fall in the glass all over the floor, so I had to release quickly.

Jake seemed to have reached a point of exhaustion. "Don't do that, man. Don't talk to my wife like that."

"Oh, I'm supposed to stay in my place, but she can throw insults like nobody's business?"

"Yeah, I can." I hurled one last time. "That's what happens when I'm the one with the common sense around here."

"I'm out." He kicked past the mess and went out the front door. As he was leaving, Vince was coming in.

"You're back since the coast is clear?"

"Whoa." Vince put up his hands. "What'd I walk into? War of the roses?"

"My place was destroyed because someone obviously is trying to send a message to my husband."

"Hey." Jake shook his head to keep me from my blabbermouth hysterics.

"I'm out of here. I can't deal with this. Vince, do you mind sweeping up?" My eyes pleaded.

"That's why I'm here. I do a mean cleanup. I already got the glass guy coming to replace the window."

"Thank you." I headed out. Jake stayed a second behind and said a few words to Vince I couldn't make out. He caught up with me at the car.

"Baby, everything's going to be fine, okay?"

"*Ohmigod.* This is not a wiseguy movie with a director to call 'Cut.' You're messing with dangerous criminals. And here I was moved by your little speech a few days ago when you said Mya and I were all that you cared about." My voice rose for the broadcast of news. "Guess what, all of us are in danger. Mya, me, you—"

"Don't forget me." Legend raised his hand. His dark skin glowed while his pearly teeth parted to a perfect smile. "I'm in danger also," he said, leaning against Jake's car.

"Good thing you don't have any loved ones who give a damn."

"Okay, stop. Don't even start, Legend, man." Jake added, "Please," then faced me for mercy. "Babe, just be patient. I swear this will be over before you know it. I promise. Have I ever steered you wrong?"

Jake had a point. He'd been the rock of our relationship from day one. Only once had he walked away and thrown in the towel, and that was after catching me at a hotel with my ex-boyfriend. When he saw Clint in my hotel room, Jake's imagination and temper got the best of him. We had gotten separate rooms, but after a brief encounter in the hallway, our keys got switched, so Clint and I switched rooms.

I'll never forget that moment of shock when Jake knocked on the hotel room door and Clint answered. He wouldn't listen to reason that the trip was innocent—if you call wanting to make Clint finally see he'd chosen the wrong woman "innocent." It was a battle I should've never picked to fight. The past should stay in the past. Trying to right wrongs or make someone regret their choice surely won't change your life or the way they feel about you. I'd found love—true love—and yet I was holding on to the pain of Clint choosing another woman over me. Jake said he didn't understand how I could still be thinking about another man while I had him. I couldn't agree more. He'd even had divorce papers drawn up. I begged for clemency, a stay of execution for our marriage. A wakeup call I never wanted to experience again. After that, I vowed never to jeopardize our love again. I did everything possible to make sure he felt the same way.

I would do anything for him. But I was worried what "anything" would entail and how much longer "anything" would continue to happen. Mya and I getting chased, Legend's presence, and Jake's determination to find Byron Steeple's real killer were as close to the limit as I was willing to go.

"All I need to do is find where Byron stashed the money he embezzled from me and this guy Ronny. The FBI, I'm not afraid of them. They're just after the money and Ronny, and they're using me to do it. That's it. If I find it, everybody wins."

"You couldn't find how he was taking the money and where he put it then—what makes you think you can find it now?"

"This time I at least know where to look." He kissed me on the forehead. "Hey, why don't I stay with you and let Legend find his way back to the house."

I was exhausted. My head hurt. My eyes hurt. "Just go." I put up a hand. I'm going back to the Stantons', then I'll see you at home."

Jake kissed me on the lips. "You're the most important thing in my life. I swear. I'll see you at home."

"Promise?"

"I promise, baby. Stop worrying. Everything's going to be all right."

❦

I didn't have any trouble getting into the Hadley Park private community this time. The security officer waved me in like we were old pals. I realized how late I was when I saw that the birthday décor had been completely removed and replaced by two teenage boys dressed in valet coats and black trousers, standing at attention.

"Good evening, welcome." My door was swung open before I could put the car gear in park.

"I'm not staying. I'm just running in to grab my daughter. Can you leave the car here?"

"Sure, no problem. Just pull up a few more feet."

Cars already lined up behind me. In the rearview mirror, a distinguished couple got out of a silver Mercedes, wearing a tux and gown. I made a dash across the cobblestone path to beat the couple. I figured the valet could move it a few more feet. I pressed the bell, out of breath. Holly Stanton was immediately not happy. "Hello, Venus."

"I'm so sorry I'm late. I had a situation at my floral shop."

She cleared her throat. "Come in. Mya is upstairs. We had a situation as well. I tried to call, but—"

Before she could finish, I hiked the stairs two at a time. Greta met me in the hall with a big white towel hugged to her chest. "Oh, Mizz Venus, you are here. Let me explain."

"Explain? Mya!" I called out. "Mya, where are you?"

"Please keep your voice down. I'm in the middle of a party if you hadn't noticed. She's fine."

Holly had eventually caught up, still holding her champagne glass. "I'll explain quickly because I have guests. She and Jory came in while I was getting ready for the party. I use a flat iron to enhance my shine. This was a thrill for Mya. I guess she'd never seen anything like it."

I covered my mouth. "She got burned."

"Not by me. I used the flat iron on a small portion of her hair. I made some cute little bangs." She twirled her finger. "When I left, I escorted them out of the room as well. Mya sneaked back into my room, plugged in the appliance, and proceeded to—" Again with the finger swirl. "—straighten her hair."

"Where is she?" I found myself screeching at the top of my lungs. Mya heard me and came out of the room with a wet towel wrapped around her neck.

"Mommy." She poked out her lip. "I hurt myself."

"Sweetie, oh baby." I kneeled down and hugged her. I unwrapped the towel to see red welts around her neck and shoulder. As if I needed this right now. As if this was the day I needed to deal with hair lessons. Daily, sometimes twice, I told Mya how beautiful she was in her natural glory. It was me against the world, trying to combat every single image from the television to the covers of magazines so boldly placed at every checkstand in the supermarket. *Look at me, I'm beautiful with long luxurious hair—and you're not.*

I was sick of it. Sick to death. It took everything in my power not to reach across and yank Holly's extensions out of her head. "Move!" I yelled, taking hold of Mya's hand.

"It's okay, Mya. You're okay." Jory was at her side, patting her shoulder like a dedicated mate. He even stroked her hair, as if he felt sorry for her.

I snatched her up and started down the stairs.

"Don't be a stranger. You're always welcome," Holly Stanton said while closing the door with a *good riddance* smile perched on her lips.

I rushed across the infinite lawn with Mya's legs banging against mine with every step.

"Mommy, ouch," she murmured into my shoulder. "My neck hurts."

We reached the car. I pulled on the door to find it locked. "Excuse me, hey." I moved toward the valet to get his attention. "My keys, the door's locked." I thought he heard me. Instead he jumped into the car of the latest guest and pulled off. "Wait . . . no!"

"Mommy, I have to go number one."

I spun around and looked at the imposing entryway, where Holly stood welcoming her guests. The thought of going back in that house was enough to make my stomach cramp. I put Mya down on her feet. I grabbed her shoulders. "The man will be back with the keys any minute. Then we're going to go home."

"I have to go now."

"Sweetie, you can hold it. You've done it before. Don't think about it. Think about something fun, like playing with your dolls when we get home."

"Mommy, I have to go." She did her little *Riverdance*. Her feet bopped and her arms crossed over her front.

The guests were piling up. Then I remembered the clubhouse, less than a minute away, if I could just get the keys. As if she could read my mind, Mya announced, "Mommy, I have to go right now."

"Okay. Fine." I took Mya's hand. There went my promise never to darken that woman's doorstep again. The closer we got, the angrier I became.

I pushed past the long gowns and coiffed hair. "Excuse me, please. Excuse me." Reaching the entrance, Holly obviously felt the same way, from her aghast expression.

"What are you doing back here?"

"Mya has to use the restroom. It's an emergency."

"Mommy . . ."

"Okay, fine. But please use the facility next to the serving area. There's no one there yet."

"Fine, which way?"

"Mommy . . ."

The next thing I knew, my baby had let go of all she was holding in. Spatters of wee-wee landed on Holly Stanton's perfectly painted toes. "Nice. Just wonderful." She was fuming mad.

Mya's big round eyes began to well up. "I'm sorry."

"No, sweetie, it's not your fault," I said, shielding her from humiliation as guests tiptoed past the spill.

"Consuelo, please, we have an emergency," Holly called out, trying to lift her gown as if she were wading in a flood instead of the small accident on her marble floor.

"Everyone, please, come in. I'm so sorry."

"Take her upstairs. She can put on something of Jory's," she said, trying not to look at either one of us. "None of this would've happened if you'd come on time." She dashed away to move her welcoming ceremony into another room. Good thing, since I was about three seconds from being all over her.

"It's okay." A man's voice came out of nowhere. "You're going to be fine, pretty girl." The hand of Robert Stanton extended to Mya.

"Come on, we'll get you into some dry clothes." He looked like he'd just stepped out of a cologne ad, with his black slacks, crisp tuxedo shirt, and bow tie hanging loosely, waiting to be tied. I followed him up the stairs.

Jory screamed with glee, "Mya, you're back!"

They rushed into each other's arms like it had been a decade since they'd seen each other.

"What do you do?" Mr. Stanton smiled. "Can't fight love."

"No, but it will sure kick the hell out of you," I was too tired to make nice talk. "Clothes."

"Let me apologize for Holly. This party was for me. It was my fault I overlapped on Jory's birthday. She's stressed, no doubt. Her rudeness should be excused." He shifted his eyes. "Well, at least this once." He handed me a pair of Jory's Hanes underpants with a picture of Superman flying through the air and some jeans and a T-shirt.

"Thank you, and I was a bit rude myself . . . to you, so I apologize as well." I pulled Mya and took her into the bathroom. She was quick lifting her arms so I could get the dress over her head. Her round tummy pushed out with the cutest belly button I was sure I'd ever seen. It was perfect from the day the rest of the umbilical cord fell off. "Step." I held the cotton underwear while she leaned on my shoulder. Her new hairdo brushed against me, the wild spikes pushed up and over in Donald Trump fashion. Her ears were tinged with red welts right along with her neck.

"Sweetie, didn't it hurt when you burned yourself? Why did you keep doing it?"

"'Cause I want to be pretty . . . for Jory."

The hairs on the back of my neck stood straight up. "You are pretty. You're beautiful. Jory likes you just as you are." I wasn't going to have this conversation in the Stantons' bathroom. I needed neutral territory. "Let's go."

The senator was still out in the room, stretched on the carpeted floor. "Everything okay?" He pushed his miniature car on the racetrack behind Jory's.

"Nothing's okay." I felt it coming—the rage, the tears, the breakdown of epic proportion.

"Hey, hey . . ." He was on his feet in a matter of seconds, wrapping an arm around me. Mya was at my thigh, giving me a comfort pat.

"It's just hair, Mommy. You say all the time. It's just hair."

"Right, just hair." I welled up and tried to keep myself from hyperventilating, or at least keep it to a minimum.

"Mommy just needs a moment. Give her a minute." His arms enclosed around me. I blubbered into his tuxedo shirt.

"I'm so sorry. Oh." I patted the wet spot. "Do you have a spare?"

"Forget about the shirt. Come on, sit."

"I'm okay, really. Don't you have to get to your party?"

"What party?" He grinned. Jory's playroom was filled with child-sized furniture. We sat in the romper-sized seats. "Tell me what's eatin' you all up inside. Besides my wife. She has that effect on a lot of people, trust me."

"I'm just tired. Nothing serious." And I meant it this time. I wasn't about to go into a soliloquy of Jake being hunted by the FBI and a local small-time criminal threatening our lives. "Really, I think it's hormonal. I'm okay."

"Okay, all right. I'm not going to press."

"I really have to go." I tried to rise. The seat was too low, so I ended up rolling to the side and squeezing out.

In between his laughter he said, "You know what, I haven't smiled this much in a long time. I can see why Jory is smitten with your daughter if she's got your personality. You are seriously a breath of fresh air."

"Always glad to entertain." I got to my feet. "Thank you for the clothes."

"We'll walk you out. Right, Jory—let's be gentlemen and walk these beautiful ladies to the door."

"No. Really, we're going to beeline it right out of here. Hopefully with as little attention as possible. Thanks again."

"That's three times."

"What?"

"You keep thanking me. You don't have to thank me." He opened the door. At the exact same time, Holly was rounding the corner.

"What in God's name. There you are. I've been looking all over for you." She looked past him, then at me. "You're still here?"

I didn't bother to answer her rhetorical question. I took Mya's hand and walked down the regal stairs. All I could hear was Jory's loud whine: "Why not? She's my best friend."

It's complicated, sweetie. Very complicated. And it never gets any easier.

Shall We Dance

"Gray Hillman, you have some nerve, absolute unequivocal nerve. Please don't think this is over. I will not rest until you are nothing but a distant memory." I took a breath only to hear the dial tone where Gray had obviously hung up before I was through. I marched back and forth across the deck of my penthouse. The chilled air was necessary if I was going to cool down. He'd masterminded the entire incident at the brunch. Delma and I fell into play like two silly puppets, fighting in front of Keisha that way.

The chime announced a security call from downstairs. At ten at night, I certainly wasn't expecting any visitors.

"Yes."

"Ma'am, Mr. Fisher is here. Should I send him up?"

"No, you may not," I sang out. "There is a note posted on your security station that specifically requests for him not to be allowed in the building." The guard was young and new, but that was no excuse. "You can read, can't you?"

"Yes, ma'am, I can read."

"Don't get snippy. I'm just asking a question. If you could read, you wouldn't be making this phone call."

He took a long deep breath. "Sorry for the interruption."

"You have a good night, and God bless." I certainly was in no mood for Airic's attitude. I'd ignored his phone call earlier, didn't even bother to listen to his message. Whatever he had to say would have to be on an affidavit declaring our divorce and me free and clear of owing him a dime.

This time the buzzing sound was coming from my front door. I moved cautiously from the deck and decided I should call to make sure they hadn't let Airic in. And if they had, I was going to make sure heads rolled.

"This is Ms. Doval, I'm calling to make sure Airic Fisher was not allowed to come up."

"Mr. Fisher was escorted out, ma'am. He left."

"Uh-huh, well someone's knocking on my door at this moment. Don't you have cameras or something where you can see who it is?"

"No, not on your floor."

"What's that supposed to mean, not on my floor?"

"Ma'am, you can only access your floor with a keycard. That means either a tenant or a security guard would have to give access to your floor. Like I said, no one here gave Mr. Fisher access."

"Fine. Thank you." I hung up, reassured but still cautious. I tip-toed gently through the living room. I spied through the peephole, greeted by a large bouquet of roses. "Who is it?"

"Dr. Perry, your neighbor." His sharp features were revealed when the flowers were shifted from one side to the other. "I have something that was left for you downstairs. Thought I'd be considerate and bring them up. I'll leave them here right outside the door if you're indisposed."

"Yes, please do." I watched him bend then stand up without the bouquet. He disappeared out of view. I waited momentarily and listened for his footsteps to fade. The penthouse he shared with his gay lover was gratefully on the other side of the building, but we used the same elevator. When the coast was clear, I opened the door.

The first thing I noticed was Airic's scent. The air of his cologne brushed past me, and then I saw him nearly eye to eye with me. "What in the world?"

"Please, we need to talk." He appeared from around the corner. He held the divorce papers he'd been served with.

"Are you serious? You sneak in here like some thieving criminal and expect me to let you in?"

He fell to his knee, holding the flowers he'd tricked Dr. Perry into delivering. "We have been through so much together. I know your faults, you know mine. We both did some hurtful things. The fact still remains that we are right for each other." He swallowed hard, as if he was going to lose his nerve. "I need you. I need you more than I've ever needed anything or anyone in my life."

"Get up. Groveling out here like some—" I yanked the flowers out of his hand. "Come inside."

The next time I saw Dr. Perry, he was going to get an earful. I marched straight to the sink and filled a vase with water. Airic knew my weakness was beautiful flowers. Lately with all that was going on, I had no time to organize weekly deliveries. That was Chandra's job before she'd slept with my husband.

"You need to put a stop to this." Airic's voice sounded different. In those few seconds, he'd gone from pitiful to making a full-on demand. He'd shifted his feet as if he wasn't sure which way he wanted to go. Then I felt him close behind me. "You have to speak with the district attorney. All you have to do is tell the D.A. the truth. The absolute truth."

"I did that already," I said, turning around with the vase of flowers to give myself some room. "But I can't talk them out of the statutory charge. Maybe it's Chandra who could lend a hand in that regard."

"The preliminary hearing is on Tuesday, Trevelle. Show them the application where she lied about her age. You are better than this. I know how hurt and angry you are, but I also know you live by the laws of the Holy Spirit. Forgiveness. Compassion. Empathy. Venus won't let me see my daughter. I have lost everything just like that." He snapped a finger. "More important, I've lost you."

I was quickly aware of his manipulation. Yet he spoke the truth. "Okay, all right. I will try one more time. But that's it. I have a lot going on right now. Keisha's wedding day is coming, and she uninvited me today. Everything that's going on has really been tough on me."

He reached out, touching my cheek. It had been an exhausting and devastating day. I was being tested; this much I knew. Even as he cupped my face and his lips met mine, I knew it was all a test. "Airic." I tried to speak, but the word no wouldn't release. He smelled so good. We were still husband and wife, and I was a woman who deserved and needed to be held.

"I've never stopped for a minute wishing for you." He began to slip his hands underneath my blouse.

I can't do this. I pulled back. I needed him in the worst way, but I knew if I gave in, I'd lose whatever dignity I had left.

"I need your forgiveness," he said, attempting to kiss me again.

"I forgive you. Now you can go. You got what you came for."

He dropped his arms to his sides. "I don't want to leave you like this. I can see you're upset."

"I'll be fine. Don't worry, I'll call the D.A. tomorrow on your behalf."

That seemed to satisfy him. He touched my chin. "When this is over, we're going to go on a long trip, somewhere hot and beautiful, just like you."

Oh brother. "Looking forward to it," I said before closing the door and securing the lock.

I called down to the manager of the building and gave him a scathing replay, starting with the security guard and ending with Dr. Perry, who may or may not have known his part in the trickery. Either way, heads were going to roll.

The Truth and Nothing But

Media vans printed with various TV channel logos lined the street in front of the courthouse. There was always a salacious case happening. No shortage of high-visibility court drama in the city of Atlanta. I moved past the crowd of broadcast journalists with my head held high. I turned to face the small news crowd.

"Ms. Doval, I understand you're testifying today in the preliminaries of your husband's trial. Does this mean there's no hope for a reconciliation?"

"My husband and I are working hard to put our differences aside. But the law is the law. These charges were brought against him by the district attorney, not me personally." I had no choice but to maintain a good front. I couldn't stand up for him publicly, at least not yet.

"You're testifying against him, is that correct?"

"I'm giving a statement, plain and simple. The truth is all that is required of me. My heart breaks in tiny pieces recalling the abuse I suffered at the hands of my husband. No woman should have to live in fear of the one who should be protecting her."

"I see. Good luck, Ms. Trevelle Doval. We at Channel Four News wish you the best."

"Luck has little to do with my fate or anyone else's. God has blessed me in abundance. Luck is for the faithless and those without Christ in their heart. But when you know better, you do better."

I closed my eyes. "Heavenly Father, guide this wonderful young woman into your light and show her your blessings, let her know your greatness, dear Lord, so she may carry on in your name, amen." I took a deep breath and walked away.

That, of course, wouldn't make it to the nightly news. I knew all too well what was considered worthy of repeating and what wasn't. Prayer time could only be bought and paid for, but if it had something to do with defaming, killing, or maiming, it would be the lead-in story.

"Ms. Doval, you are such an inspiration." The female security guard smiled while she barely searched my purse.

"Thank you. Realize I receive my inspiration and perseverance from wonderful women like you."

She handed the purse back. "Stay strong, sister."

I gave her a nod. "I have God on my side. I can do all things through Jesus Christ." I stood in front of the elevator door and said a quiet prayer. The door and my eyes opened at the same time.

Airic stood before me, dressed exquisitely in the gray Lagerfeld suit I'd picked out for him that very morning. The tie I'd bought as a Father's Day gift last year when I'd talked him into taking responsibility for his daughter, Mya. He looked amazing. I wasn't particularly well dressed. I needed to appear downtrodden and resistant to this media circus for my populace. I wore a butter-toned blouse with a few too many creases near the elbow and a pair of black pants a size too big. However, it had all been planned. What I hadn't planned to see was Chandra being escorted by Airic like a poor mistake. Her sad black pantsuit was something off a Sears clearance rack. Airic's hand dropped from her hand as soon as he realized it was me.

"Hello, Trevelle." Chandra stopped dead in front of me. "I'm so sorry about all the trouble I caused."

Anger slashed through me. My heart was broken, no denying the fact. My head hurt from holding my breath. My steely gaze was exact. I nodded but didn't speak while creating a wide distance between us.

I did my absolute best to stay levelheaded, though I was about to bust. They weren't going to see me sweat. He would be doing the sweating and soon, once I finished with the testimony I was about to deliver, he'd be doing a little begging and groveling, too.

I quickly took my space on the elevator. The stench of her cheap toilet water remained. I pushed the button and let the door close without so much as a blink of my eyes. I even curled my fingers in a baby wave to secure the effect of being nonfazed.

However, once the doors closed, I slouched against the wall, cradling my chest after having held my breath too long.

Not until the elevator stopped on the third floor and I exited did I take a long, deep inhale. I tried to stop myself. Even as I flipped open my phone, I told myself not to press Airic's number. I told myself not to. *Dear God, give me strength.*

Airic answered on the first ring.

"How dare you embarrass me like this! You bring that whore on your arm when you know there are TV cameras everywhere? You have no decency. You're the lowest scum of this earth."

"I did exactly what you suggested."

"Oh, meaning you seduced her into defending your sorry ass."

"That's ridiculous. We agreed on how this would go. Why are you acting this way?"

"The question is, how dare you run around hand in hand with that whore for full viewing. Then when you see me, you try to pretend there's nothing between you. I hate you. I hate you with all my heart."

He hung up on me. I dialed him right back. "The righteous shall rise—"

Before I could finish, the distinct silence of the call going dead stopped me. I dialed again. The phone was shut off. It went straight to voice mail. I continued with what I had to say. "Matthew 10:10. The righteous shall rise above the pious and petty."

Within seconds of hanging up, I dialed again. "Airic, your job was simply to provide and protect, and I did the damn providing. Why have you forsaken me? Why—?"

I heard movement behind me and closed my phone. Something told me when I turned around it wasn't going to be good. The smartly dressed newswoman held her microphone close to her chest, as if she'd just witnessed a crime. The cameraman kept rolling.

I swung my purse, nearly hitting her. "Turn it off. Turn that camera off."

Later that evening Channel 9 News announced the footage as an exclusive. The tagline read: RECOGNIZING ABUSED-WIFE SYNDROME. An expert psychologist, an older woman with gray-and-black wings for hair pointed at the miniature screen next to her. "You see the way her shoulders are slumped," she said, gesturing with a pen. "And the posture of her stance. She is defeated and hopeless. This is a classic case. That would explain why she still wants her husband back after what he's done to her, begging for his love. One could even say asking for more abuse by wishing for the relationship to continue. Trevelle Doval is obviously suffering from abused-wife syndrome."

Forget about the perfect testimony I'd given to the district attorney and judge, enough to seal Airic's doom. The news wasn't interested in capturing my perfect account, embellishing his attack. Their only interest was making me look like a mad fool. The Doval Ministry was at stake. I couldn't lose the support of my following, everything I'd built over the last fifteen years—not because of one man. If you didn't define yourself, someone else would. I'd learned that lesson a long time ago.

I had no choice but to call my own press conference and clear the air once and for all. I paced back and forth.

It was only a matter of time before the phone began to ring. I was hoping it was Keisha. Instead it was Gray's drawn-out voice. Tired. Or simply bored. "Interesting news footage."

"I'm planning a press conference. I have to speak publicly. Let women know they're not alone. I'd planned to spin this in my favor all along. It was all an act."

Another exhausted sigh. "I'm not telling you what to do. We don't represent you anymore, remember? That was your decision. Why I'm calling is to tell you TBN doesn't want to renew your contract."

"What? That's ridiculous. Who did you talk to? And if you're not representing me, why did you take the call in the first place? You don't have my best interest at heart. I would've been better off defending myself. I think we can call this malpractice. I smell a lawsuit, Mr. Hillman. How about that?"

"Would you really try to sue your future son-in-law?"

"That remains to be seen. If you think I'm going to let this marriage happen, you have another think coming."

"Let's not go down this road again, Trevelle." Even in his exhaustion of the subject, he sounded amused. "I'm giving you my free advice because that's what family is for."

"I would have to be six feet under before I let you marry my daughter. Especially now. Your betrayal is unforgivable."

"I didn't create this. You were on national television. This thing is unfixable. The best thing you can do is get quiet, get still, let it disappear."

"I will not get quiet. I will scream from the mountaintops. You are not going to get away with stealing my daughter and my career in one fell swoop."

More incredulous laughter. "You know what . . . you have some misplaced anger. I am not your problem. Like I said—take some time to recoup. Find a wonderful spa retreat and stay there. Your flock will understand a time-out for restructuring your life. It'll only help when you make your comeback with a revitalized message. You see, I'm not even on the clock, and I'm giving the best management advice you will ever have. Take care, dear Mom. See you at the wedding. Or perhaps not."

His laughter still rang in my ear long after I'd hung up. It felt like everyone whom I'd ever trusted had united against me, except for Keisha and, of course, God. Knowing I had God on my side, the mightiest of all warriors, gave me a minute of peace. I continued to pace back and forth.

I would not be defeated. I'd come through many fires unscathed. Raped repeatedly beginning at the tender age of twelve by grown men, my initiation into a world of drugs and prostitution. Suffered verbal and real abuse at the hands of a pimp who reveled in demoralizing the weak.

That child was gone, purified in the blood of Christ. I survived for one purpose, to live through Jesus Christ. It was time to fight as I'd never fought before.

I picked up the phone again. This time I dialed Telena Gregory, who owned the online gossip rag that seemed to be as popular and more timely than the Associated Press these days.

"Telena, this is Trevelle Doval. I know, really, you were the first person I thought of. I'd like to tell my side of the story. How's tomorrow morning's schedule?" As I guessed, the gossip hound would clear her calendar. "Very good. I'll see you tomorrow."

Sugar Daddies

"Mr. Parson, welcome. Mr. Hillman will see you now." The woman stood over him, her bountiful breasts spilling out of a pink strapless dress. All Jake could think of was Good & Plenty, the pink candies that tasted like mint and Pepto-Bismol. "This way." Her curves and full bottom begged to be followed. She didn't really have to ask.

He bet she flaunted for all the potential clients. Then again, Jake had to admit he was working the silk-blend T-shirt that showed his cuts. He wore his relaxed slacks and Bruno loafers. All the look of a man who had not a care in the world, when in reality he was bound and determined to make use of Gray Hillman.

She didn't give him much room to pass as he entered Gray Hillman's office. "Anything else, sir?"

"Not at the moment." Gray Hillman stuck out a firm hand then pulled Jake in for a shoulder hug. He winked. "She's hot, huh? A temp. Making me rethink letting the other one come back at all. Go ahead and have a seat. Looking good, man. You're looking good. I don't give male compliments lightly."

Jake grinned in appreciation of the truth. Even he had to admit that life wasn't fair—he'd been overdelivered in the looks department. While he was growing up, his mother liked to remind him good looks wouldn't pay the bills, at least not the important ones. His mother had been wrong about a lot of things. But he wasn't there for the money. He had bigger fish to fry. Still, it was nice to know he could clean up well.

"So tell me, Jake Parson, where do you see yourself? To hell with five years. I'm talking about right now."

This was no time to be shy. Jake leaned with ease in the leather chair. "I want to be highly visible." It was a loaded statement. Jake hoped he wasn't being too obvious.

Gray leaned back in his chair as if he were trying to figure out how to split an atom. "Visible." His eyes narrowed. "Commercials. I've got Pepsi's marketing team on speed dial. They've been trying to find somebody to represent them for the last two years, ever since Bill O'Reilly jacked Ludacris of his good standing."

"Pepsi, cool." Jake said, not trying to get too excited. Trying to remember he was there seriously to get information about Ronny Wilks. "Who else you workin' with?"

"You know what? Let's not limit ourselves here. Let's throw some bigger ideas on the wall. You're a recognized face. You sold eight million copies of *Juicy Lips*. Numbers don't lie. The potential is there for bigger things. I got a friend at Calvin Klein, and I know for a fact they've been shopping different people and they might give us a look. They just terminated Fifty's contract. One too many tats. How 'bout you?"

Jake patted his right shoulder. "Just one, my initials. Barely the size of a quarter."

"This might be the ticket," Gray said, writing some notes. He tapped his pen for a few seconds, beating around the bush. "I'm assuming the entire mess surrounding you and those nasty homicide charges are a thing of the past, right?"

Jake took the moment of opportunity. "Right. Buried. So you know all about that, huh?"

"I'm sorry I had to bring it up."

"It's cool. Just wish I knew who really was responsible. He had connections with a lot of people, but seems my name was the one picked in the lotto."

Gray's light eyes darted slightly to his watch then back to Jake.

"All right, man, sounds like we've got our work cut out for us, but we're about to make miracles happen."

"Thank you, man. I appreciate it. I knew if anyone knew how to jump-start a career, you could do it."

"Hey, this is what I do. Let's work, man." Gray Hillman leaned from the edge of the desk where he'd sat the whole time and met Jake's hand with a tight grip. "Let's make good things happen. I see *dream team* written all over it. I'll have a contract drawn up and ready to sign by morning. Can't wait to thank Sirena for introducing us." He still hadn't let go of Jake's hand, searching his eyes for a response.

"Sirena's been a good friend," Jake said. "Tell her I said hello."

He'd come in with an ulterior motive, simply wanting to get some quick public exposure, but the thought of getting back in the spotlight had felt better than he anticipated.

"Thank you for coming, Mr. Parson. Will you be needing another appointment?"

Before Jake could answer, Gray spoke for him: "Thursday, nine A.M., see you then, man—and do a couple of crunches in your spare time. they might want to see you with your shirt off."

"They're not the only one."

Jake turned around, looking at the receptionist undressing him with her eyes. Gray had already disappeared.

"Mr. Parson, do you need me to call you with a reminder?"

"No thanks, I got it." Jake turned and headed for the elevator. Once the doors closed, he tugged both fists in the air as if he'd won a heavyweight bout. He couldn't remember the last time he'd felt the rush of accomplishment. Only then he remembered there was much work to do. He reminded himself to stay level-headed. He had to clear his name once and for all.

"I can't go through this again. Stop whatever you've got planned." Venus entered the kitchen where Jake and Legend sat across from each other. Legend got up like a dismissed child.

"I'll leave you two alone."

"One could only wish."

Legend exited without the last word. The tension was palatable. He knew he was running out of time before the two of them ripped each other apart. But he couldn't let Legend leave until this thing was closed out for good.

No more living in fear. He stood up and took her hand. "What's your man say?" He snapped his finger to think of the bishop's name of the church she'd dragged him to the last couple of Sundays.

"Bishop Talley," she answered, folding her arms over her chest and knowing she'd fallen right into this one.

"There can be no faith where fear resides. You've got to kick 'em out." He shook his head and bounced like a Baptist preacher. "You've got to strike fear in the heart and kill it dead."

"You are so silly."

"Something I've never been accused of." His eyes lowered, and his soft breath lingered near her ear. She pushed herself closer against him, then suddenly backed away.

"What is that?"

She felt the small pistol strapped around his torso. He'd forgotten it was there. "Baby, it's legal. We're in Georgia, not California."

"I can't do this."

"Please, don't worry."

"Don't worry?"

"I hate to interrupt, but I need to make my exit," Legend boomed over their shoulders. He stood in the entryway in a close-fitting sweater, slacks, and expensive Italian loafers. His leather jacket hung over his arm as if he were simply going out for a night on the town instead of the great escape.

"You're not leaving till we get this mess straightened out."

"You're forgetting I have a business to run. The one you don't want to be involved in anymore, remember?"

"Another couple of days won't shut the place down."

"He wants to go. Let him go," Venus half whined.

Jake moved toward Legend. "Let's roll, man."

"Straight to the airport now?" she said as they were going out the door.

⟨⟨⟩⟩

"Man, you know how to push her every button." Jake drove with one hand steady. He kept his eye on the road but watched the rearview mirror for the car he knew would eventually show up.

"It's not hard." Legend adjusted his seat to get comfortable for the ride. "We've never had too much love for one another, you know that. I will admit that she's the best woman you ever had."

"Really?" Jake found this amusing. "I'm shocked."

"Seriously. She's a fighter. Not the weave-pulling kind, although I have a feeling she'd take somebody down pretty quick. I mean the kind that would fight for you, stand by you, no matter what. I respect that."

"Thanks, man. I'm surprised to hear you say that." Jake's bewilderment was sidetracked. The burgundy Ford showed up like clockwork. It occurred to Jake that his car was probably wired. The only way to explain how they could find him so easily even if they weren't following out the gate.

"So I'll leave you two the way I found you. Hopefully, man . . . no hard feelings." Legend reached out for a light finger handshake.

"We're not going to the airport. I'm putting you in a hotel. You can't drop me in the middle of this then run like some little pussy."

"You trying to blame me? You're not trying to blame me." He shook his head. "I've had your back from day one. If anything, I've shielded you long as I could."

Jake hit the brakes and pulled over. He didn't like the way the conversation had turned. Someone else listening would get the very wrong impression. "Shielded me from what? What're you talking about?"

Amends for Sins

I'm here. Can anybody hear me.

I thought I heard muffled voices. I'd fallen asleep or gone unconscious—I wasn't sure how to define my half state of delirium. Dreams or reality. I'd pictured the day my father came to my school on open house. I was eight years old. My teacher had threatened to kick me out of her class if one of my parents didn't show up. My mother had refused. She'd done her time, she said. Only eight years old, in the third grade, and she thought she'd exerted enough energy trying to straighten me out. Stubborn. Hardheaded. Fast. I'd heard it so many times, it only made sense to act the role.

My father dressed in a tweed blazer with denims before it was fashionable. He held my hand, and we walked into the classroom. He seemed so tall and gallant in a roomful of mothers. Ms. Macintosh turned giddy and red, greeting him with her big-toothed smile. He let go of my hand to shake hers. I watched her colorless knuckles gripping his hand and thought about all the times she'd dismissed me, telling me to go back to my seat. If I had something to say, raise my hand. "I raise my hand, but you keep ignoring me,"

I'd told her. But that day while my father was there and asked how I was doing, Ms. Macintosh said splendid. She only wished I could learn to keep my opinions till an appropriate time.

My father looked down at me and patted my head. "She's just too smart for her own good, I guess."

I couldn't remember if it was a compliment. I couldn't remember if being smart is what had gotten me here. Too smart for my own good. Always seeking the answer to the question everyone else was afraid to ask. Curiosity killed the cat. I had asked too many questions, it seemed.

Twice Blessed

"Most people have a hard enough time dealing with only one mother. I have two."

"It's okay, baby." Gray pushed the pillow into position under his head. Keisha scooted closer and rested on his chest.

"If I had my way, we'd just elope."

"Nah, it's going to work out." Gray closed his eyes and said a silent prayer—first for Keisha to stop talking about all the antics of the afternoon, and second to get Ronny off his case. He guessed he really had relatively minor problems compared to most of the people in the world. He drove a nice luxury car never for longer than two years running. He lived in a half-million-dollar home. He ate in the best restaurants and wore the best suits.

They should fly down to Paradise Island and have a quiet ceremony, just the two of them. Keisha could probably talk him into anything when she brushed her hair across his chest that way. She rested her chin on her hands, looking up at him with her dark lashes.

"Sweetheart, it's too late. We're going through with it. Trust me, it's going to work out."

"No, I don't think so. I can feel something bad about to happen." She slipped into the covers like a scared child. "I remember when I was little, I always knew when a bad storm was coming."

"Sweetheart, that's called lightning and thunder. Everybody can see them coming a mile away."

"No, this was even before the clouds. The sky would be bright and blue, but I could feel it. This storm, this one is going to be terrible."

"Hurricane Trevelle."

"Make fun if you want to. I'm telling you. If we go through with this wedding ceremony, I don't know if we will recover."

"If anyone dares try to disrupt our ceremony, I will take them down with my bare hands."

"My knight in shining armor. I know something else you can do with your bare hands." Keisha let him stick his fingers inside her. Usually he had to work his way there. First suckling on her breasts then nibbling at her navel. His fingers effortlessly slipped inside. He was surprised to find her ready for him. "Oh, baby, damn. We have to talk about the weather more often." He used her moisture to stroke himself. He was long and stiffer than usual. He pressed himself inside her while she arched her back and asked for more. She was wet and tighter than he remembered from a week ago. "Baby, what're you doin' to me?"

"Fuck me," she panted in his ear. "I want it hard."

He reared back, making sure it was his Keisha, his baby. Her sweet mouth uttering words like that. In all the time he'd known her, she may have cursed once, or maybe twice. He could feel her gasp from the pain. Their tongues mingled while he pushed every inch of himself inside her. He let himself go, raising her legs over his shoulders. No holding back, no treating her like the gentle princess; instead he was going to bang her back out just like she'd asked.

He slowed before it was too late. He didn't want it to end so soon. He flipped her over. Instinctively she knew exactly what to do, falling to her belly instead of staying on all fours, but keeping her derriere perched in the air. Bare back and shoulders and those firm legs sprawled open. Her wetness still begging for more. He dived in, swearing he'd gone to heaven, sweet heaven.

Maybe, he was thinking. *Possibly . . . No,* he told himself. Just because she'd gone all porno on him didn't mean she was ready to go to the next level. Mimicking the women she'd obviously spied in his DVD collection was nothing like the real thing. That's what he saved for Nikki.

But before he could stop himself, he grabbed Keisha's hair, pulling her neck back into an arch. Trailing his tongue to her ear. "You want it, baby. You want it bad?" He growled, "Tell me what you want, baby?" He massaged his rod and prepared for the real prize.

"Uh-huh," she breathed out, having no real idea of what she was agreeing to. "Yes, baby, give it to me."

He reached beneath, cupping her from the front so she couldn't get away. But before he could take hold, the annoying ring on his phone sounded off like an alarm bell. Ironically enough, he'd picked the distinct ring so he'd know not to accidentally answer, especially when his earpiece was in place, without the luxury of seeing the caller ID. More important, he could've sworn he'd turned the damned thing off.

"Don't stop," she purred. He wished he could honor her command. She had no idea how badly he wanted his body to cooperate.

The room felt suddenly hot and suffocating. He rolled over, watching Keisha and her smooth ass going to waste.

Keisha's hand slowly rose, coming to the rescue. He grabbed her wrist before she reached her target. "Don't."

"But, baby, I need you." She pressed her chest against his, letting her tongue circle the cross he wore on a chain. He inhaled her fragrance. Something stirred in him then quickly died when the phone began to ring again.

"I have to get this."

"Just turn it off."

"Too late for that," he said. "If I shut it off and he calls back, it's an instant flag that says he's being ignored. This guy does not like to be ignored." He rose out of bed, slipping on his robe and grabbing the phone. He stuck his earpiece in and headed to his den.

Gray slumped into a leather chair before answering the phone. "It's midnight, East Coast! What?" Gray found himself shouting.

"I can tell time, muthafucka, can you? Where's my money?"

"Oh, so now I'm all you got to think about, night and day?" Gray got up and closed the door. "Let me tell you something, and I'm only going to say this one time. You do whatever you have to do. Because in the end, you're still not going to have a dime if you're trying to squeeze it out of me. If you want blood, then kill me. Other than that, stop fucking with me over some bullshit I don't have any control of." He pushed the power button. This time he made sure the juice was off.

"Baby, what's wrong? I heard you yelling." Keisha came inside.

Gray's head was down, his silk robe hanging open. She rushed toward him, pressing herself against him. She raised his face and kissed him softly. She was the only thing good and right in his world. She had put on her silk negligee. He pressed his lips against the smoothness. Underneath was the smooth taut belly where he couldn't wait to plant his seed.

"I'm just about ready to take you up on the elopement idea."

"Tell me what happened?"

"Clients. Some of them need babysitters."

She spun into corporate high gear. "Who? I can help. Lloyd has me working on that baby diva girl group, but it's not that much to do. Long as I supply them with plenty of Bubblicious packs of gum, they agree to whatever I tell them to do. I can help you out, whatever you need." As an associate agent, she was eager to build her own roster. But seriously, she wouldn't be working long, not once they were married. He didn't want her to be a stray lamb for the wolves in his pack. When she'd first started at Shark and Boyd, there was a bet on the table as to who would fuck her first. Gray had won. He certainly hadn't planned to fall head over heels, to boot.

"You can't help. Trust me."

"Fine. If you say so. But if this is how you're going to start treating me once we're married, I don't like it. Suddenly I'm incapable of advice or help. When you first hired me, you acted like my every opinion was gold." She tried to pull away. He held a tight grip.

The look she gave him . . . Gray released her arm just as quickly as he'd grabbed it. "Please, I'm just not in the mood for emotional blackmail. Let's just go to bed. Everything's fine. I really don't want to bring our work home and let it get between us."

"A little late for that." She folded her arms over her pink nightie and eyed his flaccid Johnson.

"So, you do have some of your mother's quick wit. I was wondering when that side of you was going to rear its pretty little head. Let me know when you're going to start charging so I can make sure I don't waste your time," he quipped.

Keisha looked as if she'd been slapped, though it was *her* hand that had connected with Gray's face with a hard snap. She even held her own face as if the blow had come directly from his right.

He reached out. "I'm sorry. I didn't mean that."

"You meant it." She left him standing there. He listened as she slammed the bathroom door. Fuck. Ronny was messing with his head and messing with his life.

"Baby, I'm sorry. Please, please don't cry." He spoke to the closed door. "You know what this is, baby? This is our first fight. Thank goodness, right? We got it out of the way, and that's it."

He waited and listened. A couple of sniffs, and she blew. "I love you, you know that. I'm having a hard time with a client. He's making my life a little miserable," he spoke louder and eased his face next to the hinge. "But it's nothing I can't handle, baby. That's all I was trying to say. I tell you what, I can handle anything with you by my side."

Still nothing. "Keisha? Come on, now. The thing about your mother, that nonsense, now you know I didn't mean that. I was just hurt, so I lashed out."

"You will never speak like that to me again." Her stuffed nose made her sound even farther away.

"Baby, it's over. That's the end of it. I swear, never again."

"All right." The door to the soft-lit bathroom cracked. He'd had a dimmer switch installed for soothing soaks and midnight showers. Some of the most beautiful women in the world had used his bathroom. Celebrities, actresses, singers, video dancers—all knowing he wanted nothing more than their panties. He never had to pretend it was more than what it was. After a while, they all began to look alike, smell alike, feel alike. One long constant string of sameness. Same hairstyles, same clothes, shoes, and handbags. If something was left behind, he didn't know whom to call to pick it up. And then there was the expectation that once he'd had the goodies, he would give them preferential treatment in the agency. When the call came in from a media rep wanting a hip current soul artist to represent, they would be the one he'd sanction.

Too bad it wasn't that easy. He hardly felt like working that hard, trying to push a second-rate persona when he could simply suggest the current hotness of the moment. He'd had enough of wannabe-famous pussy to last him a lifetime. Especially after one-who-shall-remain-nameless refused to understand or accept the way things worked. Though she was married, she hounded him on a level that made Glenn Close in *Fatal Attraction* look like a model citizen. The long scratch all the way around his special-edition Jaguar was the last and final straw. He made sure every media outlet that gave a damn got the anonymous press release that the reality star was a thousand-dollar-a-day cokehead. After she quietly disappeared, Gray made a promise to stop fucking around and settle down with one bedmate. He chose Nikki because he trusted her and she wasn't afraid to let him do everything he'd ever dreamed of doing to a woman. Most of all, she wasn't looking for fame and wasn't going to tell two friends, who would then tell two friends . . .

Nikki was back from her visit to Trinidad.

If Keisha didn't bring her ass out that bathroom in ten seconds or less, that's exactly where he was headed.

He waited and she still didn't come out, so he knocked on the barely open door. "Keisha, baby, please. Let me hold you. Okay. Open the door."

When she appeared, her nose and eyes were as pink as her night-gown.

"Aww, baby." Enclosing his arms around her. "I'm sorry. I will never hurt your feelings again. I swear. I promise." He kissed her tender lips. She would be his answer to a better, safer, life; this much was sure. "I love you, baby. Okay? Don't ever doubt it."

TLC

Everyone thinks money will solve their problems, heal every wound, and fix every past pain. The truth—nothing could heal like a simple hug. I'd give everything I owned to feel arms around me—safe, trustworthy arms.

It was so cold. Even in the box where I should've felt suffocating heat, I couldn't stop the chill that made my teeth clatter. Cold, uncaring fear had taken over my mind. Then I heard it. The trickling sound. But it wasn't pipes, as I'd first thought. I felt the wetness seeping around me. For a moment, I thought I'd pissed on myself. Fear mixed in with trying to hold it in for more hours than I could count. How much longer could I hold it anyway? But no. This liquid was cold, and it was coming slowly but surely from the bottom slats. It pooled around my bent knees, then went on to fill every lower corner of the wood box.

In the darkness, I searched around with my fingers, trying to find where the water was streaming in. If it was open enough for a water surge, maybe I could push my fingers through and get a good grip. I stopped when I heard voices.

The moans of lovers. Hushed whispers. "No, stop. We can't do this."

The sloshing footsteps faded. The water stayed level, but I didn't know what kind of rain to prepare for. I didn't know what was supposed to happen that would save my life. Since I'd given up on the kindness of strangers, I had no one to depend on but myself. A new blast of energy pumped through my veins. I was determined to save my own damn self. Sometimes you had to realize that's all you had: yourself.

Venus

Another rough night. I woke up angry. *Get used to it*, I told myself while I brushed my teeth in the mirror. I dressed and moved quickly, grateful Jake was still sleep. I scooted Mya in the backseat. She grumbled about not having eaten breakfast. I told her we would go to McDonald's and get her favorite chicken nuggets, even though I wasn't sure they sold them at eight o'clock in the morning.

I put the baseball bat in the front seat next to me. I refused to be under house arrest. If someone followed me today, they were going to get a solid crack of my bad attitude. I was angry and knew that was no way to start the day. I tried to think of things I was grateful for. I only came up with one.

"Mya, I love you, baby."

She didn't bother to answer me back, just smiled. I checked my rearview mirror and was grateful no one was there, so that made two things to be thankful for. Jake called as I entered the McDonald's drive-through. He didn't wait for me to say hello. "I asked you to stay home. Where are you?"

"We're at McDonald's, Daddy!" Mya yelled from the backseat. She was excited to hear Jake on the speakerphone.

"You need to get back here, now."

"Welcome to McDonald's. Can I take your order?" The young lady on the intercom and Jake were speaking at the same time. I had no choice but to prioritize. I pushed the mute button on Jake.

"Yes, a order of chicken nuggets, orange juice, and a coffee."

"A Happy Meal, Mommy."

"Can you make the nuggets a Happy Meal?"

"Sorry, we don't serve Happy Meals till eleven," the intercom girl said. When she heard Mya's shrill voice, she quickly changed her mind. "I can give her the toy."

"Thank you."

I pushed the button to see if Jake was still there. ". . . right now."

"We're going to have breakfast and then I'm taking Mya to school. After that I'm heading to In Bloom. You and Legend have yourselves a good day playing cops and robbers."

"Bye-bye, Daddy," Mya said, playing right along. School meant Jory, so for the first time my baby was on my side.

"Don't you—"

I pushed the button, cutting him off. Jake would have to tell it on the mountain. Mya and I were on our merry way.

☙❧

"So you're a woman on the run." Vince grinned, showing the gap of his missing tooth. He rarely smiled. "Sexy."

"I'm not on the run. I'm right where I'm supposed to be." I pulled the tearsheet orders. The window was already fixed, and the place was good as new. I could see the deep grooved scratches in the hardwood, but felt no regret. "I'm not going to play victim. If somebody wants a piece of me, they're going to get all they bargained for and more."

"Oooh, I like it."

"Oh, quiet. You. Mr. I-can't-be-there-for-you. What was that about? Why were you afraid to report the break-in?"

Silence. Vince acted like he didn't hear me. His wide back stayed tense and unmoving.

"Okay, don't tell me. But if you did some unspeakable crime and they never caught you, you'd tell me, right?"

Still no answer. "Vince?"

"Lil' lady, I'm too much of a gentleman to burden you with bad business. Ladies should be treated with the respect of protection and the luxury of not knowing everything."

"Archaic. Okay, Vince. If you haven't heard, women aren't fragile creatures. We actually have jobs and take care of ourselves." I spoke to his back, since he still refused to face me. "Okay." I took a deep breath. "We have orders to fill." I spread the fax sheets and zeroed in on the last one. "Ohmigod."

"What?" Vince turned around alert and in defense mode.

"This order . . . it's for me." I tried not to smile. I tried not to revel in the flattery or even bask in the five seconds of joy. Why would I? A man, a married man, orders flowers to be sent to me from the flower shop I own. I shook my head. "He knew they'd never get filled. Just him being kind," I said mainly to myself. After all, I'd blubbered profusely in the man's shirt. He probably thought I was a basketcase and felt sorry for me.

Vince was behind me, reading the tearsheet. "Sounds like it's you who got some explaining to do, lil' lady."

I smiled. I seriously tried not to. I balled the sheet and tossed it in the trash. "Why, Vince—you know how sensitive you men and your egos are. Some things are best left unsaid. You know, to protect you."

Vince picked it up and unfolded it. " 'Deliver to Venus Johnston from Mr. Robert B. Stanton. You deserve to smile today,' " he read. "Nice message. Who's this guy?"

I snatched it, this time tearing it into pieces. "You've got your secrets, and I've got mine."

"If I've learned anything in my fifty-two years on this earth, it's one thing: You're either in or you're out. There's no delusions. You know from the minute you set your sights on somebody what your intentions are. So my advice, lil' lady, be honest with yourself and decide. In or out."

I threw my head back and sent a hardy laugh in the air. "Please, really. Do you know I'm running around with a baseball bat in my car? I don't have the emotional energy to expend on Senator Robert Stanton or anyone else." I got up and went to the bathroom and closed the door. I flicked on the light. I leaned over the sink and got a close-up of myself in the mirror. He was just being polite, making sure I had no hard feelings from my daughter being left in harm's way. It had been so long since I'd felt beautiful, smart, or clever. When I worked in corporate marketing, I spent my days confident or at least appearance-wise. Corporate hair to go with my suits and high heels. Now it was sandals, jeans, and wiry hair that could use a major trim and condition. What in the world . . . Mr. Stanton? I counted the freckles like moles around my cheekbones. My slanted eyes needed some eye shadow and liner.

But what I knew was that men liked to rescue and feel needed. I knew my crying in front of him had just about made the man's day. Contrary to the corporate creed, men liked to see a woman cry. It made them feel strong in their otherwise dull, uneventful lives. Also contrary to popular belief, women were the ones who hated to see other women cry. Because we secretly knew it was the ultimate dirty trick in getting attention and getting our way. What was I doing, falling into another man's arms anyway? Maybe I did need a little attention. Hell, maybe just a hug. It wasn't against the law.

"Hey, lil' lady, telephone." Vince knocked on the door. "Robert Stanton," he answered before I could ask. "Shall I tell him you'll call him back . . . like never."

I pushed the door open, nearly hitting him. "Mind your manners. I'm your superior." I took the receiver and closed myself back inside the bathroom, hiding behind the door. I waited until I heard Vince tearing open a box before pressing the line. "This is Venus," I said lightly, as if I hadn't just experienced a full fantasy starring him.

"I've sent a car over. You're going to get in that car. The car is going to drive you to the spa, where you will have a full massage, strawberries soaked in champagne, followed by lunch served in your private room. And no, I will not be joining you. I'm a married man as well as a public official. But I do know when someone needs a minute to themselves. This is not a negotiable offer. You will not tell me some other time. The car should be outside. Thank you. This is Robert B. Stanton, and I approved this message." The line went silent.

I came out, smiling ear to ear. I gently put the phone in the cradle. Vince said nothing. "I'll be back. Can you handle the orders?"

"You're making a risky decision," he sneered.

"I'll take that as a compliment." Risk used to be my middle name. Lately it was predictable. Waking up, taking Mya to school, then showing up at In Bloom had become a ritual snorefest. The little-floral-shop-that-could had me working sunup to sundown, all for the joy of self-employment. Self-fulfillment. But I wasn't fulfilled. I felt like Waldo. Where in the world had Venus Johnston gone?

The black town car sat in the red zone of the old town district. The driver waited patiently with his hands folded behind his back.

Vince was right on my heels. "You get in that car, you're dead to me."

I blew him a kiss. I got inside the backseat while the driver held the door open. There was no rearview mirror for me to check to see if I was being followed. In fact, I didn't turn or twist one way or the other. Leaned back, exhaled, and enjoyed the ride.

Orange Alert

One hot stone and reflexology session later, and I was a new woman. I'd always scoffed at women who spent their hard-earned capital in narcissistic establishments. Whether it be hair, nail, or pampering, I'd believed it a waste of money. Men would take that three hundred or so dollars and have something to show for it—stocks, CDs, a new stereo, but women were forever two paces behind, and needed to be coiffed or carry the latest designer bag when we earned 30 percent less income. Go figure.

When the car dropped me off at In Bloom, I sang a different tune. I don't know if it would've felt the same had I paid for it myself. I would soon find out, since I'd scheduled another appointment in two weeks. Addicting, to say the least.

"What was that?" Jake was standing at the back entrance with his arms folded over his chest. He was wearing a dark blue corduroy blazer over a white shirt and jeans. He'd shaved all his hair off, leaving smooth cocoa-brown skin except for the two strips of goatee that met in the middle.

"What—" I cleared my throat. "The car?"

"The car," he said, nodding with a *get on with it* expression. "Where've you been?"

"I had a spa day. It was a gift." I shifted my eyes to Vince, who was conveniently nose deep in a floral arrangement.

"From who?"

"The Stantons. I guess they felt guilty about the mishap over the weekend."

Vince sneezed mildly. *"Bullshiiiii."* I heard his undercover expletive.

"I've been calling you all day," Jake said, deciding to ignore it, but I know he heard it, too.

"I left my phone in the car. I'm sorry to have worried you."

"You don't sound sorry."

"I figured you'd be busy playing detective."

He flapped his arms up. "Well, excuse me for wanting to clear my name so we can live with a little peace of mind."

"And excuse me for needing some time to unwind. One too many car chases, one too many broken windows and vandalized places of business, and one too many houseguests."

"You know what—" He pointed his finger at me with that little dagger thing he did. "—let's go. C'mon. Get your purse."

"I'm not going anywhere."

"I've been calling you all day. I asked you not to leave the house, and Vince"—we both turned to look at him hiding behind a spiky floral arrangement—"seemed to have no idea where you went. I was two seconds from calling the police. This close. I don't need this right now."

"Nerve, a lot of nerve. I'm running around with a bat in the front seat of my car," I said slowly, so he'd understand. "For protection. And *you* don't need this right now?" I swallowed the lump in my throat. I wasn't about to let this argument close with him feeling sorry for me. I wasn't going to cry. I turned my back. "I'm not going anywhere. I have orders to fill."

"You weren't worried about filling them a couple of hours ago." Jake left, but not before going out to my car and coming back with my phone and shoving it into my jean pocket. "Answer your phone, you hear me?"

Vince stayed silent even after Jake left. We worked steadily but without our usual banter. After the day's orders were lined up, he started loading them in the van.

"Thank you, Vin." He knew what I was thanking him for. He nodded, but that was all.

Mama Said There'd Be Days Like This

As many times as his mother had warned him he was taking the plunge with the wrong woman, was equal to how many times he'd felt grateful to have someone like Venus in his life. She breathed life into his world. But damn if sometimes she didn't drive him absolutely insane. She was older than him by five years, yet he was the one who had to constantly rein her in, make her see logic and reason.

What in the world did she expect him to do? All he wanted to do was cooperate and get everybody off his back. If he went into a meeting with Ronny and could get him to somehow confess to killing Byron, he'd be cleared and Ronny would go to jail and never mess with him or his family again.

Legend had valiantly tried to talk him out of it. He said Ronny wouldn't stop—he'd send somebody from jail if he had to. Legend's argument was to just pay him the money and to hell with the Feds. They didn't have anything on Jake or they would've acted on it. Ronny was the only one he should be afraid of.

The W Hotel was dark and moody, though it was only mid-afternoon. Jake checked the time then dialed Legend again. For the second time, it went straight to voice mail. "Hey, I'm waiting for you in the lobby, man, second call."

"Sir, would you like to order a drink while you're waiting?" The hostess in a white blouse and fitted black pants leaned over to remove a glass that had been on the small table when Jake sat down.

"Ah, no. My partner's coming down in a few." He gave her a polite smile but couldn't ignore the nagging tug at the pit of his stomach. He went to the front desk. "How ya doin'?" The clerk was
female, and that was all he needed. "Can you call my buddy's room?
He was supposed to meet me down here half an hour ago."

"Sure." Her bright red nails were in position on the computer
keyboard. "What's his name?"

"Legend Hill."

She tapped a few keys then picked up the phone. Before she dialed, Jake held up a finger. "Hold on, this is him calling. Hey, I was
worried, man. Just about to have someone call. Sure, okay, I'll be
right up. No problem, man. Finish your shower." Jake slid his phone
back into the leather case on his hip. He snapped his finger. "Oh,
great, I hung up before he told me what room."

"I got it. Eleven thirty-four," she stated proudly. "Is there anything else I can do for you?"

Jake leaned in close. His dark lashes blinked embarrassment.
"You know what . . . seriously there *is*, but I don't want to get you in
any trouble."

"What?" She was young and, thankfully, not yet bitter toward
the male species, who could lie on demand.

"My buddy takes helluva long showers. You think you can just
make me a key so I can wait inside the room?" His lips softly parted,
signaling innocence. "You know what—I shouldn't have even asked."

She clicked a few buttons, then put a fresh keycard into the ma-
chine. "It's fine. Eleven thirty-four," she repeated. "Enjoy your stay,
Mr. Hill." She winked.

"I will do that. Thank you very much." He held the key to Legend's room to his chest, gracious for the hospitality. The hallway of
the eleventh floor was deathly still. Deserted. No trays outside the
room. No signs hung on doors. The half-lit hallway reminded him
of a seedy strip club instead of the upscale modernism this hotel
chain was known for.

"Legend, it's Jake." He knocked before sliding the key in. The green light flashed.

He paused, turning the knob. He knew things were about to go very wrong. Legend should've been downstairs waiting for him. He should've answered his phone. Jake never should've left him alone to his own devices. All in one moment, he was angry, frustrated. He didn't want to be responsible for something happening to his friend, let alone his wife and daughter. Venus was right, he needed to stop playing in the sand, end this thing.

He stepped inside. The curtains were drawn, blacking out everything except a sliver of light escaping down the center. He pushed them apart, then braced himself for what he might see.

The unmade bed was empty. Relieved for more reasons than he could count, Jake checked the bathroom. "Legend, man, you in there?" He pushed on the closed door, but it wouldn't move. He paused to listen.

A faint moan. "Ah shit," Jake whispered, swallowing the fear that assaulted him. With his full weight, he shoved slowly. Inside was his friend, collapsed and nearly unconscious.

Who's Your Daddy Now?

Two hundred invites sent out, and every single one of them returned by the RSVP date except one. But here it was. Delma pulled the last envelope out of the post office box. Nausea swelled in the pit of her stomach. So many people, friends, family, and work associates would witness her baby getting married in less than a week. But this one was the one that mattered: Keisha's father, the judge. HONORABLE KELLOGG LEWIS AND FAMILY, the preprinted address card read. Delma slid the tiny envelope open. In the tiny box, he'd written the number one. Meaning he would be attending alone. Neither his sons nor his wife, Linda, were coming. Delma couldn't blame her. The woman had every reason to still be bitter.

How could she so easily forgive and forget the many times Kellogg had invited Delma into their home, a few times with little Keisha in tow, only to find out she was his daughter. Right under her nose was the child he'd fathered after having an affair with a fifteen-year-old girl whom they'd let stay at their home. That girl was Trevelle Doval, teen homewrecker extraordinaire. He'd lied to Delma, too . . . by omission, of course. Delma had no idea Kellogg Lewis was Keisha's biological father. Would have never guessed it if her life depended on it.

He'd lied to all of them, even if it was by omission. He could've been forthright—he was a man of the law, for goodness' sake. Delma would've listened with an open mind. Back then, when she was a young district attorney, she'd thought the world of Kellogg. His affable personality, always wanting to do the right thing for those girls on the street. Begging for leniency in their cases, hoping they'd get sent to a halfway house instead of jail. It was understandable that he got caught up.

All he'd had to do was go to Delma and say, "I know you stole that child that night, 'cause I was right behind you. 'Cause you see, it was my child, but if anyone found out I'd gotten a fifteen-year-old girl pregnant, my life would've been ruined, so I kept it a secret for over twenty years. But now I want to be a part of her life, and if you don't mind, give her back to her biological mother . . . 'cause enough hearts have been broken in the deal."

When Keisha found out about her real parents, and especially Kellogg, a man who'd fed her hot dogs and pretzels at their July Fourth barbecue, she cried till her eyes puffed up like marshmallows. Delma held her steady and told her to let it out. It took weeks before Keisha would talk to him. "Do you think she'll ever understand, ever forgive me?" Kellogg had asked Delma. "Keisha's got a heart of gold. She'll come around," she assured him. Eventually Keisha did. They laughed and talked regularly over lunches and coffee dates until Keisha asked the big question. Would he walk his daughter down the aisle on her wedding day?

The answer was a resounding *no*. That would mean a lot of explaining to his peers. Sure it was the right thing to do for everyone else—to come clean—but not the almighty judge Lewis.

"Buzz off," Delma said to herself, tossing the card and envelope off to the side once she was in her car.

She pulled into traffic and landed at a red light. The post office was only a few blocks from the courthouse. She had a mind to walk in there and tell Kellogg personally that he needed to step up and finally take full responsibility, including walking his daughter down the aisle. Puleeze, just showing up like an average Joe—or john, in this case—would indelibly be a stain on Keisha's special day.

She'd taken a four-week leave to deal with the wedding details.

Now that Venus had stepped in, there wasn't much for her to do. Finding Venus and hiring her was genius on Delma's part. She certainly was efficient. The little spitfire had found nine ways to Sunday to save them money, but Delma had never been concerned about funds. Gray Hillman was fully capable of covering the bill—at least he was good for that much. He'd made a specific account just for the wedding expenses, and Delma was in charge of writing the checks. After the final bills were paid to the caterer, resort, and Bishop Talley, there'd be well over five grand left over. Delma was giving a great deal of thought to giving it to Venus as a bonus. To top it all off, she'd kept Trevelle out of their hair.

As if Trevelle didn't have enough to do besides ruining people's lives. One thing or another was on the news every night featuring Trevelle and her husband and their public display of hatred for one another. *Lawd, lawd, something to be said for karma.*

The light was taking forever. Delma leaned her head back on the leather rest and closed her eyes. She'd depend on the rudeness of others to honk when the light turned green.

Asleep or daydreaming, Delma pictured the perfect ceremony. Mya, the charming flower girl sprinkling red petals on the ground, leading the way for the bride. The guests standing, all eyes waiting as Keisha stepped inside the chapel, holding on to her gorgeous bouquet. The procession song beginning with those famous chords.

Then suddenly there was shouting and knocking from outside the chapel window. Hands slapping at the window, *"Let me in!"* Why, who could it be? Trevelle Doval demanding to be let in after the security enforced specific orders not to let her pass through the wooden doors and flowered arches.

Delma's eyes were still closed, but she could feel the smile across her face, satisfied to have the last laugh. She could dream, couldn't she? Only the knocking and slamming of hands across the window, the shouting sounded unbelievably real.

Soon, Delma realized it wasn't her dream, but her reality. There were two or three people pounding her window. The woman was yelling, "Are you all right in there?" Cars honked as she sat in park. She pushed the window down.

"Oh . . . I'm so sorry." Delma tried to focus, get the sleep out of her eye by blinking rapidly. "Yes, yes, I'm fine. I'm moving." She put the car in gear and hit the gas. She got more honks when she cut off another driver as she tried to get over to the side of the street. She wasn't ready to drive yet. Her eyes still blurry; she pressed a hand to her forehead. She had no idea she'd fallen into such a deep sleep. *Resting your eyes,* Hudson would've guffed. *Just resting my eyes.* Maybe after the wedding she'd finally get a good night's rest.

"Are you okay?" The same woman was back at Delma's window, where she'd followed and parked behind.

"Yes, I'm fine. Thank you. Really."

"Okay, if you're sure. I can drive you to the hospital—it's not that far. Or call the paramedics."

"No." Delma shook her head and put on a big cheesy smile to reassure the good citizen. Her phone began to ring the theme to *Star Wars,* Hudson's all-time favorite movie. "This is my husband now. Really, everything is perfectly fine." Delma answered, grateful to be left alone.

"Hey, man. I was asleep at the wheel." She chuckled. "I mean it, I literally fell asleep at the stoplight. Whew, I'll be glad when this wedding business is over."

"Well, it might be over sooner than you think. The bank called about ten minutes ago. They say you've got three checks about to bounce. Well, not you personally, but the wedding account. You been out shopping again, woman?"

"What in the world would I be buying?" Delma shook the cobwebs out of her head. "Three checks?"

"Yep. You better get on over there, find out what's going on."

"Doesn't make any sense. That account was fat and full, last time I checked."

"Maybe our friend Gray forgot he was getting married. I don't know, but you're the signer, so you need to get to the bottom of it. The wedding's next Saturday."

"Thanks for reminding me," Delma said smartly. "It may have slipped my mind."

"Save the attitude, woman. Find out what's going on—then call me back."

"Will do, Sergeant." This is one thing Delma knew and knew very well: The minute a man took on the role of husband, he felt the distinct need to start bossing.

Inside of a minute, Delma was furious and spouting words she wished she could take back. She cussed the petite bank woman upwards and sideways, telling them they'd made a major mistake and somebody had better fix it. This was her one and only daughter's wedding. Life depended on a caterer, resort fees, and a cake from a baker that swore everything he touched was a work of art.

"I can't do anything besides hope the money comes in by midnight tonight in the form of a transfer. Otherwise the checks will be denied payment." The woman put the printed-out statement on the desk for Delma to see. "Right here is the problem. A huge withdrawal was made—one lump sum."

Delma couldn't see straight from rage. But she could see straight enough to drive to Shark and Boyd entertainment law firm. She and Gray were the only ones with access to the account. She stepped off the elevator to the luxurious floor of chrome and wood. The modern fixtures and crisp floors made Delma feel out of place, landing in warp speed to a futuristic space pad.

Nikki stood up the minute she saw her. "Mama D, what a surprise."

"I'm more comfortable with Delma," she said, but her body language spoke even louder. *It's Judge Hawkins to you.* "Where's your bossman, honey? I need to talk to Mr. Hillman like now."

Nikki's eyes blinked back concern. "Sure, okay." She rushed off. Delma stood in the lobby, ignoring the odd stares of the few young associates who'd passed her. She, in her floral housedress, didn't look like the latest new R & B act. She was a solid five feet two, and the stress of the wedding had made her waistline gain some inches, so she hadn't felt like stressing about clothes. Her mother-of-the-bride suit was already being let out as far as it would go. To hell with the rest of the days of the week.

"Mother." Keisha came to her side. "What's wrong? Nikki called and said you were hostile and having some kind of breakdown." She looped her elbow through hers. "Come, come to my office." When she wouldn't budge, "Mommy, are you okay?"

Keisha looked at her like Delma were some loon who didn't know her right mind. "I came here to see Gray." If anyone knew she was not to be moved till she was good and ready, it was Keisha.

"He's at a lunch meeting. Tell me what's going on."

As much as she wanted this thing to all fall apart, she wanted her baby's happiness. Telling her that her fiancé had drained the wedding account would break her heart. "I . . . need to talk to Gray. It doesn't concern you."

"Did he do something, change something in the plans? He's like that. He doesn't mean any harm. He's just one of those men who likes to be involved." She pushed her hair behind her ear. "Come, let's go wait in my office. We'll talk to him when he gets back."

"No." Delma still was not persuaded. "I came here to speak with Gray, so I will wait for him in the lobby. I don't want to interrupt your day. Your time is just as important around here as his." This message seemed to ignite something in her daughter.

The same way she'd talked her into trying out for cheerleading after the girls had teased her, saying she had no rhythm. Or the way she'd pumped her up to demand a professor change her grade from a B-plus to an A. The B's were for blacks, Delma explained, the A's were for African American. *You let him know who you are.* She understood how the game worked and how those professors treated the students of their choosing. She'd lived through it all. She had indeed taught her daughter to stand up for herself. What didn't kill her would only make her stronger, and all that, yet Delma was thoroughly afraid of giving Keisha the straight business about her fiancé. Afraid even with full knowledge and disclosure, she'd still make the wrong decision. Still choose Gray. "You're right. Absolutely." She kissed Delma on the cheek before heading off toward her office with her shoulders back. "Have Nikki call me after your meeting with Gray."

Nikki left and said she was going to lunch, but Delma was welcome to wait right where she was. The only thing Delma didn't do was growl at the hot tamale. Who dressed like that in an office? Times couldn't have changed that much, where a red strapless fitted dress was now considered business attire. Delma checked her watch and saw the big hand closing in on 2 P.M. One hour turned into two, then three. The man sure took long lunches.

Every time the elevator doors opened, Delma got her game face on. Every time it still turned out not to be Gray, she fell into an exhaustion that made her want to ball up and cry. She knew he was wrong. *Just Wrong.*

There was no choice in the matter. It was close to four o'clock. She needed nearly fifty thousand dollars fast and in a hurry, or checks and heads were going to bounce and roll all over the place.

"Kellogg Lewis, this is Delma Hawkins."

"Delma, I don't think last names are necessary. Did you get my RSVP?" he asked solemnly. He obviously had a great deal of turmoil involved in his decision to attend but not be a part of the ceremony. The Honorable Judge Lewis still could not publicly acknowledge Keisha as his daughter without a scandal attached.

"I received it. It means a lot to me and Keisha," Delma found herself sweet-talking. She hated wasting time with niceties, but the fact remained he was her one and only last resort. "Listen, we've run into a snag. The wedding costs have gotten a bit out of hand and, well, I was wondering as the father of the bride if you could spare a loan."

He wasted no time. "Of course. Any help I can be, you know I'd do anything for her."

Except tell the world you're her father and walk her down the aisle with dignity.

"How much do you need?"

Delma swallowed hard. She didn't have enough liquid assets to cover even a fourth of what was needed. Her savings was tied up in bonds and stocks for her retirement. Somehow she knew Judge Lewis had the money. He was a white man, for goodness' sake. He and his ancestors had a four-hundred-year head start in acquiring land, property, cash, and prizes. She'd sat over enough civil family bouts to see the difference. Black families fighting over the wedding ring of their mama, needing to sell it and split the half-carat-value nine ways, while white families sued each other over million-dollar estates and tea sets from the 1800s still worth more than the house Delma lived in.

She opened her mouth and let the amount nonchalantly drop from her lips. "About fifty thousand dollars."

He coughed. "What kind of wedding y'all planning?"

"Listen, here, you haven't done nothing for that child, not a day in her life. I think it's a small price—"

"Whoa, I didn't say no."

"Well, you didn't say yes."

"Give me the account. I'll wire the money."

Relief closed around Delma like warm arms.

"Now, can we get the record straight? Don't ever say I didn't do anything for my daughter, again. You hear me? Leaving her in your care was the best thing I could've done—of that, I'm sure. You are a great mother. You raised a great young woman, and you did it all by yourself."

She grabbed a couple of tissues out of her purse and dabbed her eyes. "So noted," she said gracefully, though the tears were streaming. "It's going to be a beautiful ceremony. You're going to be so proud."

Catch a Monkey by the Toe

Ronny watched as his bodyguard finished with the count. "Two hundred grand."

"Thanks for the down payment."

Gray had put every dime he could together, begging, borrowing, and coming just short of stealing, clearing every account he had. Cash was hard to come by in a legitimate world. Unlike his present company, he'd tried to do everything the right way.

"That's it, all right. The only payment. I told you, this is my good faith effort to show you I'm on your side, but I'm not taking the fall for stealing from you." Gray pushed his silk-blend jacket back and shoved his hands deep into his pockets to keep his cool. "Look, let's focus on the future. I got some hot talent waiting to blow up. You're a creative genius, don't forget that. You're worth more than whatever Byron Steeple took from you. Time to stop living in the past and forge ahead." Gray felt his dynamic speech losing ground. He was used to a captivated audience, and this wasn't it.

It came to him in an instant. "What if I got Sirena Lassiter to step back into the studio . . . under your label, huh? Would that not be a beautiful thing?"

"Nah, she don't like me very much."

"Of course she likes you. She has a great deal of respect for your talent. She's not one to hold a grudge. Just because you gave her a little shove. Don't even worry about that. She's a tough girl." Gray could count on her to come peacefully, but he did have digital insurance, as he liked to call it. An entire safe filled with lovely naked images. Sometimes he was the costar, and sometimes not. It was amazing what even wonderfully talented women would do with a promise of becoming famous one day. Fame was a plague that had swept the nation like a virus, the disease everyone wanted to have.

"If you say so," Ronny said, slobbing on his unlit cigar. "But mostly I want my money. The economy, not so solid these days. Gotta plan for the future." His stubby fingers were covered with rings with diamonds bigger than the two carats he'd bought on credit for Keisha.

"Fuck, man, what is it with you?" Gray heard the click of the gun next to his head and cut short his rant.

"Did I say I wanted it from you?" Ronny signaled. "Put the gun down." Slash, his right-hand man, clicked the safety in place and took a step back. Ronny continued, "I figure I pick the pockets of all involved, eventually I'll have my five million with interest."

Gray hunched his shoulders. "Whatever, man. If that's how you want to spend your time and energy, what can I say?"

"Nothing. Now get the fuck out." Ronny stood up and still had to look up at Gray. "Let me know when the meeting is set up for Sirena. I already got some tracks in mind."

"Excuse me," Gray had to say to the wifebeater-clad imbecile blocking the door. *Criminals.* He was sick to death of fools trying to attain success by any means necessary. Putting guns to heads was no way to win friends and influence people.

To think he'd put in eight years of his life for an education to be dealing with these idiots. He pulled out his cell phone before he reached his car. He had to fix the mess he'd made with the wedding account. He'd gotten the message from the bank. He figured Delma had gotten word, too. No scorn like that of a woman cut off from funds.

The first person he thought of who could help, or most likely willing and able, was Trevelle Doval. She answered with dread. "Yes, Gray, to what do I owe this dishonor?"

"How are you, Trevelle?

"What do you want?"

"Snap, crack, and in a hurry. I'm down with that."

"Then be down with it and tell me why you called," she mocked, sensing he was in need. He could almost hear her gloating through the phone.

"Not everyone gets a second chance, but I'm offering this to you based on your excellent behavior in the last few days. I'm ready to go to bat for you, persuade Keisha to let you at least attend the ceremony."

"If . . ."

"I need you to do me a huge favor. There's a matter I had to deal with, so I need fifty grand. By the way, it's just a loan. I'd never take money from a woman, and definitely not from my lovely mom-in-law to-be."

"Fifty grand." She stayed quiet after that. The pause was unexpectedly long.

"Hey, you know what, it's simply an offer. You have the right to refuse service to anyone," he quipped.

"You're an asshole."

"Not very Christian-like," he sang out. "Your daughter's wedding is going to be the most beautiful event of the year. You don't want to miss it." He handed the valet his parking stub.

"I told you nothing good was going to come to you, Gray Hillman. Now you want me to come out of pocket, now you need me? Typical."

"Keisha needs you."

"What Keisha needs is the truth. I'm through. From here on out, I plan to live an authentic life. One pure in the Holy Spirit. No more pretense. You won't need the money, because there won't be a ceremony." She hung up without another word.

Gray tossed his jacket onto the backseat of his car. The day wasn't going well. He could chalk this one up as a loss—or then again. He looked up at the balcony of the room he'd just left, and came up with a brilliant idea.

He dialed the number. "Ronny, I was reconsidering our arrangement. What would you say if I told you I knew where you could get all your money, plus some. You know, like the interest you so richly deserve?" Criminals were always open for a lead. It didn't take long to convince him. Trevelle Doval was having a public war with her husband, so it could easily be made to look like a domestic crime of passion. The woman was worth a quarter of a million dollars on any given Sunday. If she left this earth a little early, she'd be glad to see heaven.

He fingered the cross on his chest. Should anyone ever question his motives, he could answer, *Two birds with one stone.* He was doing the right thing. Gray started his engine. He wanted an authentic life, too. He was done playing around. He deserved every good thing he'd worked for over the years, which included a family, a wife, and all the comforts of rich in-laws, only he didn't need the nagging mother to go along with it. *So long, Trevelle. Have a nice, short life.*

Should've Had a V8

I saw Holly Stanton waiting by the gate to sign Jory out. She wore a cream sweater over a tartan plaid miniskirt and heels to show off her long slim legs. I thought only California girls wore miniskirts past November. I kept letting people go ahead of me. I was afraid she'd see my shamed face for accepting a spa day from her very handsome husband—probably more like a warm glow, since I was still feeling as good as new.

I wasn't going to gloat. I knew exactly what Robert Stanton was up to. I wasn't about to be played and used for his amusement.

I turned my back to her and Jory when they passed. The tug on my sweater made me turn around. "Mya left early," Jory said with a sad expression. "Can she come over later?"

I kneeled down to face him. "What do you mean, Mya left early?"

"Jory, did you see Mya leave with someone?" Holly Stanton got to the point. "If so, who? Please tell her mother now."

"She had to go after lunch." He scrunched his shoulders. Holly made a *this concludes our interview* face and led Jory out.

I zigzagged my way around the waiting moms and dads to the office. I knocked on the window to get the secretary's attention. I was trying to think of her name—started with an *S*, Sherry, Stephanie. Forget it, the personal touch wasn't going to put Mya in front of me. The small circle cutout was our only communication, like a bank teller's bulletproof window. Security like Fort Knox, yet someone had walked in here and taken my child. "My daughter was taken out of here. No one is authorized to pick her up except for her father."

"Your daughter—oh, yes, Mya Fisher." The perplexed look disappeared. "Her father is exactly who picked her up. Let me get the logsheet." At the same time, I was dialing Jake. He would've told me if he had picked up Mya. Besides, I'd seen him late in the afternoon while he was harassing me about disappearing on him, so it couldn't have been—

"Airic Fisher picked her up at eleven fifty-five. You see." She slid the clipboard up to the window so I could see his name printed clearly and the signature below it.

"He's not on the consent forms, none of them. How could you just let him take my baby? Call the police, this is kidnapping."

"I'm sorry. We checked her birth certificate on file, and his name was there. His ID matched."

"Since when does that determine who a child's legal guardian is? . . . Oh my God, you people, what is wrong with you?" I slammed my hand on the glass. Now I understood why she needed it for protection. Parents. Confused, frustrated, angry parents.

"Let me get the director." She picked up the phone.

"I don't have time for you to find the director. I have to actually *find* my child. Thank you very much." I stormed out, racing to my car. I would never forgive Airic for this. He knew I would show up and lose my mind.

"Yes, Venus, how are you?" He answered without a care in the world.

"What do you think you're doing? Put Mya on the phone, right now." I pushed back the steam, ready to blow.

"Hi Mommy," she said, not too happy. In fact, the sound of her voice broke my heart.

"Hi, baby, you okay?"

"I had to leave school early. Jory started crying."

She left out the part where she'd been crying, too. Her plugged nose was a giveaway. "It's okay, sweetie. You'll see Jory tomorrow. Where are you now?"

The phone was back in Airic's hands. "We're having a great time. I'll have her back to you tonight around eight. Okay, so you can relax."

"You know this is not right, Airic. You don't have any right to pick her up from school. How could you do this?"

"You want to talk about rights? You and your husband have denied my right to see my child for the last month. I just took matters into my own hands. We'll discuss this when I drop her off tonight."

I closed my eyes and calmed myself down. I pictured my lovely massage, the scent of lavender and white tea was still on my skin. I inhaled my arm, pressing it to my face, trying to stop myself from crying like a big baby. Trying to stop myself from screaming, *I hate you!* at the top of my lungs.

"Okay, see you tonight." My stomach cramped into a knot. "Please be there at exactly eight."

"Won't be late," he said with glee, as if he'd won this one. And he had. I was helpless to do a thing. If I called the police, he'd simply flash his court order and talk his way out of what he'd actually done. *What's the problem, it's Friday.* His visitation day just happened to be Friday starting at 6 P.M. So what he was being charged with domestic abuse and statutory rape, what did those nasty little misdemeanors have to do with him spending time with his child?

I could already hear Jake screaming in my head. My anger didn't rank on the scale nearly so high as his would. I thought about not telling him. Maybe Airic would deliver Mya before Jake made his appearance. Seeing as how he was coming home later and later these days. Maybe this mishap would go undocumented on my list of faults. It was my fault I had sex with Airic after Jake and I already started seeing each other. Never mind the fact that Airic and I were engaged and Jake was considered "the other man." It was still my fault Airic existed and wouldn't go away from whence he came. Naturally, it's my fault the man can walk into her preschool and pick her up without a shred of doubt by the school gestapo.

I got myself in gear. I'd wasted enough time sitting there, berating myself. I'm sure Jake would take care of that later. Right now, I wanted to get home and curl up underneath a blanket and close my eyes. I started the car and turned up my music to an eardrum-damaging level. Jennifer Hudson's song "Spotlight" spilled out loud and full. I sang along, "Just because you think I might . . . find somebody wortheeeeee." For a minute or two, I'd forgotten to check my rearview mirror. But when I did, there was the car. The same one following me.

At the stop sign, I put my car in park and did my best to shake the steering wheel off the column. I was in no mood. *Okay.* I grabbed my bat and got out of the car. "What?" I walked to the car like a batter at the plate. The door on the passenger side swung open.

"Hold on, there. We're FBI. We're trying to protect you," the woman said, flashing her badge.

I really wanted to swing that bat. She had no idea how badly.

"Please, Mrs. Parson, put the bat down."

I hadn't talked to my friend Wendy in a few weeks. Our conversations weren't as long as they used to be, because she'd recently gotten remarried to a math teacher she'd met on a cruise. Three months married and three months' pregnant. She expected me to come and help out once the baby was born. Our conversations were strained. She was having a baby at the age of forty-one, and I couldn't have been more excited for her and jealous at the same time. I forced myself to laugh and carry on as if we were the same, but everything was different. I let her catch me up on Tia, her daughter and my goddaughter, who thought the world revolved around her. I let her complain about morning sickness and question her decision of marrying for love instead of money. "Having a second chance, I should've done at least that right. I'm too old to be pinching pennies. Girl, what was I thinking?"

"You were thinking, he's fine as hell and good in bed." I was grateful to talk about something I knew a thing or two about. "Money can't buy that. Having money without love is a waste of money."

"Okay, no. I could seriously be in love with a real millionaire. All he'd have to do is wave an unlimited credit card in front of me, and I'd probably come." She started making orgasm noises.

"And then he'd wave a prenup in front of you, and the love would sail right out the window."

"Yeah, that would just be more reason for me to stay in love. So stop stalling—tell me what's on your mind." Wendy was quick, even though she swore the pregnancy had made her drop ten IQ points.

"Legend is here in Atlanta. He and Jake are trying to solve crime like the friggin Hardy Boys. I'm being followed by FBI agents for my own protection, and Airic stole my child today from preschool." I reached out from under the covers and sipped on the glass of wine sitting by my bed.

"Oh, okay," Wendy said. "That's all."

"No, there's more. I'm feeling guilty about accepting a gift from another man. A spa day, complete with full body massage and champagne. It was magical—the massage I mean. He was nowhere around."

Wendy was quiet. She gave it a minute of thought. "Anything else?"

"Yep, pretty much covers it."

"I thought this floral shop was keeping you busy."

"Yeah, very busy. In between car chases and trying to keep the peace between Jake and Airic, I do weddings, funerals, and bar mizvahs. So forgive me if I want to escape my life for like five minutes."

"Do you like this guy?"

"Like him? Of course not."

"Liar."

"He's married. He's the father of Mya's best bud. He's just a really nice guy. Not to mention, I'm happily married. Must we go over this part?"

"Did you say something?" She laughed.

"Whatever."

"Since when does being married stop roving eyes or emotions? First thing to do is address whatever is going on with you and Jake. No one would be able to capture your attention if you guys were in happy-mode. So what's going on?"

"I just told you . . . Legend, car chases, FBI. Were you listening?"

"Absolutely. What I heard was that you were sick and tired of dealing with something that should've been done with by now. Sounds like you're mad at Jake a little bit for letting this thing interrupt your flow."

I sat up and refilled my glass. I took a sip then held the glass to my forehead. "What else do you see, oh great one?"

"I see your ass in divorce court if you keep messing with this man."

"Stop it."

"I'm serious. You know Jake does not play when it comes to other men creeping in his territory. Let him handle his business. Sounds like it's coming to a head. Maybe it'll really be over this time." Wendy paused, not sure if she'd struck a nerve. "Are you there?"

"Yeah, I'm here." I tried not to let her hear the heartache in my voice.

"Oh sweetie, don't cry. You're scared. You guys are going to get through this like you always do. It's going to be okay."

"I don't know what I'd do without you," I said, sniffing gently.

"Stop trying to find out. You never answer when I call. Then you don't call me back for weeks. Just cause I got a new husband doesn't mean I don't need you."

"I promise to call more often." I blew her a kiss into the phone. I checked the time on the alarm clock. Still an hour to go before Airic returned Mya. The two people I loved more than anyone or anything on this earth were out of my reach.

"Wait a minute. I think I hear Jake. It was good talking to you, Wen. I love you, girl. I don't know what I'd do without you promise to call more often." I blew her a another kiss into the phone. The thumping sound was in the hallway. I crawled out of bed with my new bodyguard, the bat, and cautiously peeked out our bedroom. Jake had towels and a pillow from the hall closet.

"Babe, it's me." He held up a hand, surprised to see me in my pajamas, standing with my new best friend ready to strike. "What're you doing?"

"Trying to protect this house. What're you doing?"

"It's Legend. He's hurt." I rushed down the stairs right behind him to see Legend lying on the couch. He had a huge lump on his forehead, his lip was busted and eye swollen. "Is he bleeding on my couch?"

Jake put the towel under his head.

"I'll get some ice." I went to the kitchen and filled up a ziplock bag. I came back and placed it on Legend's head.

"Mom, is that you?" Legend reached out, patting my face. I swiped his hand away. "Oh, my bad. That seventies 'fro threw me off, didn't know where I was." He let out a snarly laugh.

I snatched the ice pack back. "Nothing's wrong with him. Whatever he got, he probably deserved."

Jake just shook his head. Would the nightmare ever end? He took the ice pack and put it gently on his friend's head. He motioned for me to follow him. We went into his office. He closed the door. "I should've listened to you."

I held him and kissed his chin. "It's going to be okay. I spoke with the FBI, they're closing in on this guy, Ronny. He's the one who killed Byron. He probably did this to Legend. When they catch him, this will all be over."

"You talked to the FBI? When?"

"They're the ones who've been following me, for protection."

A look of confusion rolled over Jake's face. "They're the ones who did this to Legend."

"No," I corrected. "Wrong answer. It was a lady agent, McDonald and a man named—"

"Agent Peterson," Jake finished. "What did they say to you? Where's Mya?"

And this is how the cookie seemed to always crumble between Jake and me. Tendency for wrong answers at the wrong time. "Mya's with Airic."

"Whatthahell do you mean, Mya's with Airic?"

"Airic took matters into his own hands and signed her out of school. He was desperate because he knew we weren't going to let him pick her up, you know—with everything still pending. So, he—"

"You should've called the police."

"And said what? Just stop it, all right. Obviously it wasn't the worst thing to happen today. I mean, I'm glad she wasn't with me when I confronted those FBI agents."

"You confronted them?" He had a brief image locked in his mind, then shook it off. "Don't answer that."

"I was tired of being followed. I got to a stop sign and just mildly asked if there was anything I could do for them."

"You and your bat, right? Again, don't answer that."

"Then stop asking. Now I have a question for you, and think about it carefully before you answer. Why would FBI agents want to kick Legend's ass? I'm telling you, he knows more than he's letting on." I headed for the door.

"Where are you going? I thought you wanted an answer."

"You don't have the answer. Just get him out of my house. I'm going to call Airic, make sure he's on his way." I'd given up on trying to understand what was going on. The good guys were the bad, and Legend was an innocent victim. Couldn't quite wrap my mind around it. Especially Legend as the innocent victim—that part was way too hard to swallow. "And I'm taking my bat. So if I were you, I'd announce yourself before coming to our bedroom."

Scout's Honor

I woke up with the same instructions I had the day before: Don't leave the house. I followed those instructions the same way I had before. I packed Mya and my bat into the car. This time I said a prayer for good measure. Taking Mya back to the preschool was a lot safer than leaving her home with Jake and Legend. And I had way too much work to do for Judge Hawkins's daughter's wedding on Saturday. It was no time for hiding under the blankets.

The staff was surprised to see me. The preschool director must've been waiting on alert. She came out immediately and offered her thin hand. She had a short dark bob cut close around her ears and small apologetic eyes. "Mrs. Parson, we are sincerely dedicated to all of our children here. The thought of doing something to jeopardize them put me in a frenzy. I held an early emergency meeting this morning to go over practice and procedures. My many apologies."

"Thank you, I appreciate that." *Maybe to show how really sorry you are, I could get a free month of tuition.*

Mya unlatched herself from my hand the minute she saw Jory. I didn't take my eyes off her until they met with their signature hug. My eyes landed on his dad. *His dad!* He never dropped Jory off, or picked him up, for that matter. He kissed Jory on top of his head and said his good-bye. Seeing me, too, he started in my direction.

"Thanks again, I gotta get going," I told the director.

"Have a good day. Mya is in good hands," she called out.

"Hold on, now, wait a minute. You telling me I don't even get a thank-you." Robert trotted lightly to catch up, his khaki trench open and trailing slightly behind him.

I stopped, and ignored my embarrassment for being rude. What was I running from, anyway? "How are you?" I did a round wave. "I can't believe you're here dropping off Jory. I wanted to call, but didn't have your number in my cell phone." I held it up.

"Well, I can change that." He took the phone and put in his digits. "For next time." He handed it back. "I'm on my way to a meeting, but I've got a few minutes for coffee. How about it?"

"Coffee?"

"Uh-huh. I get the idea you spend a lot of time around people that don't mean what they say."

"Kind of like politicians." I crowned the comment with a lopsided frown.

"So noted. Come on, we can walk across the street."

I went along peacefully. The coffee shop was crowded, as I knew it would be. The mothers, having freshly dropped off their children, used it as a way station to start their day. We sat outside, the only place where there were empty seats and less staring going on. Who was the good-looking white guy dressed to kill and the Pam Grier throwback in white denim and a jean trench? We looked like sexy detectives from a crime weekly. He opened his coffee and drank without the plastic top. "In Europe this is blasphemy, drinking out of paper and plastic."

"I've never been."

"Really? I see you as a world traveler. Someone who's been places."

"I've traveled a bit, but never been to Europe."

"You'd love it." He swirled and took a sip. "Especially a tiny part of Florence, Italy. I have a house there."

"You mean, you and Holly have a house there. Married people speak in terms of *we*, not *I*."

"I have a house there, very beautiful. If you ever want to steal away, take a break from, what is it—" He leaned forward, pulling my coat open a bit to expose my white T-shirt. "—In Bloom. So have you always been a florist?"

"I was in advertising for a while. Then my own marketing firm until I decided to stay home with Mya. Then when we moved here to Atlanta, I worked at this little floral shop for a week before the owner said she was leaving, going back to Germany and selling the business, and I bought it. I didn't really know what I was getting into. But I love it."

"You say that with such conviction."

"Speaking of which, I have a huge wedding to prepare for this weekend, so I have to get going. Thank you. And I really appreciated the spa day. You have no idea how much I needed it."

"I have somewhat of an idea. You probably are working harder than you've ever worked in your life, am I right?"

"I like being busy."

"Have you thought about getting back in to marketing? Maybe work on someone's campaign, maybe someone like, say, me?"

"You don't even know me," I said, flattered.

"I know more than you think I do."

"Oh, right, you have your ways." I nodded. "Since you have that ability, do you mind helping me out on something? It's kind of touchy. I mean, you'll probably rethink your offer when I ask you this. But, can you find out if a couple of FBI agents are really agents? If I give you their names, can you—?"

Robert Stanton leaned forward, more intrigued than put off. His large face seemed always camera ready. "What's going on?"

"It's a long story, you don't have time. The names are McDonald and Peterson. McDonald is a woman agent. They claim they've been keeping tabs on me for my own protection, but turns out it might be a form of harassment. More like extortion."

"Does it have something to do with your husband's arrest a while back?"

I nodded. "If we only could wave a magic wand and make life go according to our plan, instead of the complete opposite."

He leaned back. His mood turned instantly melancholy. "I can attest to that. My first wife, Jory's mother, was diagnosed with cancer right after he was born. She was only thirty-six when she died, Jory never knew her."

"I'm sorry . . . I had no idea."

"Life is unpredictable. The best we can do is relax, buckle up, and try to take the scenic view. I live each day to the fullest and hope for the best."

I suddenly felt guilty for being so angry with Jake. *This too shall pass.*

"Write the names down," he said. "I'll see what I can do."

We walked back across the street. He escorted me to my car.

"Can you answer this probing question I've always wanted to know?"

"Fire away." He had deep-set brown eyes that concentrated too hard on me.

"What is it about men who are only interested in women who are unavailable? I mean, is it the challenge, the sport of it all? What is that?"

"Are you accusing me of being interested in you? 'Cause, like I said, scout's honor, I'm a straight shooter, married, with huge political aspirations. I'd never ever, ever, do anything dishonorable." He fought off the smile long enough. "Okay, look, I just think you're cute as hell. Nothing wrong with a little flirting, keeps your heart pumping strong. But I know the rules." He looked down at his shoes for a minute, looking like his son. "The answer to your question: I think once in a while we come across this amazing woman who just happens to be taken, and sometimes we just think, *Damn, that could've been me.*"

"You're cute as hell, too," I said. "But so is my husband. And I love him." I patted him on the shoulder.

He conceded. "I give," he said, holding up his two fingers.

The preschool was quiet and calm, not the bustle and hustle of only thirty minutes ago. The children were in their classrooms, oblivious of life's uphill journey. Robert waved as I pulled off. I kept my eye on the rearview mirror, but this time for different reasons. Not because I was afraid, but feeling safe, even as fleeting as it turned out to be. I smiled and reached down to feel my heart. It was pumping quite fast. He was right, sometimes you just needed that flittering moment of feel-good. No harm, no foul.

Pause 'n' Effect

Jake woke up to his phone ringing. He'd overslept, after swearing to himself he'd get up before Venus could make another great escape. He picked up the phone, not recognizing the caller's number. "I guess you stop keeping your promises, huh?"

"Sirena, hey."

"I hear congratulations are in order. Gray said you signed with him."

"Yeah, I did. Thanks for the hookup."

"So you're going to take me out for a thank-you celebration, right? The least you can do?"

"Of course," Jake said, rubbing the sleep out of his eyes. "I'll give you a call, set it up."

"Right," she said, not even pretending to believe him. "Jake, I'm not going to chase you. You're a big boy. You know what you want." She hung up before he could protest. He didn't want to be lumped in with those lying jokers she was used to. Then he remembered it didn't matter. He was married. There was no reason to play games. That's why he got married in the first place, to stop making shit up. Pretending he felt one way, when he didn't. He went to get up and realized he had a good-sized boner peering up at him.

Sirena's voice always used to have that effect on him; obviously his body was simply exercising muscle memory. Used to be, just the thought of her would push him to the verge of explosion. He didn't want to test that either. He lay there and let the reality of his day take hold. The erection faded as quickly as it had appeared.

Legend. Ronny. Rogue federal agents. Errant baby daddies. Airic was lucky Mya had rushed into his arms the minute she was dropped off. Had Jake's hands and arms been free, he would've been riding in the back of somebody's police cruiser. He wanted to stick his fist in Airic's long narrow nose.

There, that was better.

"J-man, you up?" Legend's deep voice reverberated through the door.

"Hold on." Jake peeled himself out of the bed. He slipped on his white drawstring boxers. He opened the door and met Legend's swollen eye. Not so bad as when Jake had found him, but still scary. "You're taking a whole lot of bruising for not having nothing to do with this."

"What are friends for?" Legend stepped inside the room. He looked around. He landed on the black-and-white family picture.

In that shot, Venus was five months pregnant with the baby they'd lost. She would try to hide it, pack it away, but Jake always dug the photo right back up. For him, it was a shame to pretend the pregnancy never existed. He'd had a *son,* even if it was only briefly. "I think if anything"—Legend put the picture back on its stand— "you should want to squash this thing. If these fools just want money, then we give it to them. Sell JP Wear, liquidate, divvy up the cash, and walk away."

"Sell JP Wear? I told you that was your choice, man. I've always said it from day one."

"Yeah, but the buyout stipulates some important small print: Like I get twenty percent and you get eighty." Legend's focus turned back to Jake. His good eye zeroed in, "That's a pretty shitty deal."

Right there, in that moment Jake saw the error of his ways.

Déjà vu. He'd had this conversation before, the very same one with Byron Steeple. He'd had it with his original partner, too, way back when. However he played it, it boiled down to the same thing:

the haves and the have-nots. He had something the other person wanted. If not the actual jewel, the essence, the perception of it, a life of substance, possibly happiness. His friend and, basically, the only father he'd known, Edgar, used to explain this distinction to him when Jake brought home the wrong friend. A have-not, the wrong type of person. Edgar was never talking about money, or material things, although it played a decent-enough role. He was talking about spirituality, peace of mind, integrity. If they didn't have their own, they eventually wanted to take yours. Drain you of your spirit, deny you your peace by planting their poison in your soul.

"Right, it's not fair." Jake agreed, "You've put in sweat and tears over the last couple of years. I appreciate it, man. Maybe we do need a new contract. But let's hash it out over a couple of brewskis before I take you to the airport."

Legend pointed to his eye. "Unless you have an eye patch, I probably shouldn't be sitting in anybody's restaurant. I'm damn sure going to get the business going through security."

"As a matter of fact, I might have you covered." He pushed the door open wide for his friend to leave. "I'll meet you downstairs in ten, man. Watch your step . . . with the bad eye."

Jake stayed in the shower longer than he should have to think things through. How many times could he have counted the signs but ignored them instead? The sidekick who was sick of being kicked. They'd joked about the women falling all over Jake and Legend getting the crumbs. The career aspirations both the same, to own their own companies. While Jake's clothing business had prospered, Legend's advertising and marketing company, Urban Works, had failed, leaving him bitter and in debt. Were those reasons enough for the thin line to cross into hate, jealousy, spite, possibly into sabotage? How many times had a sideways glance caught Legend off guard? Only to be shaken off as a friend who had his back. Putting thought into question. He hadn't wanted a bunch of yes men, an entourage of fools sucking up resources. When Legend pushed back, he appreciated his input. But at some point, the exchange became less about feedback and more about a scorecard. Checks and balances. It always boiled down to give and fuckin' take. And how much was not enough.

He dressed and rushed into Mya's room, where her closet was filled with more clothes than he and Venus had together. In the corner he found what he was looking for—Mya's pirate costume from last Halloween. He'd taken her trick-or-treating and had to carry her on his shoulders the entire time. Equipped with her sword, eye patch, and mustache, Mya was afraid to be on the ground with the ghouls, witches, and scary slasher-movie masks. He couldn't blame her. Halloween was for freaks. Some people took it a bit too far. Costumes past the age of twelve was downright psychotic. But on this day, he couldn't have been happier to have an eye patch in his possession.

"Here you go, man."

Legend took the patch. "You're serious?" The plastic black fabric had obviously seen better days.

"From a distance it looks like solid leather. You can start a new fad." Jake wasn't going to argue with him. Legend was getting on that plane or, as the old saying goes, You ain't got to go home, but you gettin' the hell outta here.

"You seriously think I'm going to wear this?"

"You asked for a patch, I got you a patch. Now let's roll."

Just an Illusion

"Mama D, I want to thank you for rescuing me." Gray put his hand to his heart, though no one was in this office to witness his humility. "I can't apologize enough. It was purely an accident. I asked my accountant to reconcile my accounts to one place so my lovely wife-to-be would have equal access—well, the mix-up wasn't all his fault, but more than anything, I'm glad you were on the case."

He waited for the preferential love he was so used to receiving from womenfolk. That absolution of any wrongdoing. But instead, she huffed on the other end of the line. "You may think you can fool all of the people all of the time, but you can't fool me. I've never bought into your perfect Gray Hillman act. I didn't tell Keisha, because I love her more than life itself and would never want to bring her a minute of pain. But you best believe I'm watching you, Gray Hillman. Believe, know, and understand it. I'm not one of these women who give a damn about your light skin and light eyes. Your nice car and clothes. I see right through all the decoration. All that matters to me is how you treat my baby, you get me?"

"Yes, ma'am," Gray said quickly. There were few things he cared about besides money, but being on Judge Delma Hawkins's bad side was not a good thing. "I swear, Keisha is my first and only priority. I want to take care of her, love her like she deserves."

"That's all I want, Gray. Long as we agree to that, we're on the same page."

He hung up, feeling victorious. Regardless of the tongue-lashing he'd received, the consequences had been mild. He was still a king in his baby's eyes. Really, what else mattered?

His phone buzzed; this time it was his office line. "Yeah, Nikki?"

"Mr. Jake Parson is here," she said, "I don't have him on the schedule." She left it open-ended. His call.

"Show him in." Gray logged out of his computer, making the screen with his accounts disappear. "It's a beautiful thing. I just got word from Calvin Klein and Pepsi—they're both interested." He put out his hand to Jake. "But I wasn't expecting you, please tell me you're not changing your mind. You gotta whole new world, my brotha, don't drop the ball now."

"Nah, haven't changed my mind. In fact, very excited."

"And you are?" Gray put out his hand.

"Legend Hill."

"Mr. Hill, a pleasure. What's the other guy look like?" He joked noticing the obvious fight wounds.

"It was a woman," Jake said.

Gray got the joke and laughed accordingly.

"Nah, seriously, a woman. Never underestimate one."

"I try not to." Gray opened his hand. "Please have a seat. So what brings this special drop-in?"

"I need a meeting with Ronny Wilks," Jake said without further explanation.

"Ronny Wilks—okay, so you're lookin' to get back in the studio. Not a bad idea."

Legend leaned near Jake's ear. "Not a good idea."

"I think it's the best idea. You see, I got a situation. You might be more familiar with it than you're letting on, so stop me if I bore you."

Gray's eyes lit up with genuine confusion. "I have no idea what you're talking about. Are you accusing me of something?"

"Not at all. Here's the situation: Ronny's your boy and all, thought you two may have had this conversation already."

"I assure you, your name has never come up."

"Well, then let me go on," Jake said. "Money went missing that belonged to Ronny via an old employee of mine, who happened to steal money from me, too. All fingers would likely point to me, that maybe I took Byron out, maybe I recovered my money and Ronny's, too. But that's not the case. I'm living off the fumes of my success. If I had an offshore account filled with the money of a gangsta like Ronny Wilks, I wouldn't be sitting here begging for a meet and greet."

"Ah, a mystery with suspense. As if life isn't complicated enough." Gray's knuckles hit the top of his desk. "Okay, time's up, gentlemen. I don't deal in business that doesn't have to do with lights, camera, and action. I wish I could help."

"You can. I need to meet with Ronny, face-to-face, neutral ground. Friendly territory for both of us."

"Me and Ronny are not that friendly. I'm sure you witnessed that the other night at Sirena's party."

"All I saw were two businessmen talking deals. Call it what you want to call it, but I need five minutes. That's all."

He nodded, threw up his hands. "What the hell, all right, a business meeting, then? At least you were honest with me. I would've seriously been pissed if you had me setting up a bogus meeting, talking about your next great hit, then you break out with this boil and trouble. Would've made me look bad. Right now that's something I can't afford."

Jake and his partner stood up, ready to leave.

Gray had to ask, "The first time you came to see me, is that what it was about, your way of getting to Ronny Wilks?"

"I'm not going to lie to you." Jake Parson managed a million-dollar smile. "Yes."

Gray shook his head. Ronny was either going to kill Jake Parson or be dumbstruck by his nerve.

"Right now I just want to figure out how to end the Byron Steeple nightmare once and for all. Once it's done, I can seriously be down with this new career."

"I feel you," Gray said, escorting them to the door. "I'll set something up, let you know where and when."

Gray had his own deal set and in place with Ronny, but if he could sweeten the bounty by delivering Jake Parson, why not?

You Have the Right

The cameraman was busy adjusting his lens while the producer's assistant felt her way up the back of my blouse with the wire of the mic. My interview was going to be aired on prime-time news. A chance to gain my name back was moments away. I was nervous for the first time. Normally being in front of a camera was like waking up and brushing my teeth. It was just something I did, but for this interview I was unhinged. So much on my mind to the point I couldn't even pray it away. Donations were down by 30 percent to the Doval Ministries. The television ratings had declined by twice as much. I was losing my following, and all because I'd loved a man.

Once the tiny unit was attached to my suit lapel, she pressed a second piece in my ear. "There, got it. Go ahead and count to three for me." She waved a hand. "Okay, we're all set." Then, she paused. "Would you like something warm, tea or coffee? You're shaking."

"No thank you. I'm fine."

"You're going to do great. No need to be nervous," the woman gave me a thumbs-up.

"We're on in fifteen seconds," the man's voice inside my ear announced.

Carla O'Brian was going to be the interviewer. She was a straightforward newswoman who I expected to be fair and classy. No longer did I want to be in the spotlight for the sake of pushing my book. CNN was the first interview of many to come. I'd planned to set the precedent of behavior, let Carla know I wouldn't be discussing Airic and his philandering ways.

Where would I begin? Start with who I was, who I'd become, and all the work still to be done. I'd spent so much time and energy healing sick hearts that I'd left my own vulnerable.

The interviewer was going to see me, but I wouldn't see her. Having watched enough of her interviews, I knew her tone and expressions. Her stiff blond hair tucked closely to her neck while she worked hard at being taken seriously. The thing to remember about these types of interviews was that they closed you up in a soundproof box to make you feel private, cozy, like talking on a phone with a good friend . . . only the whole world was listening. I wouldn't be lured in that direction. I would keep it purely about my beliefs, my faith, and the hope for a better Christian tomorrow.

"Five, four, three . . ."

"Good evening, I'm Ebony Jenkins, and welcome to the nightly news. I'm sitting in for Carla O'Brian, and we have a bustling lineup for you this evening."

I tapped on the mic attached to my lapel. "Um, excuse me. I'm supposed to be interviewed by Carla O'Brian."

The man's voice piped in, interrupting Ebony Jenkins's intro. "Not a problem. Ms. Jenkins is familiar with your story and very well read. Enjoy."

"But . . . no—"

He cut me off. Ebony Jenkins was known for entertainment gossip that destroyed reputations. She wasn't a serious journalist, not with her signature blond wig and exaggerated large bosom. The woman was an embarrassment. I couldn't see her, but I knew she was probably sitting with her breasts exposed as she usually did.

"Our first story is filled with scandal and heartbreak. Trevelle Doval, who holds the coveted title of Queen of the Pulpit, was rocked by the news that her husband of only two years had an illicit affair with her assistant, only to learn far too late that she was underage and now, we learn, pregnant. We're going to talk to her to find out how someone of such high moral aptitude picked a—" She paused briefly. "Something in my introduction seems to have shocked you, Ms. Doval."

That's when I realized she was speaking directly to me. The camera was on. I snapped out of the horrified expression she and the viewers must've seen. I plastered a calm smile on my face. However, I was seething. "No, shocked, no. I have tried to distance myself from this situation. I was hoping we could talk about my new book, *You Have the Right to Refuse Service to Anyone*."

"Absolutely, and would you say this young woman is your prime audience? This young woman who obviously didn't know she had a right to refuse service and now finds herself pregnant by a married man?"

"Yes, I'd say she was my prime target." I held my breath and waited to reclaim my position. "But let's look at the reality—women young and old, doesn't matter the age, have not learned of this right. Women are divine creations by God, yet we treat ourselves like secondhand sweaters, passing ourselves around to the first needy individual who comes along."

"Are you calling your husband, Airic Fisher, a needy individual? And if so, wouldn't that counter your stance that a woman should fulfill her helpmate by any means necessary?"

The rise in temperature in the room and the throbbing nuisance of a headache made me touch my temple for relief. "We can't always be everything to everyone. At some point, a woman must decide if she has taken on too much to bear, and maybe hand it over to God."

"If you could say anything to Chandra, the young lady who slept with your husband, if she's listening, and the many Chandras out there today, what would you tell her?"

I leaned forward, though there was no one staring back at me but the black glass of a camera lens. "You deserve good things. God made that promise when He gave his only son for your sins. Forgive yourself and begin anew. From this day forward, you have a right to refuse service to anyone."

"And you, Ms. Doval. Do you personally forgive her?"

I was filled with contempt, ready to lash out, but thoughts become words, and words become actions; this I understood. "Yes, I do. I forgive her. She is a child. She did nothing wrong."

"How apropos," Ebony Jenkins said in closing. "Most of us have not read all of Trevelle Doval's books, many are not familiar with her past history, but many understand the term 'full circle.' What you give comes back to you?"

I realized I was no longer on feed. But I still couldn't make myself get up out of the chair. So I listened to her closing remarks.

"And here we see the perfect example. Trevelle Doval had an affair with a married man when she was but a child, and this union produced a baby daughter. The wife of that man chose to stay with her husband, and fight for their marriage. The irony is for one so prophetic, how she doesn't see the similarities, how she doesn't understand that this was her test, and possibly her failure. Next we have billionaire Leon Miller—"

"Get me out of here!" I screamed. The black door opened, letting in a stream of light, hurting my eyes. "How dare she call me out like that?"

"Hold on, you're leaving with the wire attached," the assistant said as she tried to help me get loose.

I snatched every piece of wire, pulling and tugging until the unit ripped my blouse. I threw it at her and walked out.

I drove myself home, wishing I'd said and done everything differently. I should've stood up for myself somehow, demanded the last word. Ebony Jenkins would forever be on my list of neva-effa heffas. She'd never be invited to anything, and if I saw her in public, I'd pretend to not remember a thing about her.

I moved quickly through the lobby of my condominium, only to hear my name before reaching the elevators. "Ms. Doval, there's a delivery here for you."

The large floral arrangement coming toward me was probably another ploy from Airic. "No thank you. Donate them to a hospital."

"Are you sure?"

"The last time I accepted flowers, they were from my ex-husband, who you let into the building without permission. So what now, is he hiding behind a ficus somewhere?"

"These were delivered by a florist." He pulled off the huge card and handed it to me.

Embossed print with the name IN BLOOM across white linen. I opened it and read, "Your interview was great. Though you have the right to refuse, I hope you'll accept my invite to lunch. Vince Capricio, aka In Bloom Elf."

"Bring them up," I told the security guard.

"That's not all. There're four more." He threw a thumb over his shoulder. I saw the arrangements sitting lined up on the security station counter. I covered my mouth in shock. Beautiful, fresh bouquets in various colors and sizes. Long-stemmed white roses mixed with gardenias and freesia.

"Bring them up?" He asked for confirmation.

I nodded. "I'd appreciate it, yes."

The last trip up, the security guard set a glass vase on the center of my coffee table. I handed him a ten. "Thank you. I'm sorry I was so rude."

"No problem. Enjoy." He waved. I double-locked the door when he left, then faced the bounty. I inhaled and took in the calm joy of flowers freshly cut. There was no greater scent. I bent my face to the lavender and nearly came to tears. Vince Capricio, aka the In Bloom Elf, knew a thing or two about arranging flowers. I regretted having been so rude to him, too. I was noticing a serious pattern.

At 6 P.M., the place was sure to be closed, but I dialed the number on the card anyway. "In Bloom, can I help you?"

"Mr. Capricio, this is Trevelle Doval." I didn't know what else to say after that, not expecting him to answer the phone in the first place.

"You're welcome." His voice was steady.

I cradled the phone as I moved to the couch and curled myself in a ball. I didn't say a word, and neither did he. He stayed on the line, breathing quietly. When I was close enough to sleep, I said, "Good night."

"Sleep well," he answered. "If you need me, you know where I am."

⊙\◎

Marcella was standing over me. Her hand was floating above my head far too close to my mouth. I screamed. She screamed, too, then shouted, "Oh, missus!" She picked up the prescription bottle of sleeping pills that were sitting on the coffee table. "I was scared you no breathing."

I sat up, my heart still pumping hard from waking up thinking I was in the middle of a séance or something. I had fallen asleep on the couch. I had planned to take the sleeping pills, but for the first time in a long time I didn't need them. I hadn't even had a bad dream.

She left and came back with a cup of hot tea. "Here you go." She started her ritual of pulling back the curtains. I squinted from the sunlight. When my eyes adjusted, I saw all the beautiful bouquets of flowers and remembered . . . Vince Capricio. I picked up the phone again, still warm where I'd held it the entire time.

Marcella did a double take. *"Ay, bonita. Muchas flores."*

"Make sure they have plenty of water," I announced as I marched off to my bedroom. I had to get myself together. There was much to do. I had a wedding to stop.

Bitter Fruit

Gray leaned over the station and did something he'd never done before. He kissed Nikki square on the lips. "Good morning, sexy."

She put her hand to her mouth and looked in both directions. "What was that?"

"Just feeling good. You know what? I'm feeling better than good. More like on top of the world."

Nikki followed him into his office. "Guess it's the excitement of tomorrow, your wedding day." She stood next to him while he situated himself at his desk.

"Look, don't try to bring me down with more of your pouty-mouth guilt trips. How many times do I have to say it? Nothing's going to change. I'm still going to take care of you. You're always going to have a special place right here." He did a crotch grab. He couldn't help but snicker at the disgust on her face. "I'm playin' with you, girl." He tapped at his chest. "Right here, you're in my heart." He pulled her down to meet his lips. "Damn, you taste even better than last night."

Gray checked the time—it was still early. No one would be coming through for at least another hour. He slid his hands up the sides of her thick thighs. The swell of her bottom sent a bolt to his groin. "You gone have to take care of this, girl."

"I thought you said never in your office. Plus I'll mess up my hair and makeup."

"Not the full package, just a quick service, baby. Please. I was feeling so good when I came in. You brought me down. You owe me, baby."

"But what if Keisha stops in?"

"Keisha's not coming in. She's miles from here, taking care of last-minute details for the happiest day of her life, marrying me."

"What a lucky girl," Nikki said, folding her arms over her chest. "Too bad it's all an illusion."

Gray slid his hands down her dress. He patted her on the derriere. "Get out. Take the day off." He swatted his hand in the air. "Now, walk. Bringing down my day, ain't even started yet, and you're trying to ruin it," he half whined.

"What're you talking to me like that for?" She stood firm, arms crossed under her voluptuous chest.

"I've given you everything. You got the nerve to disrespect me."

"You want to talk about respect?" she huffed. "I'm the one you come to, me. I gave you everything, all of me there is to give, and you go off and marry someone else."

"Did you *ever* think it would be you?" His pitch rose with incredulity. "Leave, please. I'm not going to let you mess this day up for me."

"Tell me to leave one more time, and I will. And I'm not coming back." Her accent turned thick.

"Yeah, right."

"You can have your car, the condominium—I don't need it. I don't need you." She wiped the raging tears rolling down her cheeks. "I'm worth more than this. I deserve better than to be treated like some prostitute."

"You know what? Then go find it, 'cause I'm sick of your trick ass."

She shoved his computer to the hard shiny floor, cracking it into pieces. "You're the trick. You." She left his office.

Just as quickly, she swished back inside, her juicy thighs rubbing together. She had her bag over her shoulder and her keys in hand.

Gray rose up from his busted computer and cowered, afraid of what she would do next. "I'm not coming back. Do you hear me? I mean it, Gray. You'll not see me again. You marry your princess. I'm going to Nigeria with my Hambe and becoming a queen. Treated like I deserve to be treated."

"I hear they cut off women's passion buttons in that crew. I'd be careful if I were you. And last I heard, weave shops weren't very popular there. He may not be happy when he realizes that mop on your head isn't a real product of the colonized side of Trinidad. Take your fake ass out of here."

"So this is what it's about. You think you're getting the real thing, Miss Mulatto who knows nothing of where she comes from. I know who I am. I know."

"Yeah, I can see that. I know where you're going, too." Gray picked up the phone, pressed a button. "Security."

"I hate you. You will see, walking over people, treating them any way you want. You will see."

Gray was relieved when she finally left. He took a long deep breath. He kneeled on the ground to tend to his shattered computer. He had to call someone to save the hard drive. All the accounts where Byron had hidden money were safely there. Only problem was Gray'd never had the pass codes. Watching the money sit there, untouchable, broke his heart every single day. He kept hope that someday a miracle would set him free; until then he settled on what he already had—a good career, a wife with an inheritance, and his affable personality.

He packed up the computer and decided the day was shot. He might as well pick up his tux early and stop by the barbershop to get his fade tightened up a bit. Even after the episode with Nikki, he was still walking on high. One down, one to go. If Ronny took care of his end, there would be harmony at last. No more complications in his otherwise perfect world.

Terror Squad

"I have the information you want." Robert Stanton sounded like the mystery and espionage were the highlight of his day, or week. "Where do you want to meet?"

"We don't have to meet anywhere. You can tell me right now. You're talking to me." I held the phone to my ear while I poked baby roses into the last greenery ball for the head table arrangements.

"Phones aren't safe for this kind of information."

Vince moved behind me, slow enough to be listening. He'd been very attentive to my conversations in the last few days. I pressed the phone tighter to my mouth, "The answer is—yes, they're legit or no, they're not. You see how easy that is? Yes or no."

"It's not a yes-or-no answer." Robert Stanton's dry humor wasn't easy to detect. I couldn't tell if he was serious, or just serious about seeing me.

"Okay, but I have like three minutes . . . I'm telling you."

"Meet me at our spot," he said, hanging up before I could say, *We don't have a spot.*

"Off on another rendezvous?"

"Is Jake paying you to watch over me? I swear, you can tell me, I won't be mad."

"I wouldn't take his money," Vince said. "I'm no tattletale."

"Good. I'll be back in a flash. You won't even know I'm gone." I tossed my purse over my shoulder and ran out of there before he could give me any more sage advice. Robert wasn't at "our spot" yet. I ordered two coffees and sat impatiently. Tomorrow was Keisha's wedding. I was always nervous before a ceremony, but things were worse with the tension of my household. Jake had tossed and turned all night—once he came to bed, that is. He nuzzled next to me and said, "It will all be over tomorrow." It was two or three in the morning. I wanted to question him, but my lips wouldn't move from pure exhaustion. I made a decision to hire one more person after this wedding. I was overworked from head to toe.

"Hey there, beautiful." Robert Stanton sat down.

I pushed a wisp of dry fuzz out of my face then scooted my hands under my arms to hide my frayed cuticles. I was hardly the pampered princess. Manual labor was not my forte. I felt tired and run-down. The only thing kept me half-satisfied was knowing one thing: I had played the game of beauty, and it was an endless, thankless job that required way too much attention and upkeep. "Now, that's just plain condescending."

He laughed. "You have a strange ability to twist everything. Has anyone ever told you that before?"

"Absolutely not."

He slid the file envelope he was carrying to me. "Don't open it until you are alone, in your car."

"And burn after reading?" I said.

"Please"—he nodded—"if you don't mind."

"I appreciate it. I really do."

"No problem. They're legit," he said, easily.

"And you couldn't tell me this over the phone?"

I stood up. "But remember I said I had three minutes. Well, we're down to one. I really have to go." I took the envelope and my coffee. "That one's yours."

He popped off the lid. "Black, just like I like it." The senator gave me a dance of his eyebrows.

"You need to be ashamed of yourself."

"I'll give it a try," he said. "See you later."

"Okay," I agreed, not sure to what.

In my car, I tore open the envelope. The folded pages were pho-
tocopies of the official badges of Tonya McDonald and Tyrone Peterson, both real live FBI agents with their good standing and list of
merits and distinctions. I dialed Jake. He didn't answer. I left a message. "Babe, those FBI agents are very real and very legitimate. I have
their files right here. I don't know why they would want to hurt Legend. Something's not right." He'd have to see for himself anyway.
Nothing else I said seemed to convince him that Legend wasn't on
the up and up. Maybe now he would believe me.

The white Jaguar parked in front of my store with a license plate
that read FAVORED belonged to Trevelle. Geez, this was not the time.
I pulled in behind the In Bloom van. The doors were wide open,
filled nearly to the brim with the boxes labeled HAWKINS PARTY.
Vince had taken care of the rest of the floral centerpieces for Keisha's
wedding, thank goodness. The Witch of the East had obviously
failed at distracting him.

I expected the sound of Trevelle's haughty voice to ring with indignation. Instead I heard her laughter, then Vince chiming in like
they were on their first date. "You're kidding, right? You would've
made a great cheerleader."

"Hi," was all I could manage, looking between the two of them
as if I'd caught them with their hands in the cookie jar at the same
damn time.

"Venus, how does it look?" Trevelle was busy sticking baby's
breath in the halo that Mya would be wearing as the flower girl. She
held it up. White ribbon trailed down the back. "Exquisite, isn't it? I
had no idea I was such a talented artiste. Work of art." She continued
patting herself on the back, otherwise not needing my input after
all.

I swallowed the ball of nerves in my throat and thought about
pinching myself to make sure I wasn't dreaming.

"Glad she stopped in. I really needed the extra pair of hands," Vince said, almost daring me to say something rude.

"I came by to thank Vince for the flowers he sent. He was inundated. I really don't approve of my daughter's wedding to this man, but Vince and I started talking, and he's so wise."

I held up a finger and crooked it for Vince to follow me. I led him to the front entrance. "Huh?" I shrugged my shoulders. "What is going on?"

"Just like she said—she saw I was up to my eyeballs, and she wanted to help." He dusted his hands off. "You should be thanking her instead of being rude."

"Do not trust her. Do you hear me? She's scheming, plotting, planning. Trust me—nothing is as it seems with her."

"I think you're wrong. I think she's pretty straightforward. She says what she means. She's a good person. Got a beautiful spirit."

"Yeah, if you like voodoo priestesses. You've known her like five minutes. Please." I put both hands up to my ears.

"You should be appreciative of her help, I'm telling you."

"I can't hear you," I said. "All I'm thinking is I hope the flowers don't wilt from whatever spell she cast."

"The woman's a saint."

I covered my mouth, aghast. Then I opened my hands over his face and swirled them around. "Cast out this spell! Save my friend Vince from her evil clutches."

"Thank you for that. Now, can I get back to work? I have to deliver the order that me and wicked witch happened to fill while you were gone."

"And you sent her flowers . . . my flowers. I hope you paid for them."

"Yeah, we'll just call it a hush fund, seeing's how I got a lot to be quiet about. I wouldn't have needed her help if you hadn't run off to see Mr. Stanton, groupie of one."

"Mind your business." I put my finger close to his nose. He snapped with a bite, making me draw back in a hurry, then left me standing there grateful I still had my finger. "I'm not done with you," I said in a meek whisper.

I'll admit I was a bit more grateful when I reappeared. Vince was fitting the last of the boxes in the van. The sun was setting on the back room, so all the light shone through the right window onto Trevelle. She had on Mya's halo and looked eerily angelic. "All finished."

"It's really beautiful. Thank you." I gently lifted it off her head. I pulled down a box and began to wrap tissue around it. "Well, I guess I'll see you tomorrow at the ceremony." I was hoping she took the cue to leave.

"My daughter has banned me from the ceremony."

"What . . . from even showing up? Keisha . . . or Delma?"

"Keisha. Came directly from her mouth to mine and God's ears."

"I'm sorry to hear that," I murmured, but what I was really thinking was she'd probably done something absolutely horrendous to deserve such a punishment. I didn't even want to guess.

I set the halo wreath in the box and suddenly had a pained thought of Mya telling me not to bother coming to a school play, a birthday party, let alone her wedding. I would be crushed. "Is there a way you can talk to her, maybe one last time before tomorrow?"

"I've tried. She won't take my calls."

I felt sorry for Trevelle. I twisted my mouth and wanted to say or do something, yet had no words for such a hopeless situation. And then I remembered. "They're having the rehearsal tonight where Vince is going to deliver the flowers. Maybe you should tag along. Vince needs the helping hands. I have kind of a family emergency. I have to get home, so—" I faced Vince as he came through the back door. "—you wouldn't mind if she went with you, right?"

"I'd absolutely love it."

"Yeah, okay. Settled then."

Vince scooped up the keys. "My lady, your chariot awaits."

I touched Trevelle on the shoulder. "Please, just don't do anything, um . . ."

"Don't worry. I'm representing In Bloom. I will behave myself," she said firmly.

I snapped my fingers. "Good idea." I ran back inside and grabbed a T-shirt. I thrust it toward her.

"I have to draw the line, really." She pushed it back toward me. "I'll be fine." She sashayed out in her white knit pants and matching jacket with bright gold buttons. Vince and his black T-shirt and jeans was her complete opposite in more ways than one.

"Okay, you two kids have fun." The van pulled off. I shook my head. Unbelievable. I hoped Vince could handle her. If he thought I was bad, wait till he got a load of Trevelle.

I focused on the bigger problem looming: the FBI, Jake, and Legend. I had to find Jake. I dialed his number, prepared to leave a detailed message, but instead I heard his real live voice. "Baby, ohmigod, where are you? I've been so worried."

"I'm at the Intercontinental in Buckhead. Legend and I are having drinks. Nothing to worry about."

"No, there is something to worry about. Listen to me—"

"Babe, we have a meeting. I can't talk right now. I swear I'll call as soon as we're done."

"No, listen. Those FBI agents . . ." I was talking to myself. He'd already hung up. Intercontinental, here I come. I turned around to grab my keys and realized they weren't hanging on the plaque hook. Vince had taken the wrong keys for the van. My Range Rover sat outside. I rushed to see if the extra set was hidden somewhere, the way Jake always warned I should do. Well, I hadn't bothered, but maybe he had. Husbands did that kind of thing when you weren't looking. The car was open, thank goodness.

No, this wasn't happening. No key. I looked at the old Buick parked on the curb. Maybe Vince had left his keys. Back inside, I searched the desk drawer and anywhere there was a surface. I came across keys, but they didn't belong to me or Vince. The large gold letters read HIGHLY FAVORED..

Next thing I knew, I was fastening my seat belt in the white

Jaguar, my bat firmly locked and loaded in the front seat. I went to press the brake to start the car and realized the pedals were a mile away. Trevelle and her long legs. The electronic movement at a snail's pace made me want to scream. "C'mon."

I started the car, and the first thing I saw was the empty-gas warning. She must've needed her husband, too. The little things. I put the car in drive and stepped lightly, doing my best to conserve energy. No sudden starts and stops.

When I made it to the gas station, I thanked God. I had to give Trevelle the benefit of the doubt. That highly favored business might actually be real, running so low on gas. If it were me in my car, I surely would've been sitting on the side of the road on E, asking God, *Why me?*

"Hey, girl, you need some help with that?" A thick baggy type was standing too close, offering his assistance with the pump.

"No thank you." I pressed the lowest octane. I figured the Jag could stand one filling of the lowest gasoline. I wasn't paying nearly five dollars a gallon to feed her beast.

"You sure? Somebody fine as you don't need to be pumping gas."

"Sweet, but I have it." He was so close, I had no room to back up.

"All right, if you say so."

I watched him stroll into the convenience store. He disappeared behind some shelves. I figured I had enough gas to get me where I was going. I wanted to be gone before the guy came back outside. I knew I was in the dangerous part of town. If someone witnessed this situation, they would suggest I should've taken a chance to drive a few more miles to a better station. If someone witnessed the man coming up from behind me, they probably wouldn't have known that it didn't matter what station I'd pulled into, since he'd followed me there.

"Trevelle, I'ma go ahead and pump that gas for you." I felt an arm wrap around my neck while he dragged me over to the black Hummer that had appeared out of nowhere.

"Wait. I'm not—" I felt the hot burn of my skin twist when he tightened his grip.

"Shut up! Shut up—not a peep or I'll snap your neck."

Oh, God!

All I could remember was the show on TV, warning you never to let them take you to a second location. I opened my mouth and sunk my teeth into his arm. He yelped and released his grip. I grabbed the door handle and pushed it open. He yanked me back before I could get out.

"I'm not her!" I yelled. "Help, somebody please help me!" The disgusting hand covered my nose and mouth. I couldn't breathe. I fought as hard as I could, digging my nails into his arm then scratching at his face. *Go for the eyes, use your elbows.* How many times had I watched those women being accosted in the movies and thinking of all the right moves. None of them worked.

He barely got the door closed. "Drive, let's go. Move." The Hummer screeched out of the gas station parking lot, and the sun hadn't even set. When someone is said to have disappeared in plain daylight, it only means no one else was watching. There were no witnesses.

Made You Look

"You sure you want to do this?" Legend signed the contract on the last page. He slid it back to Jake with the pen.

Jake leaned his chin on his folded hands, watching as Legend signed. "Whatever it takes."

"You're doing the best thing. For you and your family, right? What else matters? Once the company sells, Ronny will be paid off, he'll call off his fake posse, and you'll have your life back."

"Let's hope," Jake said, putting the signed contract in his jacket pocket.

"Where's my copy, my brotha? Not that anything's going to happen to you in your meeting tonight with Ronny, but we need the deal secure."

Jake snapped his fingers. "I wasn't thinking. I should've got two copies. Sorry, man, we'll take care of it on our way to the meeting."

They slipped out of the booth of Risou. Jake left a fifty-dollar tip on fifty dollars' worth of food and drinks. He was feeling exceptionally generous. He wasn't sure how everything would play out, but knowing it was at least going to end gave him a charge of relief.

"Remember, I know this dude," Legend said, warning Jake with his eyes. "He's crazy. Just go along with whatever he says, whether you agree or not."

"Right."

"When he asks for his money back, don't defend it with the

NapPily in BloOm 251

truth. Just tell him the check's in the mail." Legend stuck his hand out to Jake; they leaned in on each other for a shoulder bump. "And this'll all be over."

"You're right about that." Jake pushed the elevator button. Ronny was in room 3012, the penthouse of the Intercontinental. The hotel was too elegant for what was about to happen. "Just to let you know, I tipped off the agents about this meeting."

Legend stopped in his tracks. "You did what? I told you they were in on this whole thing. I told you they were working for Ronny."

"I called them, told them what was going down." Jake raised his shoulders for effect.

"I've always had your back. Why didn't you listen to me?" His locs covered his face as he put his head down to think. "This isn't good."

"And why is that?"

"'Cause if you ain't wearing a bulletproof vest, you've made a death wish. If police and Feds are involved, Ronny's going to make it a showdown." Legend pointed. "Which part of my warning went over your head?" Legend paced. "I can't go up there. He's going to think it was me. I swore I'd get him the money."

"What money is that exactly? And why would you promise him money you supposedly know nothing about."

Legend was backed into a corner. "You shouldn't have gotten them involved."

"This is your last chance, man. When they get here, you might want to get your story straight. I know you want to pay off Ronny worse than I do. I know you'd sell my company to do it. The Legend I know would've thrown up his hands and wished everybody luck."

Legend didn't answer him. He turned his back to Jake.

"Tell me what I don't know," Jake said, ready to burst but keeping his calm.

"*The Legend you know,* what kind of shit is that? I was doing you a favor. I hired two homo-thugs to kick Byron's ass and get your money back. Did I know he'd stolen from some mass criminal empire or anybody else? No idea. All they were supposed to do was get him to talk and cough up the kitty he stole." Legend shook his head. "For you, all for you. And this is how you repay me."

"You want me to say thanks? Man, fuck you. I would never ask you to do something like that for me. You know that. Now you bring all this to my door, come to my house, put my family's life in danger. And I'm supposed to pay off the debt you made 'cause you did it for me? You didn't do this for me." He was holding in the urge to slam Legend against the wall. "You were going to take whatever Byron stole and keep it for yourself. You don't give a damn about me." Jake wanted to fall back and head straight out the lobby doors. Pack up his wife and daughter and get where no one would find him.

"If we go to this meeting with those agents on the case, all we're doing is admitting our guilt."

"Your guilt, not mine." Jake said. "Yours."

"Okay, mine. If they realize we're trying to strike a deal with Ronny on any level, it's an admission of guilt."

Jake shook his head. "I didn't call them. I told you that to see what you'd say."

Legend decompressed. "You'll never change. Always the prankster."

"Wish it was that simple."

"Follow through." Legend opened his hands then clasped them together. "Let's do this and end it. I swear it will be the end. Ronny's the only one we need to be afraid of. The Feds don't have nothing on us. We push the deal through to sell the business, pay Ronny off, and it's over."

"There you go using French again." Jake turned around and started walking toward the sprawling hotel lobby. "There's no *we*. You're on your own."

"So you're just going to exit stage left? What about the deal we just signed? Do I still get the money?" Legend called out to him.

Jake faced him. "If I were you, I wouldn't go up there. Go home, man. If you gotta pack your shit and hide out for a while, I suggest you do it." Jake held up two fingers for peace. He wished him well.

◎◎

For a few seconds, the evening air tasted a little fresher. Mystery solved, though he'd lost one of his best friends in the process. He started walking toward the parking lot. His phone vibrated.

"Mr. Parson," the voice said on the other end of his cell phone. "Mya Fisher has not been picked up from school. We are following procedure, calling all the numbers listed on the emergency card. We've tried Mya's mother on her cell, work, and home. If she's not picked up by eight P.M., we have an obligation to call Child Services."

Jake checked the time and couldn't believe it was seven thirty on the dot. "Please, don't. I'll be there. I'm on my way."

She would never be this late picking up Mya. Never. He faced the hotel and had the worst wave of fear. Did Ronny have something to do with this? Did he take Venus? Jake had a hard time catching his breath, not sure which way to go. Back inside, where he'd just left, or pick up Mya before the preschool went into procedure alert? Then he remembered her message, the one he'd ignored because he figured it was the usual conversation.

Her voice was shaky: *"Babe, I think you should know that the FBI agents are real. Please be careful. If they need your cooperation, give it to them. Even if it means giving up your friend Legend. Do the right thing. It'll be okay."*

Jake pulled out the card Agent Tonya McDonald had given him. He dialed the number with a shaky hand and prayed they knew something. Even if it meant they had Venus in custody for wielding her trusty bat. The only thing he knew was he couldn't move from the spot he was standing in until he knew she was safe. Otherwise, he was going up to room 3012.

Shugga Pie Hunny Bun

The oldies music was coming out past the doors and into the parking lot. Vince shut off the engine. "Looks like they're already partying in there. Remember what we talked about. If she wants to talk to you, fine, but you're not going to push it."

"Agreed." I put out my hand. He took mine and, instead of shaking it, put it to his lips. "You've been too kind to me. I'm not used to anyone wanting to simply be kind without wanting something in return—a prayer, a blessing."

"By blessing, you mean money? I thought it was the sheep that liked to give money to you, not the other way around."

"Sheep." I curled up my nose.

"Hey, I call it straight. But to be nice let's say flock."

"I have a following who enjoy my teachings—for that I am rewarded. But there's the personal side of my life that sometimes needs nourishment. When I'm always giving, I sometimes don't remember to replenish. When I reach out for a touch or caring moment, if I dare share my vulnerability, I always seem to get hurt."

"Not on my watch," he said. "Let's go and get this over with. Then we'll find the biggest juiciest steak we can get our hands on with a bottle of vino."

"Mr. Capricio, I do not drink."

"We'll pretend it's just water before Jesus made it into wine."

"You're wicked."

"And you're even more beautiful when you're vulnerable."

◌◌◌

Gray had just hung up with Ronny, who'd confirmed what he wanted to hear. Operation Get Rid of the Thorn in His Side was in effect. He felt like dancing. He snapped his fingers and sang along with the music. *"I can't help myself. I love you and nobody else."*

Keisha blushed before getting up from the table where she and Delma were going over the seating chart. She did a one-two, one-two on each side, sliding toward him. He spun around before taking her hands. The bridal party clapped and bounced with them. Even Bishop Talley got in on the action, bopping his head.

The party before the party. The celebration of the celebration. Whatever it was called, Gray was elated. Until he looked over Keisha's shoulder and saw Trevelle Doval standing there before his eyes, hand on her hip with one side of her jaw sucked in coming toward them.

Was he already being haunted by guilt? He'd gotten the news only two minutes ago. Now here she stood. Keisha stopped dancing when Gray seemed fixated on one spot. She turned to see what kept his attention.

"Oh no," she said under her breath.

Trevelle put up a hand. "I'm here to help place the flowers. Seems I have a new vocation, or temporary at least." She smiled at the floral employee who was bringing in the arrangements.

Gray was still too dumbfounded to take a step forward.

She mistook his silence for a conciliatory offering. Her determined steps on the parquet dance floor echoed with each step. "I come in peace," she said into his left ear. "I'm not trying to start trouble."

He still could not respond. Ronny had lied, point blank. But why? He understood the arrangement. Gray could pay only if he had the money directly as a result of Keisha getting her inheritance. Why would Ronny lie?

The music seemed louder than a minute ago.

Keisha was trying to get his attention. "This is bizarre, huh? The famous Trevelle Doval is delivering flowers. But kind of sweet." She watched as Trevelle carefully placed a couple of centerpieces then left out the door for a second trip, swishing in her St. John knit pantsuit and high heels.

Delma stomped her way toward them both. "Give me one of those cell phones y'all got on you. I need to call Venus. Unless somebody's kidnapped that child and tied her up good, there's no way she would allow this."

"Venus? Who's that?" Gray squinted, feeling a bad headache coming on. It had been months since he'd battled one of his off-the-chain headaches. The kind that made his stomach turn and his eyes water.

"The coordinator," Delma said, still holding out her hand for the first person who could donate a communication device. She'd announced that her phone was left in the car along with her purse.

"The florist," Keisha added. "She's Mom's friend. I don't think you met her yet. Really nice lady with the cutest little girl. Her daughter is supposed to be our flower girl. She should be here, too, for the rehearsal."

Little girl. The thought of a child and her mother landing in the hands of Slash, Ronny's fool right-hand man, made him nearly bowl over. "I'm going to the john."

"I need your phone," Mama D ordered. "Right now."

He took one step in front of the other as straight as he could, though he felt queasy. "Be right back. Use Keisha's."

"Mine is in the car, too." Keisha's eyes burrowed into Gray's back. He could feel both women staring him down as he walked away, but he didn't care. He had to find out what was going on.

⟨⟩

"Tell me you haven't done anything yet, 'cause you got the wrong woman." Gray spoke low and fast. "Do you understand me. You got the wrong person."

"Take it easy, I don't like your tone," Ronny said. "Calm your ass down."

"I'm looking at Trevelle Doval, so obviously whoever you snatched is the wrong person. What'd she look like?"

"I wouldn't know. I don't do the dirty work. I'm an outsourcing kind of guy."

"Then you need to call your subcontractor and tell him to put her back wherever he found her or the whole deal is off, you understand?"

"Might be too late for that."

"Don't even try it." Gray's head was exploding. His eyes were blurry. "Don't mess with me. You won't see a dime, not a penny, and I'll make sure your life changes real fast, you feel me?"

"Are you making threats?" Ronny was ready for the challenge.

Gray paused. "Let whoever you have go," he said calmly. "Just walk away. Better yet, the right person is here at the Callaway Resort. Make an even exchange. Tell whoever it is to come here and get her. She's got on a white suit, long hair, brown skin. . . . Hell, y'all muthafuckas don't watch the news?" Gray broke down. "You need to get here and fix this."

"I can't be in two places at one time. I'm meeting your boy JP, remember?"

"Enough with the excuses. Damn, how do you get this wrong? The woman is on TV almost every night." He hung up, realizing he'd been holding on to the cross on his chain. He put it to his lips. He did not want to be responsible for an innocent woman and child to part this earth. Trevelle Doval was another story.

The tap on his shoulder made him jump, grabbing whoever's hand, twisting it like an action hero.

"Ouch, Gray! Ohmigod, you hurt me."

"I'm sorry, sweetheart." He kissed Keisha's wrist. "Nerves, you

know. Wedding jitters. Everything all right?" He wiped the moisture off his forehead.

"Fine. I was worried about you." Keisha had had a trial run with
the makeup artist. The thick, dark liner on her eyes was too intense.
The fake lashes overshadowed her soft eyes. The pink blush, clown-
ish with her hair pulled up like the queen of England.

"Do me a favor, wash that mess off your face." He stuck his hand
behind her head and pulled the clip loose that was holding up her
hair, letting it cascade down her back.

"That's what's bothering you? It wasn't bothering you a minute
ago. Please, you can tell me. Is it Trevelle? You don't want her here.
I'll tell her to leave. My mother is trying to figure out a way to get
her out, but if it's making you sick like this, I won't hesitate."

"No." Gray held her close. "I didn't say that. All I asked you to do
is get this stuff off your face. I want you to look like the woman I fell
in love with on our wedding day. This isn't you. Okay, that's all." He
kissed her forehead. "Mama D will survive. Leave Trevelle to do
what she came to do. She wants to help. This is her way. Peace, that's
all we want, right? No confrontations. No wild accusations."

"Accusations? What would she be making accusations about?"

"Nothing, baby, nothing." He stroked her hair and inhaled the
sweetness of her. "We're going to have a beautiful ceremony. Let's
get this practice show on the road. But first . . . what did I ask you to
do?"

"Wash my face."

"All right, good girl."

When she was gone, he strolled out to the center of the room.
Trevelle was working diligently. She and the older Hulk-size dude
were exchanging smiles and glances. New liaisons were always fun.
Then the hard work began—the lies or, worse, the truths.

"The girl's not answering. I just can't figure out what this is
about." Delma closed the phone, keeping her eyes on Trevelle.
"Where's Keisha?"

"In the bathroom. Mama D, I really don't see the problem."

"She's trying to weasel her way into an invite."

"Is that so terrible?" He rested his arm over her round shoulders.

Mama D nudged his arm away. Since their run-in about the money, she dropped all pretense. "Since when are you her advocate? You know this is all an act. She's liable to go off any minute, ranting about being excluded as mother of the bride. She's only here to ruin everything."

Gray nodded and blinked understanding from his slightly watering eyes. "We're all going to be fine. Trevelle's not going to ruin anything. That's a solid promise." He felt like saying it was a money-back guarantee because he was going to have to pay, and pay dearly.

⊙⊙

"Well, we're all going to have to get started without Nikki and the flower girl." Delma waved the rest of the bridal party to the outdoor area. She was at her wit's end. What was she paying Venus for? The unwritten part of their contract specifically required a Trevelle intervention, yet here she was, delivered to the front door like an omen. The wedding was going to be a disaster.

"Are you sure, Mom?"

"Hey, your mother's right. I should've told you earlier," Gray whispered in Keisha's ear. "Nikki and I kind of had a blowup. She wanted a raise; I told her it wasn't in the cards right now."

Keisha looked stricken. "Why would she choose a time like this to ask for a raise? So did she quit, or what happened?"

"She stormed out of the office. Said she wasn't coming back. I would've thought she'd at least honor her commitment to you and be here." He rubbed a comforting hand on her back. "Show must go on, as they say."

"I could always be a stand-in." Trevelle's voice came from behind them. Keisha and Gray faced her, startled she'd been listening. "Maybe Nikki will show up tomorrow. But for now, I could stand in."

Delma came forward. "No, that's quite all right. We'll be fine."

"Right, you probably have some more flowers in the van, or

something." Gray stroked Keisha's back. For an instant, Delma saw some good in him. Not such a bad character, after all. He knew Trevelle and the fact she couldn't be trusted.

"Just thought I could help," Trevelle said, turning slowly to walk away.

"Okay, okay," Keisha said from over the shoulders of both Gray and Delma. She stepped out from their barrier. "As a matter of fact, why don't you just take her place. You have something in this color you can wear?" Keisha held up the embossed napkin with turquoise champagne glasses.

"What . . . no!" Delma felt her blood pressure rising. "Wait a minute. It's too late for changes. Nikki will probably show up. You wouldn't want to give away your new best girlfriend's spot, would you?"

"She's not here, Mother. Enough said. And you know what, I think it's time we stop being afraid of each other." She looked between Delma and Trevelle. "I just want to have a beautiful ceremony filled with love. I can't have that knowing I've kicked out Trevelle, or hurt anyone's feelings. I can't." She leaned into Gray's chest for support. "Are you all right with this decision?"

"I want whatever you want," he said, though his eyes darted to the entrance of the ballroom as if he wanted to run out of there screaming.

"All right, we have a ceremony to practice for." Keisha reached out and kissed Delma on the cheek. "I love you. You are without a doubt the best mom in the world."

Miracle at 3012

The decision was made for him. Agent McDonald regretfully informed him that she was off the case as of yesterday morning. Something about outside influence from a local official. Jake crushed the phone closed. He had to think fast.

"Sirena, hey." He tried to calm his breathing. "I need a favor. It's going to sound crazy, but you're the first person I thought of. I need you to pick up my daughter from preschool." He let her light laughter subside, then let her ask the next question he knew was coming. "It's an emergency and you're the only person I know and trust. . . ." He waited as patiently as he could. "Thank you!" He balled his fist for the small victory. He gave her the address. "Please, please, you have to get there before eight. I know that's like fifteen minutes. Please. You can't be late."

He dialed the preschool and explained that his sister was coming for Mya. He couldn't afford another minute wasted. He called the agent back and made his last plea.

Jake stood in front of the door of 3012. He listened for a second or two. His patience was at an all-time low. He knocked on the door. It flew open, and the strong scent of herb hit him square in the face.

"You decided to show up, late and shit." Ronny sat on the couch, puffing on a thick-ass cigar blunt.

"Yeah." Jake looked around, nearly afraid he'd stumble over someone's body or, worse . . . his wife. He had to keep in mind, it wasn't Ronny who was the killer, after all—now, was it?

"Have a seat."

Jake took the offer. "Whatever you thought you needed to do to get your money back, you don't have to do. You understand what I'm saying? I'll pay you back whatever Byron stole with interest. I'll find a way. But—" He choked up. He let his hands slide over his shaven head. "My wife, you have to let her go."

"Your wife?" Ronny thought this was funny. "Where she at? She here?" He leaned forward. "Go get her, man. I'm sorry. Who knew?" He pointed over his head. "Go on."

Jake's stomach turned, and he didn't think he was going to make it to the door, but he did. He twisted the knob and peeked slowly first. The naked brown bodies were pumping and flowing on top of the bed. The woman's long shiny hair flung over her head before she looked him in the eye. He slammed the door closed.

"Is that her?" Ronny called from the couch of the suite.

Jake swallowed the nausea trying to rise up. "Nah, man. Where's my wife? Did you take her? I swear to God, did you take her?"

Ronny cracked up. "Whole lotta mistaken identities goin' on around here. I got to get back to L.A. At least you can tell folks apart out West." His friends started laughing with him. "Nah, man, ain't nobody got your wife. For a minute I thought you was talking about your bitch partner."

Jake was relieved, but if he didn't have Venus, then where?

"Legend," Ronny said, "your boy. Thought you two might've took advantage of the legalities and got hitched."

Jake hadn't thought about Legend in the moments he was looking for Venus. "Where is he?"

"Good question. When I find him, I'll make sure you know." He made a finger slide across his neck for demonstration. "But as for your wifey, can't help you. Now let's talk about my money. I believe you made a nice offer and I'd like to accept it."

"That was before, when I thought you had something I wanted. Since you don't, I'm out of here." Jake headed to the door. A wide-as-hell outside dude stepped in front of him. He reached in the back of his pants and pulled out a pistol. Jake put it to the guy's head and swung him around. "I really don't have time for this, I swear."

Ronny laughed. "Ain't that cute. Look at that little gun. Where you get that, out of a cereal box?"

"Yeah, but the bullets are still real." Jake was glad the guy was so large, since now there were two guns pointed at him.

"Ay, anybody accidentally shoot my brother gone have me to deal with. Put y'all guns down. None of this is necessary, Jake. Seriously, let my brother go and be on your way. Let's just call it a truce."

Jake didn't believe him. He reached behind and opened the door. When he got it open, he used Ronny's brother as his shield, pulling him all the way to the open elevator. Ronny's entourage didn't move. Jake shoved his human shield out the elevator once the doors were closing. He nearly pissed on himself. His heart was beating so hard, he didn't feel the vibration against his hip.

He caught his breath and answered while the elevator was still moving. He knew once it stopped he'd be in war mode again. "Yeah," he let out cautiously, hoping it was really her as the name said on his screen.

"Baby!" she cried into the phone.

"Where are you?" His knees bent; he could hardly stand. A mixture of relief and fear. "Are you all right?"

"Yes," she said as clearly as she could, though still garbled with tears. She was at a gas station, too scared to move. The elevator doors pulled open slowly. He was on his way and prayed for anybody who tried to stop him.

❦

Jake pulled into the gas station and saw the white Jaguar he was familiar with from the many times Airic had driven it to pick up Mya.

He almost forgot to put his own car in park, jumping out while it was slowly rolling. He put the brake on, then walked slowly to the window, cupping his hand to see inside the tinted glass.

He saw movement in the backseat. "Open the door, baby. It's me."

"This your car? I called a tow truck." The convenience store attendant was standing a few feet away.

A click sounded, letting Jake know she'd unlocked the door. "The car is moving, don't worry about the tow." He reached inside and pulled her up where she'd been curled in the floor behind the passenger side.

She couldn't stop crying. "Shh, baby, I got you. I got you. It's okay."

"Mya!" she suddenly called out. "Oh, my God, where's Mya?"

"She's fine. I asked a friend to pick her up and bring her to the house." He rubbed her shoulders to try to calm her down. "Come on, we're home. Everything is going to be okay."

"So, these guys thought you were Trevelle. You sure you weren't hearing things, you know, at a time like that," Jake asked while he drove them home. "You could've panicked and went into imagination overdrive." He was still sure it had something to do with Ronny, but should've counted his blessings if they really had grabbed the wrong person.

He remembered Ronny's comment about mistaken identities.

"What did they want with Trevelle?" He rolled into their long driveway, mostly talking to himself. "Maybe Airic had something to do with it. Their breakup is getting pretty nasty. Maybe he paid someone."

Venus was still in shock and not paying him much attention. He had to admit he was pretty much in a similar state. The entire day seemed to stream into one long dizzying spin of events.

Inside he helped her upstairs. He started the shower water and helped her get out of her clothes. He took in the bruises around her neck and shoulders, even on her back. "Baby, maybe we should go to the hospital."

"No," she said with more resolve than anything else he'd heard from her. She wrapped her arms around him and held tight. "I don't want to go anywhere."

He helped her step out of her white jeans that were scuffed with dirt as if she'd been dragged. "Baby, did something else happen? . . . I mean, did someone—?" He didn't want to say the word.

"I fought. I fought them. They're lucky I didn't have my bat," she said into his chest, still sobbing.

He pressed his face into her wild mane of hair and inhaled. He'd never been more grateful in his life, more aware of the good with the bad, more thankful to God she was alive and in his arms.

Sacrilegious Green

I had nothing in my closet that ghastly color turquoise. With Delma in charge, I knew there would be a whole lot of ugly going on. The flowers were the one gorgeous accompaniment. I admit to being slightly biased in that regard. Mr. Vincent Capricio had made me smile, something I couldn't remember doing without it being for someone else's benefit in some time.

After we'd driven back to the floral shop, he offered the steak dinner he'd promised. I politely declined. The florist man was hardly near my standards. Besides, the last thing I was about to do was trust another man.

I told him I'd never fit into the dress I had in mind if I had a steak or anything besides the blanched salad I had waiting at home. We decided on a rain check. He offered his hand when we arrived at the floral shop to help me out of the van. I'd imagined his hands would be rough and callused from rose pricks and hard water, but instead they were soft and strong.

"I can be your date to the wedding," he said as he escorted me out of the van. I searched inside my purse for my keys to make a quick getaway, and they weren't there. "I think I left my keys inside. Wait a minute. Where's my car?"

Vince took me by the hand. "Come inside," he said quickly.

"What? What is it?" I tried to turn around to see what had spooked him.

He kept the lights off in the store and walked back to the front to peer out the window. I came to his side and looked out, too. Headlights of the large Hummer parked across the street suddenly came on. The car sped away.

"Who was that?"

"I don't know." Vince looked around, making sure the place was intact. "We had a break-in a few days ago."

"Well, you could've warned me before I left my car here. Someone obviously has stolen it."

"All I know is, I'm not letting you out of my sight till I get you home."

◎◎

The In Bloom van rattled loudly when it pulled in front of my building. Vince put the car in park, turning off the ignition so he could come and open the door for me.

"That's not necessary." I didn't want anyone to see me getting out of the van. My reputation was damaged enough.

He came and opened the door for me anyway. Worse, he insisted on walking me to the entrance.

"You're quite a gentleman. I really appreciate your kindness. I imagine you feel sorry for me. But I'm here to tell you, what you've seen of me the last few months is nothing compared to what I've been through in my life. I'm a survivor. Always have been. You don't have to feel sorry for me."

"I don't feel sorry for you. You got too much going on for me to feel sorry for you."

"Are you speaking in regards to material things?"

"No. Where I come from, money doesn't make it all better. I can see your confidence. Your heart. You're a good person."

I kept my eyes down. I didn't want him to see me foolishly fall for his line. If he saw that it was working, there'd be more where that came from, and I simply wasn't in the mood. "I have to get going. Thank you for everything."

"You're welcome. Don't forget about our rain check?"

"I promise."

He slept in the guest room, and Keisha slept in the master. He listened as the shower ran. In spite of his plan failing miserably, he was looking forward to his wedding day. Now that he was thinking straight and rational, he was glad the plan didn't go through. Trevelle obviously would hold true to her word and not try to stop the ceremony. He'd call it even Steven, since Ronny dropped the ball on his end. That meant they were square.

He still wasn't sure of the fate of the other woman Ronny had mistakenly grabbed. What Gray didn't know couldn't hurt him.

"Wake up, my handsome groom." Keisha's skin was moist and warm with only a towel wrapped and tucked. She straddled him on the bed. He moved the arm draped over his face and grabbed her for a full hug. She shrieked, "Here I thought you were knocked out cold!"

"How can I sleep in? I'm too excited for our big day."

"Me, too. Can't believe weddings are this much work. You know, when you attend a ceremony, you never guess there's this much energy put into every detail."

He ran his fingers underneath her chin and pulled her in for a kiss.

"Gray, don't be bad." She could feel the hardness underneath the sheet. "That's why we slept in separate beds last night—now you want to ruin our luck right here and right now."

"More old wives' tales and superstitions. Come on, put me out of my misery. Otherwise I'm going to be speed-reading my vows and telling Bishop Talley to get on with it so I can get you on the honeymoon, reception be damned." He pushed the sheet down. "I now pronounce you man and wife—you may kiss the bride." He flipped her over on her back and proceeded to take what was now his from this day forward and ever more.

The bridesmaids lined up side by side. From a distance they looked like a green garden worm. I came and took my place at the end as we'd agreed, since I wouldn't be matching exactly.

"What is that?" The voice screeched behind me. "You can't wear that?"

"This is all I had." I smoothed the front of my emerald green St. John suit. It was my favorite and spoke timeless class. Unlike the hideous neon pool-water green worn by the other bridesmaids.

"You stand out like a sore thumb," Delma hissed. "I knew this was a bad idea." She arched her short neck from side to side.

"What are you looking for?"

"My niece. She's wearing something pretty close to the right color. That way you can just take a seat. No harm, no foul."

"No, I will not be dismissed by you, Delma. Really, didn't you hear what Keisha said last night. Everyone has had enough. Okay, enough."

"Oh, right. You came here with your obvious mother-of-the-bride-looking suit on. You wore this to stand out."

"It's a green suit. If I wanted to stand out, I think I could've found something a little more bold. But if you're trying to compliment me on how beautiful it is, you've accomplished that. Thank you."

Gray came and stood between us. "You guys . . . you want Keisha to hear you? 'Cause I did from all the way over there. Now, calm down—both of you."

I stood firm. Delma huffed and stomped off with her cascading chiffon like a big marshmallow cloud. I smirked and tried to keep myself from a full belly laugh. I was here at my daughter's wedding. I could've told her she'd never win, she'd never keep me away.

"Please behave." Gray kissed me on the cheek. "You look stunning, by the way, Mom."

"So do you, *son*." I was feeling too good to let him bring me down.

Gray looked out over the huge attendance. It was a congregation of the who's who of Atlanta's rich and successful. Many his own clients. Family he hadn't seen in years. Most hadn't come around since the Hillman brood had lost their family fortune. Gray could taste the envy of his brother Skip, whom he hadn't seen in close to four years. A shame money could break up a family. They'd fought over the remnants and crumbs while Gray took matters into his own hands. A self-made man. He smoothed down his tux lapel and made sure his tie was straight. The music started, and the bridesmaids lined up.

The Wedding March began after everyone had already come down the aisle. It was really happening. Gray was relieved, and felt like he'd never worked for anything so hard in his life. Keisha appeared like an angel on the arm of Hudson. Her white gown billowed softly. Her smooth shoulders shimmered in the sunlight.

A tall white man stood up and moved toward Keisha. Everyone had the same puzzled looks on their faces. He whispered something to Hudson and then exchanged places with him. Her father. Gray hadn't met him, and Keisha told him the story only once and let it go. But suddenly she was in tears. He wanted to move toward her, but they were tears of joy.

Her father walked her down the aisle, proud and happy to have the most beautiful woman in the world on his arm. Gray knew the feeling.

They exchanged vows. Bishop Talley moved everything effortlessly along. The fastest-planned ceremony was now complete and a roaring success. Everyone stood and clapped as they held hands and moved down the red carpet placed on top of the grass.

The reception was just as perfect. After their first dance, toasts were made, smiles and laughter echoing through the room.

From the corner of his eye he saw a flash of green go across the lawn toward the suite where Keisha went to change her dress. Nikki. He bolted to cut her off. "Where do you think you're going?" He put out his arm, blocking her way.

"I'm here as I am supposed to be. I'm a bridesmaid, remember dat?"

"Yes, but the wedding is over. You missed out, in more ways than one, I'd like to add."

"Get your hands off me, Gray, or so help me, I will scream at the top of my lungs."

He let go. "Why are you here, huh? You're angry, I understand that, but do you want to hurt Keisha? What did she ever do to you?"

She batted her long lashes, and he thought he saw a hint of glossy emotion.

"You know I'm not perfect. You know I fly off the handle. But I've always been there for you, admit it. So we had a fight. Big deal. My only hope was that you would come back. And here you are." His eyes twinkled with sincerity. "I'm sorry I hurt you."

He led the way to the far-side cabana, where the men had gotten dressed. He made sure no one was looking. He took two handfuls of her plump breasts and kissed her full on the mouth. He left her wide open, ready to do just about anything he said. "Just go home, okay. We'll see each other tomorrow, and everything will be back to normal."

She batted her eyes in concession. He kissed her one more time, cupping the fullness of her crotch, enjoying the feel of the satin fabric of her gown. He had to be careful. He could feel his own desire building. "Go." He pulled her back. "Not that way, over there." He pointed, and that's when he saw her. She'd seen and probably heard everything.

Nikki left. He dropped his head, then lifted it up. Why. *Why now?*

"Ain't this about a blip?"

"It's not what it looked like."

"Unless this is a bad dream, it's absolutely everything it looked like." She pinched herself. "Nope, not a dream."

Gray was tired. He was about ready to throw in the towel. "All right, you got me. Now what? It's over. You could understand when two people work together, there might've been a relationship. Look at you and Hudson—you two fell in love. Got married. Only problem is that I chose Keisha instead of Nikki. I was trying to make her feel better."

Delma shook her head. "You might fool all of the people all of the time, but not me, Gray Hillman. Not me." She started toward the suite where Keisha was probably sitting, poised like a fairy princess and exchanging her veil for the tiara.

"What're you going to do?"

"I'm going to tell her everything. I spared you the embarrassment about the money, but not this. No more. I knew you were a bad seed. I knew it."

He popped in front of her. He towered over her. He hadn't realized how small she was, height wise. Her big attitude and tough talk had made her appear larger than her petite frame. "I can't let you tell her. I really, really love Keisha. We're already married. What's this going to do but cause a rocky start?" He hunched his shoulders like it was out of his hands. And it really was.

"Gray Hillman, you aren't actually looking at me like you're going to stop me from telling my daughter the truth."

"I want to go with you, is all. Okay? I want to be there just so I can explain."

"You're thinking you got a fifty-fifty shot, thinking she might not believe what I have to say, so you want to be there to clean it up. Yeah, I understand. Well, let's say we take our chances, then." She started walking ahead of him.

He saw the open utility room and tools inside hanging on the wall. His eyes drifted to the large storage crate open and empty. He'd decided in that split second that it was a really dumb idea, but for whatever reason, he couldn't stop himself. He wrapped a hand around her mouth, lifted her off her feet with the other arm, and carried her while she kicked and squirmed.

☉〇☉

"May I have this dance? Don't tell me—I know I clean up pretty well."

"Very well," I corrected, taking his hand. "I almost didn't recognize you."

"I figure you weren't going to call for the rain check. But I didn't want you to be alone on this day, however it turned out."

"It was perfect. It really was."

"So then you don't need me. Want me to leave?" He stopped their halfhearted dance.

"It's perfect because you're here," I said. "But you have to know, I'm not open for business. You hear what I'm saying?"

"I hear what you're saying." He grinned, revealing a sharp dimple. "Just so you understand. I also have a right to refuse service." He seductively whispered in my ear before dipping me backwards and spinning me around.

"You're too much."

"That's what I hear."

I was smiling again and couldn't help myself.

Gray had danced with almost every woman in the room. The DJ knew all his favorite songs, since they went way back to the days of pledging on the line and mimicking Kid N Play when they went out on the prowl.

He used a napkin to wipe his forehead. Sweat had saturated his collar and underarms. He waved for Keisha to join him. He wanted to introduce her to his buddy he hadn't seen since middle school. He sipped on champagne and offered solutions to the world's ills. He was feeling good, bottom line. Gray Hillman couldn't recall a time in his life when he felt more on top of the world. He was always scratching, calculating, anticipating his next move. Not tonight. He was free-falling, landing amongst friends and even strangers who simply appreciated his presence.

"You got a good woman, son. Congratulations." His uncle Jerry was a crackhead. He'd been on the drug for twenty years and still going strong.

"Thank you, Uncle. I appreciate you coming."

"Aberdeen, is that you?" Gray gave his cousin a hug. She'd gained a whole other person. He forced himself not to ask if there was a baby in there. "You sho looking good, girl. Yeah, God bless." He headed toward the direction he'd last seen Keisha. It was a good run, but the party was closing out. All the celeb clients had already left. He knew the envelopes were filled with checks of gratitude. He had his eye on a beautiful estate in Buckhead, large enough to raise the three or four kids he'd hoped for. He planned on paying cash. Dropping a million or so just like that. He never wanted to be on the bubble again, hoping something came through just so he could meet his obligations.

If only that damn Byron had given him the pass codes. He'd set him up with nearly all his important clients, and the deal was simple. He got 10 percent off the top. Byron did all the hard work, the thinking, the execution. Now he was dry as a bone. The programs were in place, the money piling up, and he couldn't touch it.

"Mr. Hillman." A hand landed on his back. "I just want to say, you sure know how to throw a party." His drunk cousin Nedra smelled like vinegar. She'd tried to suck his dick when he was ten and she was thirteen. Only three years apart, but now she looked like she could be his mother. "You want a dance?" She slurred the question. Then answered it herself. "No. You think you too good for your old cousin now. You wasn't too good for me when I licked your monkey."

Gray patted her on the back. "I need to call you a taxi."

She hugged him back, both her hands falling on his backside. "Damn, you still fine."

"Thank you, cousin. So are you."

"Liar. You always was a liar. Tell the truth. You think I'm sexy?"

Gray stopped and turned around. He stared her down. "No,

cousin. I don't think you're sexy." He wasn't a liar. He told the truth when he could. He tried to be honest when he could. No one wanted to hear the truth. Was that his fault?

He finally made it through the throng of people to the other side of the ballroom. There before him was Nikki in the green dress, leaning into Keisha's ear.

"Hey, you guys having a good time?"

Neither one of them answered him. Keisha directed her eyes to the ground. Nikki smiled. "I told her about everything." She touched Keisha's arm. "Ask your mother if you want confirmation. She saw us. She knows the truth."

Keisha slapped Gray hard across the face. He gripped her wrist. "Don't believe her. Do you hear me? I love you."

She snatched her arm away. "I'm going to give you one chance. One only. Were you with her the entire time we've been engaged?"

Gray felt the eyes staring him down. "Can we please talk about this in private?"

"No. Why should we be in private? Everyone here seems to know you but me."

"You know me. You know the best part of me."

Keisha moved past him. "Has anyone seen my mother? Delma, has anyone seen Delma Hawkins?" She pulled the crystal crown off her head. The saltwater pearl earrings she held in each hand dropped to the ground. "She's about this tall." She faced him. "Where's my mother?"

The sky seemed to have darkened and opened up within minutes. Rain started pouring. The pummeling sound of drops outside the open door made everyone conclude the party was over. The bride and groom were staring each other down, one with a ferocious hate and the other with a passion too deep to call love.

Keisha walked out into the rain and called her mother's name. She stood still and waited for a response. Something, an inkling of a stir. Thunder jolted the sky. Keisha's tears mixed with the rain, and all she wanted was her mother.

"Did you hear that?" I put my fingers to my lips.

"What? I don't hear anything except the rain and now thunder. It's coming down." Vince ran a hand through his wet hair. His nice suit was sprinkled with dark droplets.

"Listen." We'd gotten caught in the rain, then ran to take cover. We were close, taking in each other's air, hearing only each other's breathing, then, "There it is again. Did you hear that. Like someone's crying."

"Or something like a puppy." Vince nodded then took my hand. We followed the muffled sound. Rain poured down a gutter spout and splashed around our feet. We tiptoed best we could, but the water was deeper than we thought.

"Oh, great. Do you know how much these shoes cost?"

He pressed his ear against the locked door. Vince slipped off his jacket. His shirt fit close and tight. "How do you get a body like that?" I asked spontaneously.

"It's something called having too much time on your hands."

I knew the lingo. "You were in prison?"

He shook his head. "Lets just say I was separated from the people I love, who loved me, for their sake. I was afraid to get to know anyone else, start over. Until now."

I held his jacket close and appreciated the scent of him. The moaning sound came again, and I focused. "It's a woman."

"Yeah." He looked around briefly, then lunged into the door. The wood cracked but didn't give way. He pushed three or four more times before it let go. He rubbed his shoulder. "I'm going to need a serious massage."

I smirked but didn't offer. If I'd learned anything at my age, it was start how you planned to finish. If anyone was going to be getting the massages, it would be me. He stepped inside. The room was filled with water from the cracked spout pouring directly onto the walkway.

"Please, somebody. Can you hear me?"

Vince lifted off the heavy boxes that were placed on top of a storage crate. When he got it open, I screamed from shock. Never in a million years could I have expected to see her bent, tattered, and defenseless. "My Lord. What happened? Who did this?" I took Vince's jacket and draped it over her shoulders. She stepped out, weeping uncontrollably. I held her by one hand, and Vince took the other. She could barely stand.

"He's going to take her, he's going to take Keisha."

He didn't try to run. When the police came, he was still sitting in the ballroom, long after most everyone had cleared out. His shirtsleeves rolled up. He held his Rolex in his hand and twirled it around. He tossed it to the worker who was cleaning up plates and glasses.

"Serious?" The young man shoved it into his pocket.

"You want to stand up, please?" An officer snapped on handcuffs. Maybe by the time he got out, he'd figure out those pass codes. Interest would've built up nicely, and whatever was left of his life would be spent well.

He was escorted past Keisha, flanked by both mothers at her side. All three women refused to look in his direction. He guessed it wouldn't be long before they were at one another's throats.

The Sun and the Rain Make Flowers Grow

It took a couple of weeks to digest everything. Jake wasn't talking much since coming back from his meeting with the FBI. He couldn't bring himself to tell them about Legend, who seemed to have disappeared overnight. But the biggest mystery was still plaguing me.

I'd tried to keep silent on the issue. After all, there was so much to be grateful for.

Jake was relieved to know what really happened to his accountant, and that was all that mattered. He was also relieved to have his company back. JP Wear was solid and profitable. The only problem was, we were going to have to move back to Los Angeles, just when I was in my groove.

Business was booming. Vince was happy, and a happy employee makes for a happy business. He was seeing someone religiously, no pun intended, and I refused to ask for details. The less I knew, the better. My new friend and fan, Senator Stanton, made sure all his associates called In Bloom if they needed flowers, and they needed them often.

Then Jake got a call from Keisha Hawkins, who was taking over new clients at Shark and Boyd Associates, letting him know they still wanted to work with him. So we had good options. Things were looking way up.

The decision was a toss up: heads we move back to Los Angeles and run JP Wear; tails we stay in Atlanta and smell the roses. The decision wasn't going to be that easy. We had a lot to think about. Uprooting Mya was a major factor. Best friends were hard to come by, even if you were only four years old.

I came up and wrapped my arms around Jake from behind. I planted a kiss in the center of his back. "You all right?"

"I am, or I will be," he said. "Why aren't you rushing off to In Bloom?"

"I wanted to have a full day alone with you. Just us."

"I like it." He turned around and kissed me on the lips.

"What are we going to do?"

"Flip a coin."

"We already flipped. Seems either way we both feel like we're losing. I want you to be happy. You want me to be happy."

"The decision should be about what makes us both happy," he said. "I don't have any ties here in Atlanta. But you do. You have Vince; Mya has Jory."

"And you have Sirena Lassiter."

He tensed his muscles then caught himself and tried to relax to a *not a care in the world* stance, but it was too late. "I guess I was wait-ing for this." He shook his head. "I don't *have* Sirena Lassiter. I knew her way back when. We ran in to each other when I was out with Legend. We exchanged numbers. Luckily she was there to pick up Mya. End of story."

I kissed his chin. "She's enough of a reason to pack up and move. Could she be any cuter?" If I wasn't mistaken, I felt something move between us before he loosened his grip for a little distance.

"We have some time. Let's see how commuting will work out for JP Wear. I'll fly out and get some good people in place, maybe we can even take turns going."

"Okay, I guess we'll see."

"So how about our day, just us?" His thumbs pressed with his grip around my lower waist.

"How about we go see that new movie, *Sharp Edge*, starring our friend Sirena?" I checked his vitals. Nothing shifted.

He let out a deep sweet laugh. "At least I know I'll have your undivided attention for a while."

"Oh, you can believe that."

"But, babe, please don't make me go see that movie. It was horrible."

I slapped his shoulder. "Ah-ha . . . you saw a preview, a private screening."

He took off running. "You'll have to beat it out of me." Of course, he was headed to the bedroom. I knew a trap when I saw one. Thank goodness he was the only one I'd ever let capture me again.

Kristi Fontamillas

TRISHA R. THOMAS is an NAACP Image Award for Outstanding Literary Work finalist. She's a Literary Lion Award honoree by the King County Library System Foundation and was voted Best New Writer by the Black Writers Alliance. Her debut novel, *Nappily Ever After*, is now a Netflix movie. *O, The Oprah Magazine* featured her novels in "Books That Matter" for delving into the self-esteem of young women of color and the insurmountable expectations they face starting at an early age. She lives in California with her family where she continues to write the Nappily series.